TO MAKE THE PUNISHMENT FIT THE CRIME

is definitely not Alfred Hitchcock's idea of the proper medicine for murderers. If he had his way, silver loving cups instead of solitary cells would be awarded to champion killers, medals instead of manacles would be offered to standout slayers, and there would be a Nobel Prize for the finest fiend of the year.

Unfortunately, Hitchcock still has a long way to go in accomplishing these enlightened reforms—which leaves a lot of his favorite people at the end of their ropes. And all the lovable master of the macabre can do is offer his very good advice to those for whom no noose would be good noose:

"I hate to leave you dangling, but you'll just have to try to hang loose. And whatever you do, be sure you don't choke up!"

A HANGMAN'S DOZEN

Stories to tie your nerves in knots!

ALFRED HITCHCOCK'S

A
Hangman's
Dozen

A Dell Book

Published by DELL PUBLISHING CO., INC.
1 Dag Hammarskjold Plaza
New York, New York 10017

Previous Dell Edition #3428
New Dell Edition
First printing—January 1976

ACKNOWLEDGMENTS

BOMB#14 by Jack Ritchie—Copyright 1957 by H. S. D. Publications, Inc. Re-
printed by permission of Larry Sternig Agency.
THE FORGIVING GHOST by C. B. Gilford—© 1961 by H. S. D. Publications, Inc.
Reprinted by permission of the author and the author's agents, Scott Meredith
Literary Agency, Inc.
THE CHILDREN OF NOAH by Richard Matheson—Copyright 1957 by H. S. D.
Publications, Inc. Reprinted by permission of Harold Matson Company.
AN ATTRACTIVE FAMILY by Robert Arthur—Copyright 1957 by H. S. D. Publica-
tions, Inc. Reprinted by permission of the author and the author's agents,
Scott Meredith Literary Agency, Inc.
LET THE SUCKER BEWARE by Charles Einstein—Copyright 1958 by H. S. D. Pub-
lications, Inc. Reprinted by permission of Lurton Blassingame.
FAIR GAME by John Cortez—Copyright 1957 by H. S. D. Publications, Inc. Re-
printed by permission of the author's agents, Scott Meredith Literary Agency,
Inc.
THE CURIOUS FACTS PRECEDING MY EXECUTION by Richard Stark—© 1960 by
H. S. D. Publications, Inc. Reprinted by permission of the author and the au-
thor's agents, Scott Meredith Literary Agency, Inc.
YOUR WITNESS by Helen Nielsen—Copyright 1958 by H. S. D. Publications, Inc.
Reprinted by permission of the author and the author's agents, Scott Meredith
Literary Agency, Inc.
BLACKOUT by Richard Deming—© 1961 by H. S. D. Publications, Inc. Reprinted
by permission of the author and the author's agents, Scott Meredith Literary
Agency, Inc.
THE OCTOBER GAME by Ray Bradbury—Copyright 1948 by Short Stories, Inc.
Reprinted by permission of Harold Matson Company.
STOP CALLING ME "MISTER" by Jonathan Craig—Copyright 1956 by H. S. D. Pub-
lications, Inc. Reprinted by permission of the author and the author's agents,
Scott Meredith Literary Agency, Inc.
THE LAST ESCAPE by Jay Street—© 1960 by H. S. D. Publications, Inc. Re-
printed by permission of Theron Raines.
NOT A LAUGHING MATTER by Evan Hunter—Copyright 1958 by H. S. D. Publica-
tions, Inc. Reprinted by permission of the author and the author's agents,
Scott Meredith Literary Agency, Inc.
MOST AGREEABLY POISONED by Fletcher Flora—Copyright 1957 by H. S. D.
Publications, Inc. Reprinted by permission of the author and the author's
agents, Scott Meredith Literary Agency, Inc.
THE BEST-FRIEND MURDER by Donald E. Westlake—Copyright 1959 by H. S. D.
Publications, Inc. Reprinted by permission of the author and the author's
agents, Scott Meredith Literary Agency, Inc.

Contents

PREFACE

As you know, I have long been a student of the criminal method; and I have been told recently, by certain well-informed persons, that the crime rate in this country is beyond belief.

On the face of it, this is an inexact statement and one which might force me to seek other employment. However, I can assure you that the crime rate may be much greater than the local and national law enforcement agencies believe. The reason for this sad state of affairs, you see, is due to the fact that no one can properly enter the *perfect crime* into the body of the statistical quotient.

It is because the *perfect crime* goes unsung that I have decided to write this little essay for your enlightenment and edification. I have great respect for crime and the people involved with it, and such being the case, I deplore the careless crime. It has no finesse, no sense of balance, no feeling of accomplishment.

If one is to undertake a "job," it is well to remember that it should be done well. I remember reading that the first recorded crime was the murder of a young man by his brother. The brother did a poor job of it, his act was soon known to one and all, and he received his just deserts. Therefore, one should consider all possibilities. Over the years, in my line of endeavor, I have had the pleasure of viewing many criminal types: embezzlers, pickpockets, assassins, and oh! so many more. These gentlemen—and gentlewomen—have led me into a unique way of life. I have made their crimes pay . . . for me . . . but I have always cherished in my bosom the wish to emulate them in their chosen profession.

At last, I can report that I have done so; I have committed a *perfect crime*. Without fear of contradiction, one can state that one wishes to be the best in one's field—and in that profession which operates outside the laws of our society, the *perfect crime* is the ultimate. The *perfect crime* is the royal flush, the hole in one, the home run in the ninth with bases loaded.

I planned for many years, worked ceaselessly to perfect myself, to establish a reputation without blemish, all this bearing on that one act, that one great moment. At last I achieved my goal, at last I . . .

At this point in my little essay it was my intention to illustrate through personal experience how very difficult it is for one to commit such an act—the hardships and dangers one must face when one sets foot on this most difficult of roads—but, unfortunate to relate, my attorney informs me that any such illustration on my part would be tantamount to a confession. The local district attorney is a great follower of my modest writings.

I fear, therefore, that I must halt further discussion on this subject; but since we have come so far together, I hope you will do me the pleasure of continuing through the following pages. I can assure you a shudderingly good time.

Alfred Hitchcock

BOMB #14

●

Jack Ritchie

Lightning only strikes once—so I was informed years and years ago by a lightning-rod salesman. That matches aren't to be played with—if memory serves me correctly—was something told me by my mother when I was a child, and shortly after I had playfully attempted to burn to the ground the very satisfactory house in which we were then living. To this store of man's wisdom, our story makes its contribution: bombs may prove a shattering experience. And they have also been known to disrupt associations of long standing.

The big square package was alone in an island of space near the baggage windows. It was number fourteen in the last six years and we were supposed to see that it didn't kill anybody.

Pete and I studied the faces of the crowd behind the ropes. That was part of our job—to see if maybe somebody was licking his lips a little wetter than anybody else.

Pete chewed on his cigar. "I see the same eager types every time we're waiting for an idiot to jump out of a twentieth story window. Bet half the city knows about this by now."

The ropes kept the curious ones forty yards away from the box. I thought it should have been more than forty, but I wasn't running that part of the show.

A detail of men finished laying the twelve-by-two planks on the concrete steps and the bomb disposal truck drove up the improvised ramp and into the terminal's big lobby. It was an unwieldy vehicle, a thing of steel mesh and wickerwork with high sides that would divert the force of an explosion upwards where it would do the least harm.

The truck stopped within fifteen feet of the box before O'Brien and Hastings climbed out of the cab.

Pete stepped on his cigar. "The main event," he said and walked over to them. I hesitated a few moments and then followed, keeping the truck between me and the box.

O'Brien grinned. "They're setting up cameras. I'll have to remember my right profile's my fortune."

Pete helped him strap on the front harness. "I admire these hero boys. They're devil-may-care all right. And cute too."

O'Brien stepped closer to the box.

"Hold it," I said quickly. "If nobody's got any objections, I think Pete and I'll take our bodies a little farther away from here first."

We went back to our station behind one of the big marble pillars.

One of the patrolmen left the ropes and joined us. He talked close to our ears. "That guy with the light hair and tan jacket over there near the candy stand. I'll swear I saw him in the crowd at the library last week."

We looked at the faces behind the line and found him. He was a small man with a light complexion. His bright eyes had no attention for anything but what was going to happen near the truck.

Pete started to move, but I touched his arm. "He can wait a minute."

O'Brien and Hastings were alone on their stage. They went to the truck and got the long pole with the steel mesh basket.

The emptiness of silence took over as O'Brien bent over the package. He looked up for a moment and I thought I saw a grin through his mask. Then he put both hands gently on the package and began to lift it.

The explosion was a giant's roar that echoed and re-echoed through the big terminal.

I heard Pete curse. And when I stepped from behind the pillar, O'Brien and Hastings were two costumed dolls that lay twisted grotesquely on the marble floor.

I bulled my way through the screaming crowd and got to the little man. He didn't know I was there. Not even when I put a hand around his thin arm.

He was still in his own world. His protruding eyes were on the two broken men on the floor and he smiled.

Captain Wilson moved his ash tray back and forth a few times before he looked up. "Hastings died right away. O'Brien's still hanging on, but if he makes it, he'll be retired for life."

He picked up the report sheet. "The suspect's name is Irwin James Stuart, 1368 98th St. I left him for you two to work on, considering that you picked him up."

Wilson rubbed the back of his neck. "Stuart is thirty-six, a bachelor, and living with his mother. She thinks we're beasts. Her boy never did anything wrong in his life. He's a good son and he never forgets Mother's Day."

He rummaged through the papers on his desk top until he found the slip he wanted. "We went through Stuart's house. Four lead pipes, ten cappings, the works of three cheap wrist watches and a small keg of powder. It's the kind of powder you use when you go in for reloading your own cartridges. But Stuart doesn't own a gun and there aren't any cartridges in the place."

Wilson got up and moved about restlessly. "We also found a scrapbook of newspaper clippings. It covers all the bombs, all the way back to the first one."

There were deep lines in his face. "Besides the big damage, three people got hit by fragments. Nothing serious, but they're probably talking to their lawyers now. Five more got trampled, some in the rush for the exits, and I guess we'll hear from them too."

I tapped a cigarette from my pack. "Somebody should have seen the box put there."

Wilson shrugged. "Fifty thousand or more people go through that terminal every day. Stuart must have counted on that." He exhaled a tired breath. "We got seven witnesses and seven descriptions. Five claim it was a man and two that it was a woman."

Pete thought it over. "Did they get a look at Stuart yet?"

Wilson's laugh was short. "Three identified him, including one who was sure it was a woman. Any good lawyer could tear them apart on the witness stand."

He looked at us. "A confession would be a help. A real dandy help."

Pete and I got up and went out into the corridor. We walked down to room 618.

Pete stopped a moment before he turned the doorknob. "You go on being the kind, understanding detective, Fred—if you want. My heart wouldn't be in it. I'll feel a lot more comfortable being mean."

Stuart was handcuffed to one of the steam pipes and he had a patrolman to keep an eye on him.

Pete walked close to Stuart and grinned. "Everybody around here's been treating you too gentle. I'm here to change that."

I unlocked Stuart's handcuffs. "Rub your wrists a little, Mr. Stuart. They'll feel a lot better." I put my hand on his shoulder. "And please take a chair. You must have been standing for hours and you're tired."

Stuart sat down and Pete leaned over him. His voice was a growl. "How do you feel now? Nice and comfortable?"

Stuart's lips trembled and he looked away.

"Mr. Stuart," I said. "All we ask of you is that you answer our questions in the best way you know. How soon after you plant those bombs do you make the phone call?"

Stuart shook his head. "I know nothing about those bombs."

Pete rubbed his knuckles. "Tell us what you were going to do with all that powder we found in your basement. And how about the pipes, the caps, and the watches?"

Stuart flushed slightly. "You had no right to search my mother's house. You had no right at all to go through my things."

Pete blew cigar smoke into his face and laughed.

The door opened and Captain Wilson came in. He stared at Stuart for ten seconds and then turned to us. "O'Brien died a few minutes ago."

Pete handcuffed Stuart to the steam pipe again and we went into the corridor. "Where's Eileen?" he asked. "At the hospital?"

Wilson shook his head. "There wasn't anything she could do there. I told her to go home about an hour ago."

He smiled tiredly. "I guess you two are elected to break the news."

He walked us to the elevators. "The lab boys have been putting things together. This time the bomb was a lot stronger. They figure at least three pipes were used."

Pete grunted. "I guess Stuart got tired of having his things go off without killing anybody."

Wilson pressed the elevator button. "Another thing. It wasn't a time device. It was rigged to go off when somebody lifted the package."

Eileen O'Brien opened the door of her ranch-style home. Her face was calm as she studied us and then she spoke softly. "It's all over, isn't it? Jerry's dead?"

I nodded.

She turned and walked away. Pete and I followed and closed the door.

We stood there awhile watching her stare out of the window and then Pete cleared his throat. "Maybe we'd better go, Fred."

Eileen turned. "No. I don't want to be alone now. I think it's better if somebody's with me." She smiled weakly. "I know this is hard on you too. You were Jerry's best friends."

Pete's hands played with the brim of his hat. "At least we got the guy who did it. That's something on the good side."

Eileen bent over the silver cigarette box on the cocktail table. "Has he confessed?"

"He'll get to it," I said. "We'll see to that."

Eileen sat down on the davenport. "Just what kind of a man is he?"

I shrugged. "I wouldn't know. I'm not his psychiatrist."

"He's weak," Pete said. "But he likes to feel important. He likes the idea of a whole city being scared."

Eileen was thoughtful for a moment. "Why don't you fix us all drinks, Pete? I think I could use one."

I listened to Pete moving about in the kitchen. "We got the right man, Eileen," I said softly. "We found everything we need to make it stick."

She smiled slightly. "That was luck, wasn't it?"

"Yes," I said. "Some luck."

Pete came back with mixed drinks for Eileen and me and then opened a bottle of beer for himself. "There wasn't any beer in the refrigerator, so I went down into the basement and got some from the case. That was all right wasn't it, Eileen? Jerry always said to help myself if the refrigerator was empty."

He poured his beer carefully. "I guess Jerry really liked his job. The bomb work, I mean."

Eileen watched him. "Yes. I think so."

"While I was getting the beer, I noticed that he's got a sort of workshop down there. It looks like he did a lot of homework on those bombs." Pete smiled. "Didn't it worry you that he might blow up the house some time?"

Eileen shook her head. "He never brought any powder or dynamite home with him. He just studied the mechanics of the bombs."

Pete and I stayed another half hour and then we said good-bye.

Pete slipped behind the wheel of our car and turned on the ignition. "How long were they married, Fred?"

"Two years," I said. "You know that as well as I do."

He nodded. "Did you ever realize that most of the time you see people only when they're wearing their Sunday clothes? You never know what they got on when you're not around."

"They got along all right," I said. "If they didn't, they could always have gotten a divorce, couldn't they?"

Pete turned into the traffic at Eighth. "All kinds of diagrams lying around there. In the basement, I mean."

He stopped for a traffic light. "It's a terrible thing, Fred. But at least O'Brien was a considerate man. He once told me that he was insured up to the hilt. I think he said fifteen thousand."

I tossed my cigarette out the window. "We'd better get back to Stuart before he gets a chance to see a lawyer."

Stuart had had time to think, but his thoughts must have been bad ones. He flinched when Pete and I entered the room.

Pete took off his suitcoat and draped it over the back of a chair. "Well, here I am, Stuart. Have you been thinking about me?"

The movement of Stuart's head was jerky. "I tell you I know nothing at all about the bombings."

Pete put his face close to Stuart's. "You never got anything big like this before. Just a few cripples. Now you're big time. Everybody's going to read about you."

There was a flicker in Stuart's eyes.

"Mr. Stuart," I said. "All we ask is a simple statement from you. After that you may talk to the reporters if you want to. I'm sure you'll be on the front pages for weeks."

He licked his lips. "No," he said finally. "I have nothing to say."

"Mr. Stuart," I said patiently. "We didn't just pick you out of the crowd at random. We've seen you other times. Last week at the library, for instance."

Pete tapped him lightly on the shoulder three or

four times. "You're a cop killer now, boy. You're going to fall down a lot of stairs if you don't co-operate."

"Mr. Stuart," I said. "We are not here to judge you. Perhaps you had some kind of legitimate grievance. Is that it?"

He almost spoke.

Pete broke the silence. "You know what's waiting for you, Stuart? You know what happens to killers in this state?"

Stuart's face went white.

I stepped back to where he couldn't see me. I looked at Pete and shook my head warningly. "Mr. Stuart," I said gently. "There is no danger of your going to the electric chair. I think we all realize that. You are a disturbed person and the state will recognize you as such. The worst that can happen to you is a few years in an institution for treatment."

We gave Stuart a full minute to think, but he shook his head stubbornly. "No. I refuse to say anything."

Pete moved closer and grabbed a handful of Stuart's shirt. He slapped him hard. This was the only way he could operate.

"Now, Pete," I said. "You know we can't allow anything like that."

Pete wiped the palm of his hand. "Why don't you go downstairs for a cup of coffee, Fred? Come back in fifteen minutes."

I shook my head. "No, Pete." I studied Stuart. "Your scrapbook is quite comprehensive. Apparently bombings were your favorite subject."

Pete grinned. "But that book of yours isn't complete, Stuart. Your picture isn't there."

"I really must admire you, Mr. Stuart," I said. "You were quite clever to escape detection all these years."

I thought I saw smugness in his eyes.

"You'd be surprised how many confessions we get," I said. "Right now there are three men downstairs who're clamoring to get their pictures in the papers. They want credit for this bombing and for all those that preceded it."

I believe it was indignation that made him flush.

"There's that, Mr. Stuart," I said softly. "And more. You know I won't always be here. Pete'll get to see you alone some time—and he gets what he's after the tough way. There's nothing I can do to prevent it unless you give me a statement."

I lit a cigarette and let Stuart think.

I could almost see his thoughts reflected in his face, the idea of someone else getting the publicity, the idea of being alone with Pete. I didn't know which fear was stronger.

Stuart rubbed his hands on his trousers and stared at the floor. Finally he sighed. "All right. I'll tell you everything."

Pete smiled tightly. "I'd especially like to hear about the last bomb."

Temper flared in Stuart's face. "I won't say a word as long as you're in the room." He pointed to me. "I'll talk only to him."

Pete looked at me and shrugged. He went out and sent the stenographer in.

When Stuart finished telling about the thirteenth explosion, I lit a fresh cigarette. "About this last one," I said. "The fourteenth. What made you use three pipes instead of one? Was it because you weren't satisfied with the effects of the other bombs?"

He glanced at me slyly. "Yes. That was it."

I let some smoke dribble through my nose. "This time you didn't use a timing device. You had the package primed to explode when it was lifted. I don't suppose you could possibly explain that, could you?"

He frowned for a moment. "I thought it would be more efficient that way."

When the stenographer returned with the typed transcript, Stuart read it carefully and signed all the copies.

And then the two of us were alone again.

I went to the window and opened it. I leaned out and breathed the fresh early evening air.

Stuart came beside me. "Suppose I said I was just

lying when I confessed. I could do that, couldn't I?"

"Yes," I said. "I suppose you could."

"Two policemen killed," he said, relishing it. "My picture should be on the front page of every newspaper in the country."

I nodded.

A note of craftiness came into his face. "Suppose I denied setting off that last explosion? Suppose I admitted all the others, but denied that? Would my picture still be in all the papers?"

I pointed down below at the street. "I'll be damned. Did you ever see anything like that?"

He leaned over the ledge and squinted.

It took me a second. Stuart screamed all the way down.

Pete took a stool at the counter and ordered a cup of coffee. "I learn something every day. I could have sworn Stuart wasn't the type to jump out of a window."

I shrugged. "Let's not cry about it. We got the confession and that's enough. He saved the state money."

Pete watched the counterman draw the coffee. "You know, Fred, all the time I was riding Stuart I had other ideas about that last explosion. I still have and I'm going to work on them—just to satisfy my curiosity."

"You're wasting your time, Pete."

"It's my time, Fred. I won't charge it to the department." He put cream in his coffee. "I'm not saying Stuart wasn't guilty. There's too much to show he was. I just got the feeling that maybe he wasn't guilty all the way down the line."

He stifled a yawn and glanced at the wall clock. "I'd like nothing better than to be in my little old apartment now with my shoes off, but I promised my folks I'd drop in for a couple of hours."

He sipped his coffee. "But I'll be snug in bed by ten tonight. You can bet on that."

It was nine o'clock when I got to Eileen's house.

There was eagerness in her voice. "How did it go?"

"We got the confession," I said. "It covered all fourteen of the explosions."

Eileen smiled slowly. "You must have been persuasive."

I tossed my hat on the couch. "Stuart jumped out of the window a little while after he signed the confession. I was the only one there when it happened."

She was pleased for a moment and then she frowned. "Maybe it's not all over yet. There's Pete. I don't think he'll be satisfied. He's a pryer. He's the type who likes to be sure of the answers."

I took her in my arms. "Don't worry about it, honey."

She met my eyes. "Oh?"

"I made another package," I said. "And let myself into Pete's apartment while he was gone. The first time his phone rings, he'll be blown to there and back."

At eleven o'clock I dialed Pete's number.

Just to make sure.

THE FORGIVING GHOST
●
C. B. Gilford

Not all ghosts, I assure you, are friendly or forgiving or translucent. Some are ghostly. Others are just plain ghastly —and give ghosts, generally, a bad name.

The murder—although Claude Crispin, the murderer, was the only one who knew that that's what it was—occurred in broad daylight, in bright sunshine. But not, of course, within view of any casual spectators.

Nobody saw it; so everybody took it for what Claude Crispin said it was, an accident.

The first that any outsiders knew of it was when Claude Crispin raced his motor boat in from the center of the lake, and started shouting and waving his arms at the nearby joy riders and water skiers. He told them something about his wife's falling in the water and his not being able to find her.

Immediately, all the boats—some with their skiers still dangling behind them—raced for the spot. They found it when they found the swimming dog. Momo was the belligerent little Pekingese which had belonged to Mrs. Crispin. Claude babbled something to the searchers about how the dog had fallen into the water, and Mrs. Crispin had jumped in to save her. Here was the dog still swimming, of course, but there was no sign of the mistress.

Somebody apparently thought that as long as they were there, they might as well save the dog. So Momo was pulled aboard one of the boats, where she showed her gratitude by shaking the water out of her fur rather indiscriminately and snarling at her rescuers. Claude looked especially askance at that part of the operation. Now that the Pekingese had provided the visible reason why Mrs. Crispin, a poor swimmer, had been in the water at all, he would really have preferred to let her drown.

Meanwhile, nearly all the other occupants of the boats had jumped into the water and were doing a lot of diving and splashing around. Claude, watching them, wrung his hands, wore an anguished expression, and generally gave the appearance of an anxious, worrying, tragic husband.

They were at it for some twenty minutes. But at the end of that time everyone was pretty well exhausted, and even the most enthusiastic divers were ready to admit that they weren't going to find Mrs. Crispin either dead or alive. When they related this fact to Claude, he burst into tears and started to shake so violently that a stranger had to climb into his boat and steer it back to shore for him.

Thereafter, it became an official matter. The sheriff was summoned and he came out to the lake with a couple of his deputies. Preparation got underway for a dragging operation. The sheriff himself, a kindly, sympathetic man, sat down with Claude and got the whole story from him.

Yes, the Crispins were city folks, Claude said, and they'd vacationed for several summers at this lake. One of their favorite pastimes had been to rent a motor boat and cruise aimlessly around. Claude was a pretty fair swimmer, though he didn't get much practice these days. Mrs. Crispin wasn't afraid of the water, but she'd been a very poor swimmer.

"Why didn't she wear a life jacket, like the rules say?" the sheriff demanded, but without too much harshness.

Claude shrugged his shoulders helplessly. "You know how women are," he answered. "My wife had a very good figure, looked fine in a bathing suit. So she was always interested in getting a tan. If she'd worn one of those jackets, it would have covered her up and she wouldn't have gotten the tan. So she just left the jacket in the bottom of the boat. Vanity, I guess you'd call it."

The sheriff nodded sagely. "And you say she jumped in on account of the dog?"

Claude let himself sound bitter. "She loved that dog as much as if it had been a kid. Took it with her everywhere. Don't ask me how the dog fell overboard, though. Usually my wife carried it around in her arms. But this time she was letting it ride up front by itself. I don't know whether it fell or jumped. The thing never seemed to have much sense. But there it was in the water suddenly, and my wife started screaming. Now, I'd have stopped the boat and jumped in after it myself, but my wife didn't wait even to ask me. The next thing I knew she was gone too. I slowed the boat down and did a U-turn, but by the time I got back to the place, my wife had already disappeared. I cut the motor and went in after her, but I never did see her. I don't know what happened. She was just gone."

The sheriff seemed to understand. "Sometimes," he said, "when a poor swimmer jumps into deep water, gets a cramp or something, he just sinks to the bottom and never does come up. I guess it was one of those cases."

And that was the verdict. Probably because the idea never once crossed his mind, the sheriff didn't even mention murder.

Though he'd gotten rid of his wife, Claude Crispin still had his wife's prized possession, Momo. Sometime later that same afternoon Momo's rescuer returned her to Claude, clean, dry, but in no better humor.

The instant the dog was brought into the one-room cottage, she began an immediate sniffing search for her mistress. When the mistress couldn't be found, she set up a mournful, yelping wail. Claude, alone now and able to vent his true feelings, aimed a kick which almost landed, and which was close enough to send the animal scurrying into a safe corner to cogitate upon what had gone wrong with the world.

"Alvina is dead," Claude explained happily and maliciously.

The dog blinked and stared.

"I guess for the moment," Claude went on, "I've got to endure you. I'm supposed to be so broken up about the accident that I've got to pretend that I'm cherishing you as my remembrance of my poor dead wife. It won't last though, I can promise you that. Your days are numbered."

Momo whined softly and seemed to be looking around for a route of escape.

Claude smiled. He felt good, very satisfied with himself. "Ought to be grateful to you though, oughtn't I, Momo? You were a very convenient gimmick. But don't think that's going to do you any good once we're away from this place. You swim too well, Momo, so I won't try a lake on you. Some little something in your hamburger maybe, and then you can fertilize my garden. As soon as we get home, Momo."

The dog cringed and lay down with her head between her paws. She'd endured unkind remarks from Claude before, and now the threat in his tone was unmistakable.

Claude lay back on the bed and closed his eyes. He had really and truly had a hard day. There'd been the strain and excitement of planning, the deed itself, and then the display of grief all afternoon. It had been rewarding, but quite wearing, too. He felt like sleep.

That was when the dog yelped. Claude had begun to drift off, and the noise woke him. Cursing, he sat up and looked toward the corner where he'd last seen Momo. The dog was still there, but not cringing any longer. Instead, Momo was standing up shakily on her hind legs, her tail wagging, her eyes shining. In fact, she was the very picture of canine ecstasy.

"Hello, Claude."

The voice was a familiar one. Alvina's voice. At first he was sure that he was either dreaming or imagining. He blinked his eyes, striving to come fully awake. But then he knew somehow that he was already awake, and he looked in the direction the dog was looking.

Alvina was standing there!

Not all wet and dripping, her hair tangled with seaweed. Not even in the bathing suit and bandana she'd last worn. This Alvina was quite dry, lipsticked and powdered, and in a gay little flowered frock he'd never even seen before. Her blue eyes were bright; her blond hair was shining; and she stood just inside the door of the cottage, although Claude was quite sure that the door had neither opened nor closed.

"Claude, I said hello, and you haven't even answered me." Then she smiled, as if she'd suddenly remembered something. "Oh, of course. You're dreadfully surprised. You hadn't expected to see me ever again."

Claude stated the incredible. "You're alive!"

"Oh no, Claude, I'm a ghost."

Instinctively he looked to Momo for confirmation. She wasn't, however, howling with fear as dogs are supposed to do in the presence of the supernatural. Instead, she was still wagging her tail, quite as if she too saw and recognized Alvina. But the strangest fact of all was that, although Momo obviously was aware of the presence of her mistress, and would normally have run to Alvina to be picked up and petted, now she seemed to realize that this visitor was not the sort who could pick up and pet even the smallest dog. In other words, Claude reflected as he tried to sort out his thoughts—Momo knew it was Alvina and yet wasn't Alvina, a friendly spirit but a spirit nevertheless.

But Claude still found this hard to believe. "Are you sure you're a real ghost? I mean . . ."

"Of course I'm a real ghost. I'd have to be, wouldn't I? I'm certainly not alive. Because you killed me. Remember, Claude?"

"It was an accident," he started to say automatically.

"Oh, for pity's sake, Claude," she interrupted him. "I should know, shouldn't I? I was there. It was murder. You pushed me in, dear, and then you held my head under water."

It wasn't till then that Claude began to wonder, not whether this was really Alvina's ghost, but more as to what Alvina's ghost was doing here. And with the curiosity came just a little tingle of fear.

"I swear to you, Alvina," he began again.

"Darling, I know it was murder, and everybody where I came from knows it was murder. Only people who've been murdered get to come back as ghosts. Or didn't you know that?"

"No, I didn't know that," he admitted.

She threw back her head and laughed. It was Alvina's old laugh, tinkling and silvery. Momo barked in happy accompaniment to it. "Maybe you wouldn't have murdered me if you'd known that, eh, Claude?"

tingling in him again. Not from incipient fear as before. From what then? He wasn't quite sure. But when someone is so generous and tolerant . . . well, it just gives one a funny feeling, that's all.

"Gee, Alvina . . ." he started to say.

But she was gone. Momo was whining piteously, and frantically running about the room from wall to wall, searching for something that was surely no longer there.

"Don't bring that dog in my apartment," Elise said. She was in purple toreador trousers today and stood with her hands on her hips barring the passage. Her dark hair waved behind her as she shook her head.

"But, angel," Claude Crispin said, "it's my wife's dog."

"I know that," Elise snapped. "But I don't like dogs, and I liked your former wife even less."

"But, angel, I couldn't leave the dog at home alone. And I've got to take care of it."

"Why?" The electricity in Elise's dark eyes crackled. "Why don't you just get rid of it?"

"I promised . . ."

"You what?"

"Well, I sort of made a secret promise after my wife died. It was the least I could do. After all, I owed her something. Try to understand, angel. Don't be cruel. We have gained quite a bit, you know. There'll be no more interference. I'm free. Just the two of us . . ."

"Three," she corrected him. "You and me and the dog."

"But we're better off than before, aren't we? We've made progress. Please let me in, angel."

She hesitated for another long moment, scorning him with her eyes. Then, abruptly, she turned and walked away, leaving the passage free for him to enter. He slipped in, bringing Momo on her leash, and closed the door behind him.

Gaining admittance didn't make Momo happy. She lay down just inside the door, watching Claude reproachfully, and making small glum sounds. But Claude ignored the dog, and followed Elise to the sofa, where he sat down close but without touching her.

"You took your sweet time coming to see me," Elise said viciously.

"Angel, I had to be discreet. I'm a widower. I'm supposed to be in mourning. I explained that to you."

"Three whole months. Did it have to be that long?"

"Maybe I was trying to be too cautious."

"You certainly were."

"Forgive me, angel." He put his arms out for her, but she squirmed away. "Won't you forgive me? I was torn between caution and passion, believe me, angel."

"And the caution won."

"All right. But it's over now. Let's make up for lost time."

"I'm afraid I'm not in the mood, Claude."

"Elise, I went through an awful lot for you. I took big chances. Seems you ought to forgive me a little caution in a case like this."

"I'll forgive you nothing. You'll have to learn you can't toy with my affections this way, Claude Crispin. You can't leave me dangling for three whole months . . ."

Elise's bitter speech was interrupted suddenly by a sharp bark from Momo. Distracted, Claude looked at the dog. He found her sitting up, eyes bright, tail wagging. And Alvina was sitting in the chair opposite them.

"So this is the woman you murdered me for, Claude," she said.

"Alvina!" he breathed.

"Did you call me Alvina?" Elise demanded.

"Darling," Alvina explained, "she can't see me. So don't make her think you've gone crazy by talking to someone she doesn't know is here. I'll be very quiet. You just go ahead with what you were doing."

"Claude, what's the matter with you?" Elise wanted to know.

"Nothing. I'm just a little upset, I guess."

"She's very pretty, Claude," Alvina commented. "Much prettier than I was. Different type, too. More exciting and romantic."

"Look, Elise," Claude said, hastily rising from the sofa, "I think I'd better go home. I don't feel well."

"Go home? You just got here, and I haven't seen you for three months."

Alvina sighed audibly. "She's the demanding sort, isn't she, Claude? I guess that makes women more desirable. I wish I could have been more that way."

"Elise." Claude was confusedly fumbling now. "Maybe some other time . . ."

"Claude, you stay here, or it's all over with us."

"But you don't want me, Elise. You're angry with me."

"You're so right. And I'm going to keep on being angry with you till you apologize."

"All right, I apologize."

"That's better."

"Am I forgiven then?"

"That will take some time. You'll have to make it up to me. I've sat around here waiting for you for three long months, and you'll have to make that up to me."

"She's very demanding, isn't she?" Alvina said. "Is that what makes her so interesting, Claude?"

"That doesn't make her interesting!" Claude shouted.

"Claude," Elise screamed, "don't shout at me! And besides, I don't know what you're talking about." Then she stood up, too, facing Claude angrily. "You don't show up for three months. Then you come here without a decent explanation and you talk gibberish."

"Angel . . ."

"Don't angel me!"

"Is it presents you want, Elise? What can I do? Just tell me. I want to take up where we left off. I went through so much. You know what I did."

"I know nothing of the sort, Claude. Don't try to implicate me."

"But you're in it as much as I am."

"Oh, no, I'm not. It was your idea, and you went through with it all alone."

"But you approved, angel. You wanted me to do it."

"Claude, if that's what you came here for, to tell me I'm just as guilty as you are, then you can leave."

Without waiting for him to accept her invitation, she turned from him and walked away, through the bedroom door, which she slammed behind her. Claude stood open-mouthed in the center of the living room, and Momo barked joyously.

"Poor girl," Alvina said, "she feels guilty. That's what's upsetting her so. I'm sure she's not like this normally. Claude, I want you to tell her that I've not only forgiven you, but I've forgiven her, too."

Claude sat down on the sofa again, heavily, wearily. "Thanks, Alvina. That's mighty decent of you."

"I'm sure the impression I just got of her is inaccurate."

"I'm afraid it isn't," Claude admitted with a frown. "She's headstrong. She's quarrelsome. She's tremendously selfish."

"But, darling, those are the very things that were wrong with me. Oh, I wish there was something I could do. The trouble is, you see, that ghosts can haunt only their murderers, and strictly speaking, Elise isn't even an accomplice. But I wish I could talk to her, and tell her everything I've learned. Because basically I think she must be a very nice girl. When are you going to get married, Claude?"

"Married?" The word startled him somehow.

"You did intend to marry her, didn't you?"

"Oh, yes, she's always insisted on it. On her own terms, of course. The trouble is that now I don't know what her terms are."

"That makes her mysterious, darling. And mystery is so attractive."

"Look here, Alvina." He rose from the sofa again, greatly disturbed. "Are you trying to encourage me?"

"Darling," she remonstrated, "you went to an awful

lot of trouble murdering me. I think you should get
your reward. And if Elise is what you want, then I
want her for you. You see, Claude, I still have your
interests at heart. And, well, I must confess . . ."

"What, Alvina?"

"A little soft spot, I guess you'd call it."

"Really? That's very generous of you."

"Oh, no, it's still selfish, I'm afraid," she answered
softly. "Sometimes, Claude, I have the very selfish
yearning for another chance. If I could just get another body or something and come back to you, I'm
sure I could do a much better job of making you happy
than I did before."

He felt terribly embarrassed, felt he ought to do
something or say something, but he didn't know what.
Poor Alvina . . . but he didn't want to say that.

She was gazing tenderly up at him. "Oh, darn," she
said, "I'm afraid I'm going to cry. Good-by, darling.
Good luck, too."

Then once again, and as suddenly as before, she was
gone. Momo began to whine pitifully and lonesomely.
And Claude Crispin felt pretty much the same.

Alvina was home waiting for him, when he returned
from one of his many unsatisfactory visits to Elise's
apartment. He'd left Elise in a rage, but here was
Alvina placidly curled up in her favorite old chair and
giving him a smile of welcome. He felt almost glad to
see her. It had been over two weeks.

"How's Elise, darling? I didn't want to be a busy-
body and poke my nose in there, but I am concerned."

"Well, she still can't stand the dog."

Momo barked in confirmation.

"And even though I've gone to see her every day
since, she still hasn't forgiven me for staying away for
three months."

"Darling, she's just as unreasonable as I was, isn't
she? That's too bad. I wish you could find someone
more suitable. You know, it's too bad you can't murder
Elise. Then she'd learn her lesson like I have." She

paused, crestfallen. "Oh, darn, that wouldn't work
either, would it? The dead and the living can't get
together very well."

He crossed the room and sat down on the hassock
in front of Alvina's chair. Momo followed him and
hopped up onto his lap. He petted the dog.

"You know something, Alvina?" he said. "If murder
were the proper way of managing a woman, I wouldn't
have to bother with Elise at all. Because I would have
already found the perfect woman in you."

"That's sweet of you, Claude." Her smile was
radiant. "Isn't it too bad that things have to work out
this way? That we couldn't reach our perfect understanding until it was too late? Oh, I wish there were
some way. I've asked about borrowing another body
somewhere, but they say it can't be done."

"Yes, I wish there were some way too, Alvina," he
said.

Momo agreed, barking enthusiastically.

"You know," Claude said suddenly, "I've just had a
happy thought."

"What, darling?" Alvina's ghostly eyes lighted with
hope.

"Well, though you can't join me, I could join you."

"Claude!"

"Yes, it's rather drastic, I know."

"What about Elise?"

"I don't think she'd mourn more than a day or two."

"But there are other things to consider, too. You're
still a young man, Claude. You have so much to live
for."

"What? Just tell me what? I lost everything when I
lost you."

"Claude, darling. Oh, I wish I could kiss you."

"Can't you? Have you really tried?"

"I know I can't. I've been told. There's a barrier
between us."

"Then if you can't cross it, I certainly shall!"

"Oh, Claude, do you mean it?"

"Of course I mean it. There must be something appropriate in the medicine cabinet. I'd go up to that lake again and use it, darling, for sentimental reasons. But that would mean an awful delay. And I'm impatient to be with you again."

"Claude, dearest . . ."

He stood up. "I'll go see what's in the medicine cabinet right now."

He rushed off, but her voice stopped him. He turned back.

"Claude, get something for Momo too, will you?"

"Certainly. I don't want to be separated from Momo, darling, any more than I want to be separated from you."

When they met on the other side, Momo jumped down from Claude's arms and went running to Alvina. She leaped into her mistress's arms and cuddled there, giving off small, ecstatic squeaks.

"That's a lucky dog," Claude said. "When do I get my welcome kiss?"

But for the moment, Alvina and Momo were lost in the contemplation of each other, hugging and squealing and kissing. Claude was patient. He spent the time glancing around at his new surroundings.

"I never thought to ask you, darling," he said, "but what kind of place is this anyway?"

What prompted the question was the fact that a couple of strangers were approaching. They were wearing a sort of uniform, like doormen, or perhaps guards. The uniforms had a red and black motif.

"Claude Crispin?" one of them asked.

"That's me," Claude said.

"Come with us, Mr. Crispin."

"I'm afraid you don't understand," Claude objected. "This is my wife here. I intend to stay with her."

It was Alvina who explained the difficulty. "Claude darling, Momo and I really would like to have you stay with us. But there are those old rules, darling.

You're a murderer, you know. You'll have to go to the other place."

And Alvina and Momo went back to hugging and kissing.

THE CHILDREN OF NOAH

•

Richard Matheson

While your corpulent correspondent is among the first to admit he would be willing to shed a few pounds, he is shudderingly averse to losing them as did Mr. Ketchum in the sleeping town of Zachry, pop. 67!

It was just past three a.m. when Mr. Ketchum drove past the sign that read *Zachry: pop. 67*. He groaned. Another in an endless string of Maine seaside towns. He closed his eyes hard a second, then opened them again and pressed down on the accelerator. The Ford surged forward under him. Maybe, with luck, he'd reach a decent motel soon. It certainly wasn't likely there'd be one in Zachry: pop. 67.

Mr. Ketchum shifted his heavy frame on the seat and stretched his legs. It had been a sour vacation. Motoring through New England's historic beauty, communing with nature and nostalgia was what he'd planned. Instead, he'd found only boredom, exhaustion and over-expense.

Mr. Ketchum was not pleased.

The town seemed fast asleep as he drove along its Main Street. The only sound was that of the car's engine, the only sight that of his raised headbeams splaying out ahead lighting up another sign. *Speed 15 Limit.*

"Sure, sure," he muttered disgustedly, pressing down on the gas pedal. Three o'clock in the morning and the town fathers expected him to creep through their lousy hamlet. Mr. Ketchum watched the dark buildings rush past his window. Good-by Zachry, he thought. Farewell, pop. 67.

Then the other car appeared in the rear-view mirror. About half a block behind, a sedan with a turning red spotlight on its roof. He knew what kind of car it was. His foot curled off the accelerator and he felt his heartbeat quicken. Was it possible they hadn't noticed how fast he was going?

The question was answered as the dark car pulled up to the Ford and a man in a big hat leaned out of the front window. "Pull over!" he barked.

Swallowing dryly, Mr. Ketchum eased his car over to the curb. He drew up the emergency brake, turned the ignition key and the car was still. The police car nosed in toward the curb and stopped! The right front door opened.

The glare of Mr. Ketchum's headlights outlined the dark figure approaching. He felt around quickly with his left foot and stamped down on the knob, dimming the lights. He swallowed again. Damned nuisance this. Three a.m. in the middle of nowhere and a hick policeman picks him up for speeding. Mr. Ketchum gritted his teeth and waited.

The man in the dark uniform and wide-brimmed hat leaned over into the window. "License."

Mr. Ketchum slid a shaking hand into his inside pocket and drew out his billfold. He felt around for his license. He handed it over, noticed how expressionless the face of the policeman was. He sat there quietly while the policeman held a flashlight beam on the license.

"From New Jersey."

"Yes, that . . . that's right," said Mr. Ketchum.

The policeman kept staring at the license. Mr. Ketchum stirred restlessly on the seat and pressed his lips together. "It hasn't expired," he finally said.

He saw the dark head of the policeman lift. Then, he gasped as the narrow circle of flashlight blinded him. He twisted his head away.

The light was gone. Mr. Ketchum blinked his watering eyes.

"Don't they read traffic signs in New Jersey?" the policeman asked.

"Why, I . . . You mean the sign that said p-population 67?"

"No, I don't mean that sign," said the policeman.

"Oh." Mr. Ketchum cleared his throat. "Well, that's the only sign I saw," he said.

"You're a bad driver then."

"Well, I'm—"

"The sign said the speed limit is fifteen miles an hour. You were doing fifty."

"Oh. I . . . I'm afraid I didn't see it."

"The speed limit is fifteen miles an hour whether you see it or not."

"Well . . . at—at *this* hour of the morning?"

"Did you see a timetable on the sign?" the policeman asked.

"No, of course not. I mean, I didn't see the sign at all."

"*Didn't* you?"

Mr. Ketchum felt hair prickling along the nape of his neck. "Now, now see here," he began faintly, then stopped and stared at the policeman. "May I have my license back?" he finally asked when the policeman didn't speak.

The policeman said nothing. He stood on the street, motionless.

"May I—?" Mr. Ketchum started.

"Follow our car," said the officer abruptly and strode away.

Mr. Ketchum stared at him, dumbfounded. *Hey wait!* he almost yelled. The officer hadn't even given him back his license. Mr. Ketchum felt a sudden coldness in his stomach.

"What *is* this?" he muttered as he watched the policeman getting back into his car. The police car pulled away from the curb, its roof light spinning again.

Mr. Ketchum followed.

"This is ridiculous," he said aloud. They had no right to do this. Was this the Middle Ages? His thick lips pressed into a jaded mouth line as he followed the police car along Main Street.

Two blocks up, the police car turned. Mr. Ketchum saw his headlights splash across a glass store front. *Hand's Groceries* read the weather-worn letters.

There were no lamps on the street. It was like driving along an inky passage. Ahead were only the three red eyes of the police car's rear lights and spotlight; behind only impenetrable blackness. The end of a perfect day, thought Mr. Ketchum; picked up for speeding in Zachry, Maine. He shook his head and groaned. Why hadn't he just spent his vacation in Newark; slept late, gone to shows, eaten, watched television?

The police car turned right at the next corner, then, a block up, turned left again and stopped. Mr. Ketchum pulled up behind it as its lights went out. There was no sense in this. This was only cheap melodrama. They could just as easily have fined him on Main Street. It was the rustic mind. Debasing someone from a big city gave them a sense of vengeful eminence.

Mr. Ketchum waited. Well, he wasn't going to haggle. He'd pay his fine without a word and depart. He jerked up the hand brake. Suddenly he frowned, realizing that they could fine him anything they wanted. They could charge him $500 if they chose! The heavy man had heard stories about small town police, about the absolute authority they wielded. He cleared his throat viscidly. Well, this is absurd, he thought. What foolish imagination.

The policeman opened the door.

"Get out," he said.

There was no light in the street or in any building. Mr. Ketchum swallowed. All he could really see was the black figure of the policeman.

"Is this the—station?" he asked.

"Turn out your lights and come on," said the policeman.

Mr. Ketchum pushed in the chrome knob and got out. The policeman slammed the door. It made a loud, echoing noise; as if they were inside an unlighted warehouse instead of on a street. Mr. Ketchum glanced upward. The illusion was complete. There were neither stars nor moon. Sky and earth ran together blackly.

The policeman's hard fingers clamped on his arm. Mr. Ketchum lost balance a moment, then caught himself and fell into a quick stride beside the tall figure of the policeman.

"Dark here," he heard himself saying in a voice not entirely familiar.

The policeman said nothing. The other policeman fell into step on the other side of him. Mr. Ketchum told himself: These damned hicktown nazis were doing their best to intimidate him. Well, they wouldn't succeed.

Mr. Ketchum sucked in a breath of the damp, sea-smelling air and let it shudder out. A crumby town of 67 and they have two policemen patrolling the streets at three in the morning. Ridiculous.

He almost tripped over the step when they reached it. The policeman on his left side caught him under the elbow.

"Thank you," Mr. Ketchum muttered automatically. The policeman didn't reply. Mr. Ketchum licked his lips. Cordial oaf, he thought and managed a fleeting smile to himself. There, that was better. No point in letting this get to him.

He blinked as the door was pulled open and, despite himself, felt a sigh of relief filtering through him. It was a police station all right. There was the podiumed desk, there a bulletin board, there a black, pot-bellied stove unlit, there a scarred bench against the wall, there a door, there the floor covered with a cracked and grimy linoleum that had once been green.

"Sit down and wait," said the first policeman.

Mr. Ketchum looked at his lean, angled face, his swarthy skin. There was no division in his eyes between iris and pupil. It was all one darkness. He wore a dark uniform that fitted him loosely.

Mr. Ketchum didn't get to see the other policeman because both of them went into the next room. He stood watching the closed door a moment. Should he leave, drive away? No, they'd have his address on the license. Then again, they might actually want him to attempt to leave. You never knew what sort of warped minds these small-town police had. They might even— shoot him down if he tried to leave.

Mr. Ketchum sat heavily on the bench. No, he was letting imagination run amuck. This was merely a small town on the Maine seacoast and they were merely going to fine him for—

Well, why didn't they fine him then? What was all this play-acting? The heavy man pressed his lips together. Very well, let them play it the way they chose. This was better than driving anyway. He closed his eyes. I'll just rest them, he thought.

After a few moments he opened them again. It was damned quiet. He looked around the dimly lit room. The walls were dirty and bare except for a clock and one picture that hung behind the desk. It was a painting—more likely a reproduction—of a bearded man. The hat he wore was a seaman's hat. Probably one of Zachry's ancient mariners. No; probably not even that. Probably a Sears Roebuck print: *Bearded Seaman*.

Mr. Ketchum grunted to himself. Why a police station should have such a print was beyond him. Except, of course, that Zachry was on the Atlantic. Probably its main source of income was from fishing. Anyway, what did it matter? Mr. Ketchum lowered his gaze.

In the next room he could hear the muffled voices

of the two policemen. He tried to hear what they were saying but he couldn't. He glared at the closed door. Come *on*, will you? he thought. He looked at the clock again. Three twenty-two. He checked it with his wrist watch. About right. The door opened and the two policemen came out.

One of them left. The remaining one—the one who had taken Mr. Ketchum's license—went over to the raised desk and switched on the gooseneck lamp over it, drew a big ledger out of the top drawer and started writing in it. *At last,* thought Mr. Ketchum.

A minute passed.

"I—" Mr. Ketchum cleared his throat. "I beg your—"

His voice broke off as the cold gaze of the policeman raised from the ledger and fixed on him.

"Are you . . . That is, am I to be—fined now?"

The policeman looked back at the ledger. "Wait," he said.

"But it's past three in the mor—" Mr. Ketchum caught himself. He tried to look coldly belligerent. "Very well," he said, curtly. "Would you kindly tell me how long it will be?"

The policeman kept writing in the ledger. Mr. Ketchum sat there stiffly, looking at him. *Insufferable,* he thought. This was the last damned time he'd ever go within a hundred miles of this damned New England.

The policeman looked up. "Married?" he asked.

Mr. Ketchum stared at him.

"Are you married?"

"No, I—it's on the license," Mr. Ketchum blurted. He felt a tremor of pleasure at his retort and, at the same time, an impaling of strange dread at talking back to the man.

"Family in Jersey?" asked the policeman.

"Yes. I mean no. Just a sister in Wiscons—"

Mr. Ketchum didn't finish. He watched the policeman write it down. He wished he could rid himself of this queasy distress.

"Employed?" asked the policeman.

Mr. Ketchum swallowed. "Well," he said, "I—I have no one particular em—"

"Unemployed," said the policeman.

"Not at all; not at *all*," said Mr. Ketchum stiffly. "I'm a—a free-lance salesman. I purchase stocks and lots from . . ." His voice faded as the policeman looked at him. Mr. Ketchum swallowed three times before the lump stayed down. He realized that he was sitting on the very edge of the bench as if poised to spring to the defense of his life. He forced himself to settle back. He drew in a deep breath. Relax, he told himself. Deliberately, he closed his eyes. There. He'd catch a few winks. May as well make the best of this, he thought.

The room was still except for the tinny, resonant ticking of the clock. Mr. Ketchum felt his heart pulsing with slow, dragging beats. He shifted his heavy frame uncomfortably on the hard bench. *Ridiculous,* he thought.

Mr. Ketchum opened his eyes and frowned. That damned picture. You could almost imagine that bearded seaman was looking at you.

Almost . . .

"Uh!"

Mr. Ketchum's mouth snapped shut, his eyes jerked open, irises flaring. He started forward on the bench, then shrank back.

A swarthy-faced man was bent over him, hand on Mr. Ketchum's shoulder.

"Yes?" Mr. Ketchum asked, heart jolting.

The man smiled.

"Chief Shipley," he said. "Would you come into my office?"

"Oh," said Mr. Ketchum, "Yes. Yes."

He straightened up, grimacing at the stiffness in his back muscles. The man stepped back and Mr. Ketchum pushed up with a grunt, his eyes moving automatically to the wall clock. It was a few minutes past four.

"Look," he said, not yet awake enough to feel intimidated, "Why can't I pay my fine and leave?"

Shipley's smile was without warmth.

"We run things a little different here in Zachry," he said.

They entered a small, musty-smelling office.

"Sit down," said the chief, walking around the desk while Mr. Ketchum settled into a straight-backed chair that creaked.

"I don't understand why I can't pay my fine and leave."

"In due course," said Shipley.

"But—" Mr. Ketchum didn't finish. Shipley's smile gave the impression of being no more than a diplomatically veiled warning. Gritting his teeth, the heavy man cleared his throat and waited while the chief looked down at a sheet of paper on his desk. He noticed how poorly Shipley's suit fitted. Yokels, the heavy man thought, don't even know how to dress.

"I see you're not married," Shipley said.

Mr. Ketchum said nothing. Give them a taste of their own no-talk medicine he decided.

"Have you friends in Maine?" Shipley asked.

"Why?"

"Just routine questions, Mr. Ketchum," said the chief. "Your only family is a sister in Wisconsin?"

Mr. Ketchum looked at him without speaking. What had all this to do with a traffic violation?

"Sir?" asked Shipley.

"I already told you; that is, I told the officer. I don't see—"

"Here on business?"

Mr. Ketchum's mouth opened soundlessly.

"Why are you asking me all these questions?" he asked. *Stop shaking!* he ordered himself furiously.

"Routine. Are you here on business?"

"I'm on my vacation. And I don't see this at all! I've been patient up to now but, *blast it,* I demand to be fined and released!"

"I'm afraid that's impossible," said the chief.

Mr. Ketchum's mouth fell open. It was like waking up from a nightmare and discovering that the dream was still going on. "I—I don't understand," he said.

"You'll have to appear before the judge."

"But that's ridiculous."

"Is it?"

"Yes, it is. I'm a citizen of the United States. I demand my rights."

Chief Shipley's smile faded.

"You limited those rights when you broke our law," he said. "Now you have to pay for it as we declare."

Mr. Ketchum stared blankly at the man. He realized that he was completely in their hands. They could fine him anything they pleased or put him in jail indefinitely. All these questions he'd been asked; he didn't know why they'd asked them but he knew that his answers revealed him as almost rootless, with no one who cared if he lived or—

The room seemed to totter. Sweat broke out on his body.

"You can't *do* this," he said; but it was not an argument.

"You'll have to spend the night in jail," said the chief. "In the morning you'll see the judge."

"But this is ridiculous!" Mr. Ketchum burst out. "*Ridiculous!*"

He caught himself. "I'm entitled to one phone call," he said, quickly, "I can make a telephone call. It's my legal right."

"It would be," said Shipley, "if there was any telephone service in Zachry."

When they took him to his cell, Mr. Ketchum saw a painting in the hall. It was of the same bearded seaman. Mr. Ketchum didn't notice if the eyes followed him or not.

Mr. Ketchum stirred. A look of confusion lined his sleep-numbed face. There was a clanking sound behind him; he reared up on his elbow.

A policeman came into the cell and set down a covered tray.

"Breakfast," he said. He was older than the other policemen, even older than Shipley. His hair was iron-gray, his cleanly shaven face seamed around the mouth and eyes. His uniform fitted him badly.

As the policeman started relocking the door, Mr. Ketchum asked, "When do I see the judge?"

The policeman looked at him a moment. "Don't know," he said and turned away.

"Wait!" Mr. Ketchum called out.

The receding footsteps of the policeman sounded hollowly on the cement floor. Mr. Ketchum kept staring at the spot where the policeman had been. Veils of sleep peeled from his mind.

He sat up, rubbed deadened fingers over his eyes and held up his wrist. Seven minutes past nine. The heavy man grimaced. By God, they were going to hear about this! His nostrils twitched. He sniffed, started to reach for the tray; then pulled back his hand.

"No," he muttered. He wouldn't eat their damned food. He sat there stiffly, doubled at the waist, glaring at his sock-covered feet.

His stomach grumbled unco-operatively.

"Well," he muttered after a minute. Swallowing, he reached over and lifted off the tray cover.

He couldn't check the *oh* of surprise that passed his lips.

The three eggs were fried in butter, bright yellow eyes focused straight on the ceiling, ringed about with long, crisp lengths of meaty, corrugated bacon. Next to them was a platter of four, book-thick slices of toast spread with creamy butter swirls, a paper cup of jelly leaning on them. There was a tall glass of frothy orange juice, a dish of strawberries bleeding in alabaster cream. Finally, a tall pot from which wavered the pungent and unmistakable fragrance of freshly brewed coffee.

Mr. Ketchum picked up the glass of orange juice. He

THE CHILDREN OF NOAH

took a few drops in his mouth and rolled them ex-
perimentally over his tongue. The citric acid tingled
deliciously on his warm tongue. He swallowed. If it
was poisoned it was by a master's hand. Saliva tided in
his mouth. He suddenly remembered that, just before
he was picked up, he'd been meaning to stop at a café
for food.

While he ate, warily but decidedly, Mr. Ketchum
tried to figure out the motivation behind this mag-
nificent breakfast.

It was the rural mind again. They regretted their
blunder. It seemed a flimsy notion, but there it was.
The food was superb. One thing you had to say for
these New Englanders; they could cook like a son-of-a-
gun. Breakfast for Mr. Ketchum was usually a sweet
roll heated, and coffee. Since he was a boy in his
father's house he hadn't eaten a breakfast like this.

He was just putting down his third cup of well-
creamed coffee when footsteps sounded in the hall.
Mr. Ketchum smiled. Good timing, he thought. He
stood.

Chief Shipley stopped outside the cell. "Had your
breakfast?"

Mr. Ketchum nodded. If the chief expected thanks
he was in for a sad surprise. Mr. Ketchum picked up
his coat.

The chief didn't move.

"*Well . . . ?*" said Mr. Ketchum after a few minutes.
He tried to put it coldly and authoritatively. It came
out somewhat less.

Chief Shipley looked at him expressionlessly. Mr.
Ketchum felt his breath faltering.

"May I inquire—?" he began.

"Judge isn't in yet," said Shipley.

"But . . ." Mr. Ketchum didn't know what to say.

"Just came in to tell you," said Shipley. He turned
and was gone.

Mr. Ketchum was furious. He looked down at the
remains of his breakfast as if they contained the an-

swer to this situation. He drummed a fist against his thigh. *Insufferable!* What were they trying to do—intimidate him? Well, by God—

—they were succeeding.

Mr. Ketchum walked over to the bars. He looked up and down the empty hallway. There was a cold knot inside him. The food seemed to have turned to dry lead in his stomach. He banged the heel of his right hand once against the cold bar. By God! *By God!*

It was two o'clock in the afternoon when Chief Shipley and the old policeman came to the cell door. Wordlessly the policeman opened it. Mr. Ketchum stepped into the hallway and waited again, putting on his coat while the door was relocked.

He walked in short, inflexible strides between the two men, not even glancing at the picture on the wall. "Where are we going?" he asked.

"Judge is sick," said Shipley. "We're taking you out to his house to pay your fine."

Mr. Ketchum sucked in his breath. He wouldn't argue with them; he just wouldn't. "All right," he said, "if that's the way you have to do it."

"Only way to do it," said the chief, looking ahead, his face an expressionless mask.

Mr. Ketchum pressed down the corners of a slim smile. This was better. It was almost over now. He'd pay his fine and clear out.

It was foggy outside. Sea mist rolled across the street like driven smoke. Mr. Ketchum pulled on his hat and shuddered. The damp air seemed to filter through his flesh and dew itself around his bones. Nasty day, he thought. He moved down the steps, eyes searching for his Ford.

The old policeman opened the back door of the police car and Shipley gestured toward the inside.

"What about *my* car?" Mr. Ketchum asked.

"We'll come back here after you see the judge," said Shipley.

"Oh. I . . ."

Mr. Ketchum hesitated. Then he bent over and squeezed into the car, dropping down on the back seat. He shivered as the cold of the leather pierced trouser wool. He edged over as the chief got in.

The policeman slammed the door shut. Again that hollow sound, like the slamming of a coffin lid in a crypt. Mr. Ketchum grimaced at the simile.

The policeman got into the car and Mr. Ketchum heard the motor cough into liquid life. He sat there breathing slowly and deeply while the policeman out-choked warmth into the engine. He looked out the window at his left.

The fog was *just* like smoke. They might have been parked in a burning garage. Except for that bone-gripping dampness. Mr. Ketchum cleared his throat. He heard the chief shift on the seat beside him.

"Cold," Mr. Ketchum said, automatically.

The chief said nothing.

Mr. Ketchum pressed back as the car pulled away from the curb, V-turned and started slowly down the fog-veiled street. He listened to the crisp sibilance of tires on wet paving, the rhythmic swish of the wipers as they cleared off circle segments on the misted windshield.

After a moment he looked at his watch. Almost three. Half a day shot in this blasted Zachry.

He looked out through the window again as the town ghosted past. He thought he saw brick buildings along the curb but he wasn't sure. He looked down at his white hands, then glanced over at Shipley. The chief was sitting stiffly upright on the seat, staring straight ahead. Mr. Ketchum swallowed. The air seemed stagnant in his lungs.

On Main Street the fog seemed thinner. Probably the sea breezes, Mr. Ketchum thought. He looked up and down the street. All the stores and offices looked closed. He glanced at the other side of the street. Same thing.

"Where is everybody?" he asked.

"What?"

"I said where *is* everybody?"

"Home," the chief said.

"But it's Wednesday," said Mr. Ketchum. "Aren't your—stores open?"

"Bad day," said Shipley. "Not worth it."

Mr. Ketchum glanced at the sallow-faced chief, then withdrew his look hastily. He felt cold premonition spidering in his stomach again. What in God's name *is* this? he asked himself. It had been bad enough in the cell. Here, tracking through this sea of mist, it was altogether worse.

"That's right," he heard his nerve-sparked voice saying. "There are only sixty-seven people, aren't there?"

The chief said nothing.

"How . . . h-how old is Zachry?"

In the silence he heard the chief's finger joints crackle dryly.

"Hundred fifty years," said Shipley.

"That old," said Mr. Ketchum. He swallowed with effort. His throat hurt a little. Come *on*, he told himself. *Relax*.

"How come it's named Zachry?" The words spilled out, uncontrolled.

"Noah Zachry founded it," said the chief.

"Oh. Oh. I see. I guess that picture in the station . . . ?

"That's right," said Shipley.

Mr. Ketchum blinked. So that was Noah Zachry, founder of this town they were driving through—

—*block after block after block*. There was a cold, heavy sinking in Mr. Ketchum's stomach as the idea came to him.

In a town so big, why were there only 67 people?

He opened his mouth to ask it, then couldn't. The answer might be wrong.

"Why are there only—?" The words came out anyway before he could stop them. His body jolted at the shock of hearing them.

"What?"

"Nothing, nothing. That is—" Mr. Ketchum drew in a shaking breath. No help for it. He had to know.

"How come there are only sixty-seven?"

"They go away," said Shipley.

Mr. Ketchum blinked. The answer came as such an anti-climax. His brow furrowed. Well, what else? he asked himself defensively. Remote, antiquated, Zachry would have little attraction for its younger generations. Mass gravitation to more interesting places would be inevitable.

The heavy man settled back against the seat. Of course. Think how much *I* want to leave the dump, he thought, and I don't even live here.

His gaze slid forward through the windshield, caught by something. A banner hanging across the street. BARBECUE TONIGHT. Celebration, he thought. They probably went berserk every fortnight and had themselves a rip-roaring taffy pull or fishnet-mending orgy.

"Who was Zachry anyway?" he asked. The silence was getting to him again.

"Sea captain," said the chief.

"Oh?"

"Whaled in the South Seas," said Shipley.

Abruptly, Main Street ended. The police car veered left onto a dirt road. Out the window Mr. Ketchum watched shadowy bushes glide by. There was only the sound of the engine laboring in second and of gravelly dirt spitting out from under the tires. Where does the judge live, on a mountain top? He shifted his weight and grunted.

The fog began thinning now. Mr. Ketchum could see grass and trees, all with a grayish cast to them. The car turned and faced the ocean. Mr. Ketchum looked down at the opaque carpet of fog below. The car kept turning. It faced the crest of the hill again.

Mr. Ketchum coughed softly. "Is . . . uh, that the judge's house up there?" he asked.

"Yes," the chief answered.

"High," said Mr. Ketchum.

The car kept turning on the narrow, dirt road, now facing the ocean, now Zachry, now the bleak, hill-topping house. It was a grayish-white house, three stories high, at each end of it the crag of an attic tower. It looked as old as Zachry itself, thought Mr. Ketchum. The car turned. He was facing the fog-crusted ocean again.

Mr. Ketchum looked down at his hands. Was it a deception of the light or were they really shaking? He tried to swallow but there was no moisture in his throat and he coughed instead, rattlingly. This is so *stupid,* he thought; there's no reason in the world for this. He saw his hands clench together. For some reason he thought of the banner across Main Street.

The car was moving up the final rise toward the house now. Mr. Ketchum felt his breaths shortening. *I don't want to go,* he heard someone saying in his mind. He felt a sudden urge to shove out the door and run. Muscles tensed emphatically.

He closed his eyes. For God's sake, *stop* it! he yelled at himself. There was nothing wrong about this but his distorted interpretation of it. These were modern times. Things had explanations and people had reasons. Zachry's people had a reason too; a narrow distrust of city dwellers. This was their socially acceptable revenge. That made sense. After all—

The car stopped. The chief pushed open the door on his side and got out. The policeman reached back and opened the other door for Mr. Ketchum. The heavy man found one of his legs and foot to be numb. He had to clutch at the top of the door for support. He stamped the foot on the ground.

"Went to sleep," he said.

Neither of the men answered. Mr. Ketchum glanced at the house; he squinted. Had he seen a dark green drape slip back into place? He winced and made a startled noise as his arm was touched and the chief gestured toward the house. The three men started toward it.

"I, uh ... don't have much cash on me, I'm afraid," he said. "I hope a traveler's check will be all right."

"Yes," said the chief.

They went up the porch steps, stopped in front of the door. The policeman turned a big, brass key-head and Mr. Ketchum heard a bell ring tinnily inside. He stood looking through the door curtains. Inside, he could make out the skeletal form of a hat rack. He shifted weight and the boards creaked under him. The policeman rang the bell again.

"Maybe he's—too sick," Mr. Ketchum suggested faintly.

Neither of the men looked at him. Mr. Ketchum felt his muscles tensing. He glanced back over his shoulder. Could they catch him if he ran for it?

He looked back disgustedly. You pay your fine and you leave, he explained patiently to himself. That's all; you pay your fine and you leave.

Inside the house there was dark movement. Mr. Ketchum looked up, startled in spite of himself. A tall woman was approaching the door.

The door opened. The woman was thin, wearing an ankle-length black dress with a white oval pin at her throat. Her face was swarthy, seamed with thread-like lines. Mr. Ketchum slipped off his hat automatically.

"Come in," said the woman.

Mr. Ketchum stepped into the hall.

"You can leave your hat there," said the woman pointing toward the hat rack that looked like a tree ravaged by flame. Mr. Ketchum dropped his hat over one of the dark pegs. As he did, his eye was caught by a large painting near the foot of the staircase. He started to speak but the woman said, "This way."

They started down the hall. Mr. Ketchum stared at the painting as they passed it.

"Who's that woman," he asked, "standing next to Zachry?"

"His wife," said the chief.

"But she—"

Mr. Ketchum's voice broke off suddenly as he heard

a whimper rising in his throat. Shocked, he drowned it out with a sudden clearing of the throat. He felt ashamed of himself. Still . . . Zachry's wife?

The woman opened a door. "Wait in here," she said.

The heavy man walked in. He turned to say something to the chief. Just in time to see the door shut.

"Say, uh . . ." He walked to the door and put his hand on the knob. It didn't turn.

He frowned. He ignored the pile-driver beats of his heart. "Hey, what's going on?" Cheerily bluff, his voice echoed off the walls. Mr. Ketchum turned and looked around. The room was empty. It was a square, empty room.

He turned back to the door, lips moving as he sought the proper words.

"Okay," he said, abruptly, "It's very—" He twisted the knob sharply. "Okay it's a very funny joke." By God, he was mad. "I've taken all I'm—"

He whirled at the sound, teeth bared.

There was nothing. The room was still empty. He looked around dizzily. What was that sound? A dull sound, like water rushing.

"Hey," he said automatically. He turned to the door. "Hey!" he yelled, "cut it out! Who do you think you are anyway?"

He turned on weakening legs. The sound was louder. Mr. Ketchum ran a hand over his brow. It was covered with sweat. It was warm in there.

"Okay, okay," he said, "It's a fine joke but—"

Before he could go on, his voice had corkscrewed into an awful, wracking sob. Mr. Ketchum staggered a little. He stared at the room. He whirled and fell back against the door. His outflung hand touched the wall and jerked away.

It was hot.

"*Huh?*" he asked, incredulously.

This was impossible. This was a joke. This was their deranged idea of a little joke. It was a game they played. Scare The City Slicker was the name of the game.

"Okay!" he yelled. *"Okay! It's funny, it's very funny! Now let me out of here or there's going to be trouble!"*

He pounded at the door. Suddenly he kicked it. The room was getting hotter. It was almost as hot as an—

Mr. Ketchum was petrified. His mouth sagged open. The questions they'd asked him. The loose way the clothes fit everyone he'd met. The rich food they'd given him to eat. The empty streets. The savage-like swarthy coloring of the men, of the woman. The way they'd all looked at him. And the woman in the painting, Noah Zachry's wife—*a native woman with her teeth filed to a point.* The banner:

BARBECUE TONIGHT.

Mr. Ketchum screamed. He kicked and pounded on the door. He threw his heavy body against it. He shrieked at the people outside.

"Let me out! *Let me out!* LET . . . ME . . . OUT!!"

The worst part about it was, he just couldn't believe it was really happening.

AN ATTRACTIVE FAMILY

●

Robert Arthur

Because I have a beret, I feel that perhaps I should get a sports car—one my size, naturally. I could, of course, save myself all the trouble by getting rid of my beret. Getting rid of something—a perfectly good individual, in this case—is the primary problem of our little tale.

The Farringtons were a rather attractive family, if you don't mind overlooking a few bad habits—such as committing murder. And it is probably not fair to speak of murder as being a habit with them. After all, they had only committed it twice.

However, they were well on the way to making it a habit. Even now they were planning to make the figure two into a three. But they were not looking sinister, or whispering to each other. They were discussing the subject frankly and openly as they sat in the parlor of East View, the summer home they had rented on the Massachusetts coast at a spot where the rather steep, rocky cliffs fell away to the brawling waves of the Atlantic.

They were even drinking tea as they talked. At least, Marion Farrington was—tea with lemon. Bert Farrington, her uncle, was also drinking tea, but his was laced with Jamaican rum. Dick, her younger brother, was drinking Scotch and soda, which looks like tea but isn't.

"It's really a pity the child must have her birthday in two weeks," Marion Farrington said. "It forces us to act."

Dick, who was thirty-two, well built, tanned and handsome, obviously accustomed to living well and spending money freely, glanced out the window. Jinny Wells was visible across the open field, just at the edge of the woods. She seemed, from a distance, almost the child that Marion had called her, although Jinny was almost twenty-one—a twenty-one that, based upon past performance charts of the Farrington family, she was not likely to reach. At the moment Jinny seemed to be searching the ground for small objects which she popped into a basket on her arm.

"She's quite a pretty thing," Dick commented. "And I do think she admires me." He straightened his tie. "If we could only put it off for a little longer—"

"Ah ha!" Bert Farrington, who was plump and red-featured, twenty years older than his nephew, wagged a finger at him. "Mustn't get sentimental, Dick. The future of the Family is at stake." He said it that way, with a capital F, as if he were speaking of the British Empire or the State of Texas.

"Bert's right." Marion sat erect, a full-bodied forty-two, attractive if you overlooked the set of her chin and the determination that glinted in her pale blue eyes. "On Jinny's twenty-first birthday we have to make an accounting of the estate, under the terms of Alice's will. We might manage to postpone it for a few weeks, but eventually her lawyer would force the issue. You know what the result would be."

Dick drained his glass in a nervous sort of way while he thought of all the money Alice had left him that was now gone, including half of what she had left Jinny. "Money certainly doesn't go far these days," he said.

"The inflation," Bert said, in a philosophical manner. After all, if anyone went to jail it would be Dick, as trustee of Jinny's estate, rather than Bert. Just the same, Bert, having sponged off his niece and nephew for fifteen years now, and hoping to continue to do so indefinitely, was willing to go to any reasonable lengths to help keep Dick out of jail. After all, Dick would soon have to find another rich wife to marry, and that was seldom accomplished in jail.

Dick refilled his Scotch and soda. "I could take her out for a sail in the bay and capsize."

Bert frowned. "I think not," he said. "After all, Alice went by drowning."

"And Harry too, when we capsized fifteen years ago," Marion said. "Three drownings would seem entirely too many to be coincidental."

Harry had been Marion's first, and only, husband. A wealthy apple grower in Oregon, whom she had married at a time when the family finances were at rock bottom, he had survived only seven weeks of matrimonial bliss. The waters in Puget Sound can also be quite tricky, and when the sailboat overturned Marion had been too concerned with helping her younger brother Dick (who was a splendid swimmer) to give her non-swimming husband a hand. Soon he was out of reach. He had been only forty feet away, but unhappily the forty feet had all been straight down.

Alice, Dick's only wife—to date—had drowned only two years before, while swimming off a lonely beach at Acapulco, Mexico. Alice had been a dull, rather homely girl with a thin, curveless body, but she had been a splendid swimmer. When she met Dick—whose car had broken down in the small midwestern town where she lived and who had visited the local swimming pool to while away the time until it was fixed—she had been overwhelmed with wonder that he found her attractive. No other man ever had, though possibly some might have if they had known, as Dick did, that she had a half interest in a two hundred thousand dollar estate, left in trust for her and her sister Jinny by their father.

Dick had been hoping for a better figure, using b/it meanings of the word, but a balance in the bank always been worth two on the wing. He had there seized the opportunity and eloped with her, an but and Bert and Marion had jointly taken her off to Mexico to honeymoon. Alice had exulted in long swims out into the blue Pacific. Sometimes, when Dick was weary, she had swum alone. From one of these lonely swims she had not returned.

Cramps, said the Mexican authorities when her body finally washed ashore. But it may have been the overpowering lethargy brought on by sedatives mixed with the black coffee she loved to drink before starting a swim.

Anyway, now her money was gone; Jinny was almost 21, and the share Alice had left her pretty sister, and which had been nibbled at, must be accounted for. The Farringtons, if a little provoked at Fate for forcing another murder upon them, were nevertheless facing up to their burden.

"It must be clearly an accident," Marion said.

"Don't give any gossip a chance to get started," Bert agreed.

incident of school life. But she, finally, put the dish firmly before her and started eating. She had eaten at least three of the mushrooms, from her side dish of fatal and non-fatal types, when the phone rang. As bouncy as a small boy, Jinny leaped up to answer it. And the dish of mushrooms had fallen to the floor and scattered across the rug.

Jinny was painfully embarrassed, but there had been nothing to do save throw the mushrooms in the garbage can. As for the phone call, it had only been from their tiresome neighbor, Mr. Downey, inviting them to tea the following afternoon.

They had waited hopefully for Nature to take its course, if the three mushrooms Jinny had eaten were of the fatal type. But Jinny had gone up to bed quite healthy and now the Farringtons were under the annoying necessity of figuring out some other way to dispose of her. It was really very thoughtless of the girl to put them to so much trouble.

"It will have to be a fall from the cliff," Marion said. "I told Mr. Downey we couldn't come to tea because we were going on a picnic. Very well, we will go on a picnic. Jinny will see a very special flower she wants to pick, clinging dangerously to the side of the cliff. She will start down for it and slip and— Well, we just weren't close enough to catch her."

She spoke very convincingly. It almost sounded as if Jinny were already lying broken and lifeless on the cruel rocks, and as a consequence, they all felt much better. Then suddenly a piercing scream from the bedroom above them made them look up. Again came the scream—and again, a tremolo of horror that made the cut glass chandelier tinkle timorously.

Hope sprang in Marion's eyes.

"The mushrooms!" she exclaimed.

"Dash it!" Bert said. "She'll wake the whole neighborhood. Can't she die quietly?"

Screams from above continued to indicate that she couldn't.

"Amanita virosa!" Marion exclaimed, with awe. "Why that's the name I couldn't think of. It—it just came to me. No mushroom is deadlier."

There was another scream.

"We'll have to go up," Marion told them. "Mr. Downey is sure to have heard her by now. Come on, Dick."

She and Dick ran up the stairs and flung open Jinny's door. Jinny was sitting up in bed, her hands pressed to her mouth, trying to stifle another scream.

"Jinny!" Marion hurried to her. "What is it? Do you feel bad?"

Jinny shook her head, her breath coming in ragged gasps.

"No pain?" Marion was eager, rather than solicitous.

"It was—another nightmare. The—the worst of all."

They heard a window go up. A voice called, "Hello! Anything wrong over there?"

"That you, Mr. Downey?" Dick stepped to Jinny's window. "Jinny had another nightmare, that's all. She's all right now."

"Oh," Mr. Downey said. "Oh."

The window went down again. Dick came back and sat on the side of the bed, holding Jinny's soft hand in his.

"Tell us about it, Jinny," he urged. "That's the best way to get over it."

Jinny's breathing was more normal now. She flushed delicately, and tried to pull the sheet up around her.

"It was—so real," she said. "I was in a great, dark room, in some strange old house all tumbling down and full of shadows. And the shadows suddenly came to life and started creeping toward me. There was a terribly high ceiling and down from the darkness came a rope. It had a noose in the end of it. And the shadows all pushed me toward the noose and I knew they wanted me to put it around my neck, and they pushed closer and closer until I couldn't breathe. Then all of a sudden the noose twisted itself right around my throat and—and—"

She gasped and began to tremble. Marion produced a pill and a glass of water.

"Take this, Jinny," she said. "Get some sleep. It was just a dream, that's all."

"Yes, of course," Jinny whispered. "Just a—dream. Thank you, Marion."

She took the pill, drank, lay back on the pillow. Dick gave her hand a little squeeze.

"See you in the morning, Jinny."

He went out softly. And Marion and Bert followed him on tiptoe, like loving parents leaving the side of their sleeping child.

It was a perfect summer morning. The horoscope in the daily paper said *Today is a good day for carrying out projects you have been putting off*. Bert, who always read the horoscopes, showed it to Marion.

"Yes, we've waited too long," Marion said, and frowned. "We'll finish this thing up today. Jinny's nightmare last night has given us just the opportunity we need." She reached for the phone.

"Hello," she said to the operator. "I want to make a long distance call to Boston. Person to person to Dr. M. J. Brewer. He's a famous psychiatrist. I don't know his address, but I'm sure you'll be able to locate him. It's very important . . . Yes, call me back."

She hung up and turned to Bert.

"I already phoned Dr. Barnes," she said. "Told him about Jinny's nightmares and said I was dreadfully worried. He suggested Brewer. I'll make an appointment with Brewer and explain all about Jinny's fits of depression and the time she took too many sleeping pills—"

"When was that?" Bert asked.

"Don't be tiresome, Bert. The thing is, the child is melancholy, subject to depression, thinks of suicide. After all the buildup I gave the call, the operator is sure to listen in and spread the story. So will Mrs. Graves and Miss Bernham, on the party line—I heard their receivers picked up. Jinny is over now, apologizing to Mr. Downey for waking him up last night. By evening, the whole town will know about Jinny's dream, her suicidal tendencies, instability, everything. Then this afternoon, for the picnic, we'll go to Black Point. You know the old house in the woods there?"

"Yes," Bert nodded. "What about it?"

"Why, it will be the most natural thing in the world— Oh, there's the phone . . . Hello? Dr. Brewer? . . . Dr. Brewer, it's urgent that I make an appointment with you for as soon as possible. You see—"

The Farringtons were a rather attractive family, especially on an occasion such as this, all of them off to a picnic.

Marion had packed a hamper with food, and Bert had packed a smaller hamper with wine and other drinks. Dick drove the car far out on the lonely cliffs to the region known as Black Point. The evergreens grew tall with cathedral-like shade and quiet beneath them. Dick helped Jinny tenderly over the rough spots. His fingers caressed her bare arms as he helped her sit down on the edge of the rocky cliff, in the sunshine, the Atlantic combers crashing on the rocks far below. Sea gulls screamed; there was a smell of salt spray in the air. Jinny breathed deeply.

"It smells so fresh and clean," she whispered. "It makes me forget all about last night—that horrible nightmare—" Her eyes clouded, but Dick's admiring gaze brought her good spirits back. "But there, I'm not going to talk about it any more. Let's eat. I'm starved!"

They ate. Bert told humorous stories of his travels in Europe, neglecting to mention that he had been in Europe because of an embezzlement in the U. S. A. Marion was witty, and her stories about the towns-people were also malicious. Dick sat close beside Jinny and held her hand whenever he could, leaning close to her and whispering in her ear from time to time that she was lovely. Jinny flushed, and her eyes laughed, and she looked more than ever like a child on the happiest day of her life.

The sun sank behind the pines. Shadows grew longer. A chill seeped into the air.

"Why don't you two take a walk?" Marion asked. "Bert and I will clean up."

Dick was on his feet at once, helping Jinny.

"Come along," he said gaily. "We'll explore."

Laughing, Jinny allowed herself to be drawn along. Dick slipped her small hand into his large hand.

"Glorious day," he said with a wide gesture. "Enjoying it?"

"Oh, yes. Except that—looking at the sea—made me think of Alice."

"I know." Dick looked solemn. "She loved the sea—too much. Couldn't keep her out of the water."

"Did you love her very much, Dick?" Jinny asked.

"Very much indeed," Dick said, nodding. "They were the happiest three weeks of my life. Then—she was taken from me."

"She loved you, too," Jinny told him. "You should have seen her face when she told me she was going to marry you. It was transformed. She couldn't imagine what you saw in her. She was so plain."

"Plain?" Dick was indignant. "I never thought of her as plain. To me she was lovely, lovely . . ."

"I always thought she was rather dull," Jinny said ingenuously. "All she could do was swim. She couldn't talk well and she didn't like books or music or—"

"Please, Jinny!" Dick's voice was suddenly brusque. "You forget that we were in love. It upsets me to talk about her. I still—miss her terribly, terribly . . ."

"Of course," Jinny said, with swift contrition. "I'm sorry, Dick. Oh, look—isn't that a house ahead of us?"

"An abandoned house!" Dick exclaimed. "Maybe it's haunted!"

The house they had come upon, buried in the woods, was huge and a dismal brown in color. Part of the roof had fallen in. The wide veranda was sagging.

Most of the windows were broken. An air of dark desolation hung over it, brooding.

Jinny drew in a deep breath. "I don't like it," she said. "Let's go back, Dick."

But Dick had hold of her hand and was pulling her toward the old ruin with masculine enthusiasm.

"Let's look inside," he coaxed. "Say hello to the ghost. No telling what we'll find."

Jinny tried to hold back, but willy nilly she came along with him, half running.

"Dick, it—scares me. It's so dark—and gloomy. It's like my nightmare last night—"

"Aw, that was only a dream. Now don't be a child, Jinny. Come on, let's see what's inside."

Reluctantly Jinny followed him onto the veranda, which swayed and creaked beneath them. Together they peeked through the doorless doorway. Inside was darkness, a smell of moldy plaster and termite-infested wood, the tiny chittering of rats, curious creaks and rustlings.

Jinny shivered. "Please, Dick! I feel—so scared. I know it's irrational, but please let's go back."

"That would be the worst thing you could do, giving in to your fears. Come on inside."

Dick pulled, and Jinny went in with him.

Inside the gloom was worse. But they could see the holes in the plaster, the leprous stains on the walls, the broken stairway leading to the next floor—and the rope that hung from an old hook in the ceiling.

It was an old rope, a frayed rope, but it seemed to twist and curl gently, as if alive, as if hungry, as if waiting. And it ended in a noose.

"My dream!" Jinny cried in terror. "It's happening. This old house—this room—the rope. Dick!" She tugged to free herself. "Let's run!"

Dick held her tightly.

"Don't be silly," he said. "This is how to cure yourself. Go over, touch the rope, prove to yourself it's just an old rope someone left hanging there."

"No, oh no! See how it—twists."

"Sure. It's drafty. The windows are all busted in this place."

And Jinny found herself almost lifted across the creaking floor, to stand below the dangling noose that waited like an open mouth.

"Jinny," Dick said softly, gently. "Here's an old stool. Stand on it—put the noose around your neck. Then take it off again. Do that, and you'll never have nightmares again. You'll be too brave for them. I promise you."

"No, I can't." Jinny shuddered and then with a sudden do-or-die effort wrestled free of Dick's arms. "I can't."

"You must, Jinny." This time it was Marion who spoke. Somehow, Marion and Bert had materialized in the doorway, like two shadows coming out of the woodwork. Soon they stood close behind Jinny, touching her, hemming her in. She stood there, trembling violently, like a wild thing caught in a trap.

"This is for your own good, child." Marion's voice was soft, almost gentle. "It will help you get over the nightmare habit. The doctor suggested it. Dick, put the stool in place. Bert, lift her up."

In a moment the three of them had Jinny on the old stool, the noose around her neck, the rope harsh against her tender throat. Pressed close about her like ugly, waiting shadows, they held her so she could not move—could only tremble uncontrollably.

"You're going to kill me," she said, looking down at them, her eyes enormous in her small white face. "You want me out of the way. So you're going to kill me. And you killed Alice, too. I can see it in your faces."

"Yes, you tiresome child," Marion answered. "I put a sedative in her coffee before she went for a swim. But we're not going to kill you, child. You're going to kill yourself. You're moody, inclined to suicide. Last night you had a nightmare. Today you went wandering, found this old house, found the rope, tied it to an old hook in the ceiling, and you acted out your dream. You killed yourself. We should have watched you, but you slipped away from us, and in a fit of melancholy you killed yourself.

"Dick, take away the stool. Bert, lower her gently. This must look natural. Let her grab the rope to support herself—her hands should be abraded—and grabbing the rope would be the instinctive thing to do. She'll tire soon enough."

Dick took away the stool. Bert lowered Jinny and then let go of her. Jinny hung there, her small hands clutching at the rope in an attempt to support her weight, but the hemp cut deeper and deeper into her throat. Slowly, her body turned about, throwing crazy shadows on the wall as a final shaft of sunlight broke into the room and as her breath choked in her throat.

"All right, put the stool back."

But it was not a Farrington who spoke. It was Mr. Downey, who stood in the doorway with a shotgun in his hand. Beside him was Sheriff Lamb, a large, silent man who seldom spoke, but whose expression now conveyed displeasure.

"Put it back, I said!"

Little Mr. Downey's voice sounded like a trap snapping shut. Bert put the stool back beneath Jinny's feet. Jinny stood very straight and with steady fingers loosened the noose. Then she stepped down.

"For a frightened moment," she said, "I almost thought you weren't coming, Mr. Downey." She no longer sounded like a child.

"Oh, we were there," Mr. Downey said. "Right on the dot, just like you said. But what took us a little longer, we were listening at the window and we had to come around to the door so you wouldn't be between them and us."

Jinny looked coldly at the three Farringtons, who were like grotesque shadows frozen in the act of trying to move.

"You killed Alice," she said. "I knew all along you must have killed Alice. I loved her, but she was dull and plain and nobody would marry her, I knew, except for her money. So I promised myself I'd get you somehow. Since you'd killed her in a foreign country, the only way I could get you was by making you try to kill me—before witnesses.

"It was risky. Sure it was. But I studied psychology in college and Mr. Downey is a crackerjack private detective, and I thought I could do it, one way or another. I pretended to have dreams so you'd think I was a real nervous kid. Last night when you were willing to let me eat poisonous mushrooms, I knew I'd better do something. So I tried putting this hanging idea into your heads. I didn't want you to try to drown me or push me off a cliff—I might not have been able to have stopped you if you'd done that. Well, it worked out as I hoped it would. You were so gullible, so easy to lead around. You should have seen your faces when I spilled that dish of mushrooms on the floor. Of course, the ones I'd eaten were the harmless ones."

But she did not laugh at the memory. She only turned to Mr. Downey and Chief Lamb.

"Take them away, please," she said.

The Farringtons went, followed by the two men with shotguns. Last of all came Jinny Wells. Behind her the noose, stirred by the air currents, twisted and curled.

As was mentioned earlier, the Farringtons were a rather attractive family, if you don't mind overlooking a few bad habits.

But Jinny Wells was one individual who apparently did.

LET THE SUCKER BEWARE

●

Charles Einstein

I, if memory serves me right, have never purchased a bridge from anyone. But then I have never felt that possessing a bridge is essential to the good life. And now let me present Mr. Holland and his *confrère* Arch, who might conceivably try to sell you something of consequence, like the Mississippi River, its bridges and tributaries.

Well, we were riding this boat from Liverpool when Arch, my old buddy with whom I grew up together on the sidewalks of New York, brought up the matter of O. Henry.

"The trouble with you," Arch said to me, "is you're not up on your reading. You think all suckers have to come from some place else. Fifty years ago O. Henry knew better."

"Quote me some O. Henry," I said.

"Quote," Arch said. "'In the west a sucker is born every minute; but in New York they appear in chunks of roe. They lie down on the floor and scream and kick when you are the least bit slow about taking money from them.'"

"That was fifty years ago," I said.

"Exactly," Arch said. "People like you forget that the old ways were frequently the best ways. I think we should bear this in mind this trip. Instead of prowling the main salon for little old ladies from Nebraska and Toledo, I suggest we hunt up a live New Yorker."

"New Yorkers are up on all the latest things," I said.

"I personally cannot imagine selling uranium stock to a fellow New Yorker, or offering our popular air-coach funeral service. Can you?"

"No," Arch said, "but I think maybe we ought to try some of the older techniques. As I said to you only recently, the old ways are frequently the best ways. I got to thinking about this because of that uncle of yours who used to conduct that small but well-attended game of three-card monte on top of an unfolded newspaper on the subway platform at Seventh Avenue and Fourteenth Street."

"You mean my uncle Herbert Holland," I said. "I always thought his technique a little crude. He thought he could escape the police merely by switching from the uptown to the downtown sides of the subway.

"It was his name I was thinking about, not his technique," Arch said. "For the remainder of this voyage, I suggest that you adopt your uncle's name. You will be Mr. Holland. Tonight we are going to have a small game of cards with a gentleman I met on this boat. He is Worthington T. Jones, chairman of the board of several New York banks, and he seems friendly. The idea is to let Mr. Jones win some money at cards and remember at all times that your name is Holland. Leave the rest to me."

Even after a lifetime in this particular trade, there are certain people whose money you dislike to take. Thus it was with Mr. Worthington T. Jones, who was a sociable, lonely old fellow with a crinkly face and a kind smile for all. He was so grateful to have somebody to play cards with that he nearly burst out crying.

"Money isn't everything, boys," he said, drawing one card to fill an inside straight. "Here I am worth several millions negotiable, and what good does it do?"

"Well," Arch said to him, "don't knock money. Ain't that right, Mr. Holland?"

"That's right," I said.

"Mr. Holland here is a member of the Holland

Tunnel Hollands," Arch said. "A fine old New York family. In June 1958, when the 30-year public bonded indebtedness is paid off, Mr. Holland here will become owner of the tunnel outright."

"You don't say?" Mr. Jones said to me.

"Yes," I said. "I can hardly wait."

"Permit me," Mr. Jones said to me, "as a banker with considerable experience, to offer you a suggestion. You should set up a corporation and peddle stock. Consider the tax benefits."

"This," Arch said to Mr. Jones, "is precisely what Mr. Holland has in mind. However, there are other members of the Holland family to consider."

"Well," Mr. Jones said, and exhibited fives full over treys, "of course if he has relatives to consider . . ."

"However," Arch said hastily, "the decision is his to make. Right, Mr. Holland?"

"Right," I said. "I can hardly wait till June 1958. There is a lot of revenue from a thing like a tunnel."

"If Mr. Holland could make a quick sale," Arch said to Mr. Jones, "I would be willing to bet he would do it. Of course, it would have to be done quietly so as not to alert the rest of the family."

"You don't say?" Mr. Jones said. "How many vehicles a year use the tunnel, might I inquire?"

"Including westbound and eastbound tubes, some 60 million," Arch said. "After salaries and upkeep that is quite a bit left over."

"You'd be asking quite a fancy figure if you were to sell," Mr. Jones said to me. "Or so I'd imagine. Did you have a price in mind?"

"It would be a distress sale," Arch said hastily. "Remember, the tunnel doesn't start paying off until June 1958, and Mr. Holland here can use a little ready scratch."

"Well, boys, it's my bedtime," Mr. Jones said, and reached for his winnings. "It certainly has been fascinating talking to you two boys." And he smiled and nodded and got up and went his way.

"Saints-at-large," I said to Arch, "are you really going to sell him the Holland Tunnel?"

"He's panting for it," Arch said. "Does a hundred thousand sound like a fair score?"

"You were right about that part where I could use the money," I said. "Meanwhile, what is the next step?"

"One or two more losing evenings at cards should do it," Arch said. "And in between times I shall visit the ship's printing office and have the necessary documents brought into being."

We met Mr. Jones for a few hands again the following evening. The conversation concerned everything except the Holland Tunnel, and I wondered how Arch was going to bring the subject up. But he was just biding his time. The opening came when the waiter brought a round of drinks. Arch left a bountiful tip on the tray.

"I always say," he said, "better to overtip than undertip." And he kicked me under the table.

"Not me," I said. "Personally, I believe waste not, want not."

"I agree with Mr. Holland here," Mr. Jones said to Arch. "I like to count my pennies."

"Well," Arch said, "it just so happens I have a small article here which might please you, sir." He took out a little embossed card. "Mr. Holland's signature is on it, and we'd like you to have it with our compliments. It entitles you to ride through the Holland Tunnel for nothing."

"You don't say?" Mr. Jones said, and laid down three eights and accepted the card. "Well, this certainly is wonderful. I don't know how to thank you boys."

"Mr. Holland," Arch said to me. "So long as we find ourselves talking about the tunnel, why don't you run down to the stateroom and bring up those ownership papers? I'm sure Mr. Jones here would like to see what they look like."

I went down to the stateroom and got the papers Arch had had printed up. When I got back, the two of them were talking about something else entirely.

Arch took the papers and casually handed them over to the other man. "Look these over at your leisure, Mr. Jones," he said. "We've got another night on shipboard yet."

"Well, thank you," Mr. Jones said. "So long as we've reached this point, I might as well warn you boys, not a word about this to anyone. We don't want it to get back to the Holland family in New York."

"Heavens no," Arch said.

At the card table the following evening, our last night at sea, the matter of the tunnel came up at once.

"Boys," Mr. Jones said, "I've been thinking over your proposition. Your business adviser here drives a hard bargain, Mr. Holland, but I've decided the terms are acceptable."

"Well, sir," Arch said to him, "I trust you brought your checkbook with you and you won't be sorry. If Mr. Holland here didn't need the money, you could never have scored like this. I believe you'll make that hundred thousand back in the first month's operation."

"I'm counting on it," Mr. Jones said. "I have the check all written out. As soon as I've seen the property, the money is yours."

"Seen the property?" Arch said.

"Why, yes," Mr. Jones said. "Soon as we get to New York in the morning, I hope you boys won't mind driving through the tunnel with me, just so I can look it over. It's a standard practice of mine in all real estate deals."

"Why, certainly," Arch said. "We can conclude our deal at the New Jersey end of the tunnel if you like. Meanwhile, should we have a hand or two of poker?"

"My pleasure," Mr. Jones said. "I certainly hope your luck changes, boys. You've been holding miserable cards."

Later, back in the stateroom, Arch started to beat himself on the right side of the head with the palm of his hand. "Come on," he said to me. "Think. Put your brain to work."

I said, "What's the nature of the problem?"

"We've got to go through that tunnel for nothing," Arch said. "He's got that card I gave him, so we've got to make it work."

We doped it out finally on a timetable basis. Arch cabled ahead to have two rented cars waiting for us at the dock in New York. I had to figure out some excuse to get away, ahead of Arch and Mr. Jones, so I could take the first car. Everything had to be right.

It was agreed that we both would use the farthest right-hand toll booth at the tunnel entrance on Canal Street. When I got there in my car, I handed a dollar bill to the collector. He tried to hand me back fifty cents, but I wouldn't take it.

"What's this?" he said.

"Look," I said, "there's going to be a car come along in a couple of minutes with a nut inside. He's going to show you a card and tell you he owns the tunnel. Don't charge him anything. Just salute him and let the car go through. The extra half dollar I'm giving you now will pay for that car. Understand?"

"Sure," the toll booth guy said doubtfully. "You say he owns the tunnel?"

"He thinks he does. We're taking him to an asylum in Jersey. I'm going ahead now to cement the necessary arrangements."

"He ain't going to do something crazy, is he? Like stop the car in the middle of the tunnel?"

"Oh, no," I said. "There'll be a gent with him doing the driving. Don't worry about a thing."

"I shouldn't, huh?" the toll booth guy said.

I waited and waited in the hotel room without any sign of Arch. After a while it occurred to me that it had been my money we'd lost at poker, playing with Mr. Jones on the boat, and Mr. Jones' check for the tunnel had been made out to Arch, as it had to be since I'd been using the assumed name of Holland, and that maybe Arch just wasn't going to show up at all.

But then I figured no, Arch was too honest to do a thing like that. And sure enough, finally there was a knock on the door and Arch was standing there. He had a big grin on his face.

"Well?" I said.

"Worked fine," he said. "We rode free."

"Where's the money?"

Arch set down his briefcase. "No money. He got a good look at the place and decided it just wasn't his kind of tunnel."

"It wasn't his kind of . . . Wait a minute! We lost five thousand dollars playing cards with him and went to all this trouble with the printing and the toll booth and now . . ."

Arch held up his hand. "He realized all that. He's a splendid citizen, this Mr. Jones. Comes from an old distinguished New York family. All kinds of tradition and honors and so forth. Said he felt he should do something for us." Arch opened the briefcase. "And so, my friend, in exchange for just five thousand dollars more, we . . ."

"You gave him *another* five thousand?"

"Please," Arch said. "Look what we wound up with."

He handed over a batch of documents.

No doubt about it, he is a fine and upstanding character, this Mr. Jones, from an old and honored New York family.

Arch and me, we own Jones Beach.

FAIR GAME

●

John Cortez

Not so long ago a relative asked me if I'd like to go hunting with him. I was about to say yes when a line in this story, which fortuitously I was reading at the moment, leaped out at me: ". . . there's no thrill like shooting your own."

She had a kind of sad face. The gray eyes were set wide apart and they had a way of taking on a gaze as though she were thinking of something far away and forever lost. Her high cheekbones gave her the hollow look of pining away and the long, rose-colored lips were almost always grave. She seldom smiled. Still she was beautiful, beautiful in a haunting, unforgettable way. I know.

She was not tall or short for a woman, and she was slim, very slim. You could see the fine bone structure beneath the skin when she closed her hands. She was like a piece of delicate china. Even her voice had a fragile quality, like the last echo of some forgotten whisper.

Every time he took her in his arms, it seemed as if he would crush the breath, maybe even the life, out of her for he was a big brute of a man; but I suppose he could be gentle because she seemed to like it. These were the few times that something like a smile would touch her lips and she'd hug him in return and then kiss him. I always tried not to watch, but no matter how quickly I averted my eyes the picture was there, sharp and lasting.

She had seen us coming and had stepped outside and was standing there, bare-headed, in the snow. She waved and that was enough to send him on ahead with long, fast strides. I hung back looking out over the hard rippling blue of the lake which was still unfrozen after this first light snowfall of November.

I heard them murmur things to each other, sweet, tender things, I imagine, and I tried to pay no attention to them.

What's eating you, Ludlow? I asked myself. Why let it get you like this? There's been nothing, not even a hint of it, between you and her. She scarcely knows you're alive. Besides, she's married, and he's a good joe.

I circled around them and heard her say, "Please, Elroy," and sensed her pushing away from his embrace, then I was on the steps, which she had swept clean, stamping snow from my boots. I looked to the south and west, seeing the expanse of leaden sky and the endless stretch of the evergreens for this was what we call big country up here, miles and miles of wilderness.

Endicott said: "Aren't you coming in, Ludlow?"

I shut the door behind me. Endicott had shed his red hunting jacket and she took it from him and hung it on the rack. His big chest swelled as he inhaled deeply.

"That coffee sure smells good, Rosemary," he said. "Get the whiskey, won't you, hon? I feel like a good stiff slug of it."

I stepped into the room where I bunked and unloaded my rifle and stood it in a corner. I dropped my jacket and cap on the bed and then sat down on the edge. I don't know how long I sat there like that with my hands clasped between my thighs, staring at the floor.

Endicott's voice brought me out of it. "Coffee, Ludlow?" he called from the next room.

"I'll be right there," I said.

He had a cup half full and the whiskey bottle in his hand. "Hold it," I told him. "I'll take mine plain."

His brows went up. "I've seen you drink coffee royals before. How come?"

"I don't feel like it today."

He shrugged. "Suit yourself."

I could feel her watching me, like she often did, but I pretended to be unaware of it. She went on staring, however, and finally she said, "No luck today either, Sam?"

I shook my head.

"I don't know whether to be sorry or glad," she said. "Those poor little deer aren't hurting anybody. Why must you men be so brutal? Why must you slaughter them?"

"Don't mind her, Ludlow," Endicott said. "Never known anyone as soft-hearted. She'll walk around a bug on the ground rather than step on it." His laugh boomed in the room. "You've got to get more spunk, hon."

"It isn't that, Elroy," she said. "You know it. I just can't stand the thought of anything being killed."

Endicott's laugh boomed again. "You'll get over it. Just come out with me and watch me knock one over. That'll cure you."

She shuddered. "You know I couldn't stand that, Elroy. I'd be sick for a week. I hope you don't even get a shot at one."

He was a big man and, I suppose, like a lot of big men he was attracted to women who were small or seemingly helpless. If that was all there was to it then I guess they were a perfect match. But he was much older than her, fifteen or twenty years older, I'd say.

There you go again, Ludlow, I told myself, getting mad. What business is it of yours their difference in age? Just because she looks at you sometimes— He's crazy in love with her. Can't you tell?"

He had asked her to get chow ready but he did most of the cooking. "My only chance, Ludlow," he said, winking and grinning. "At home she won't even let me in the kitchen."

After we'd eaten he washed the dishes while she wiped. I went to my room. I lay down on my blankets with a magazine but I couldn't read. I could hear them talking, low and soft, and his pleased chuckles and once the sound of scuffling followed by her tone of reproach and his light laugh. I lay there, pretending not to hear, remembering how I'd got into this.

When he'd offered me an even hundred bucks rent plus my wages as a guide during the nine-day deer season I'd marked him for what he obviously was, a rich guy from the southern part of the state who owned a construction business down there or was it a small factory? I never bothered to make sure. He paid the rent in advance and that was enough for me. When he said his wife would be along I said okay because I figured it would be someone middle-aged like him and probably built like a tank, but then it turned out to be her.

I had put the magazine aside and was lying there staring, just staring, at the ceiling when she looked and then came in.

"Am I bothering you?" she said in that small, almost timid voice.

"Not at all," I said. I swung my legs over the side of the bunk and sat on the edge.

She stared at my carbine and my rifle, both of which were leaning against a corner. She pointed a long, slim finger. "How come you've got two guns?" she asked.

I cursed the quickened beating of my heart. She's just bored, I told myself, she's just tired of being alone during the day while you and Endicott hunt. She's probably used to shows and night clubs. She's not used to being cooped up way out in the wilderness miles away from any doings.

I tried to be flippant about it. "I'm a two-gun man," I said, "like in the western movies. One for each hand."

She glanced at me sharply and showed me that shadowy smile. "You're making fun of me," she said, reproachfully. "I'm really serious. Is there any difference between the two?"

I went over and picked one up. "One's a rifle," I told her. "This is a carbine. It's a little shorter and lighter and so it's easier to carry around in the woods all day. I prefer the rifle, though. There's no difference in caliber. They're both .30-.30s."

"Would you show me how it works?"

I stared at her.

For a moment a little color showed under the becoming pallor of her features. "I—I'd really like to know. Because of Elroy. He likes so much to hunt and I—I'd like to be a part of that. I like sharing things with him. But he won't take me seriously. He makes fun of me when I ask him certain things and that gets me rattled. Would you show me how that gun works?"

I went on staring at her. Her glance started to shift but then she brought those gray eyes back and the moist appeal in them decided me.

"When the hammer's back slightly like this it's on safety," I said. "When you want to shoot you cock it with your thumb like this. Then you squeeze the trigger. To eject the empty shell and get a fresh one in the breech you work the lever like this. Then you squeeze the trigger again or if you aren't shooting any more you let the hammer down like this and set it back on safety. See?"

She nodded.

"Here," I said. "Take it and try. It's unloaded."

Her eyes went wide as if I had thrust a poisonous snake at her. "Oh, no, Sam. I can't make myself touch one."

"Then how are you going to learn to shoot?"

"Give me time. Will you do that? When I'm alone tomorrow I'll try. You'll leave it unloaded, won't you? I'll try when I'm alone so no one will make fun of me. I know it's silly to be like this but that's the way I am. I so much want to learn to shoot a gun—for Elroy. You'll teach me, won't you?"

I knew a moment of a strange, new loneliness and a hopeless yearning. "Okay, Mrs. Endicott," I said. "I'll teach you."

The deer came out of the thicket and stood still a moment. I caught him in the sights and then I hesitated, thinking, if he'll go over that rise he'll be set up just right for Endicott. After all, that's what he's paying me for. I could drop it for him but there's no thrill like shooting your own.

The deer was a big buck with a large rack of antlers but he was far enough away so that I couldn't count the points. Probably as tough eating as an old inner tube, but he'd make a fine trophy. I tightened my finger around the trigger. If he wasn't going to move soon I'd shoot.

Just then the buck stirred and started up the slope. He moved without hurry, ambling up the hill. A moment he was silhouetted against the gray sky. Then he was gone.

I waited. The shot cracked out loud and sharp in all that stillness. The echoes rolled past me and beyond me, far into the evergreens and into silence. Then came another shot and on the heels of that a third one. These echoes, too, rolled and faded and died.

A strange reluctance gripped me as I started up the slope. I could not understand it. All I knew was that it unnerved me. Was it the temper of the day, the low, dismal clouds, the first hush of winter like the deep, eternal silence of the tomb? Then her image crossed my memory and I knew what it was.

I stopped on the crest of the hill. He was there below, sitting on a stump with his back to me. I stood there and watched. And I felt it begin in me, mildly at first, just swirling around in the dark depths of me and I didn't know what it was, then something nurtured it and it grew and I felt it rise overwhelmingly in me and at the last moment I caught myself and forced it back to whatever depths had spawned it. I lowered the rifle from my shoulder, aware that I was trembling all over.

When I had myself in hand again I went down to him. He heard me coming and he rose to his feet and picked up his rifle. His face wore a disgusted look.

"Missed him," he said bitterly. "Three shots and every one a miss. I suppose you heard?"

I said nothing.

"He came over that rise," Endicott went on, "walking slow and easy. I couldn't have asked for a better target. But I missed and he really took off. I tried two more on the run but what can you expect when I can't even hit a walking target?" He peered at me. "You listening, Ludlow?"

I hauled myself out of it, out of the black thoughts and the fear, the numbing fear of the great and dark evil that I had never known existed in me until a few minutes ago.

"I heard you shoot," I said woodenly. "Tough. But you'll get another chance. Better luck then."

He was still peering at me. "You don't look so good."

I stared off at the green ring the balsams and spruces and hemlocks made around this clearing. "I'm all right."

"You look all in," he said. "I'm pretty well bushed myself. How about calling it a day?"

I didn't like the thought of going back to the cottage and seeing her move around and hearing her voice and feeling her eyes on me every now and then. I didn't like that at all but there was no way to run from it.

So I said, "Okay, Endicott. Let's start back . . ."

That evening I didn't even try to read. I lay on my blankets with my hands under my head and my eyes closed and straining everything in me to keep from remembering the incident of that day and trying not to pay attention to their voices beyond the curtain.

They were playing cribbage and she squealed delightedly every time she won and he grumbled but you could tell it was good-natured grousing and that he was really glad she had won. Maybe he had even let her win. There wasn't a thing he wouldn't do for her.

I didn't hear her come in. My eyes were closed and it was the fragrance first of all, and then an awareness of her and I opened my eyes and there she was, staring at me with that grave, faintly wistful look in her eyes, the lamplight turning the ends of her dark hair to golden brown.

Endicott was moving about in the next room and the radio began to blare, loudly, and though I've always hated loud radios somehow I liked it loud right then.

"Aren't you feeling well, Sam?" she asked, and I thought there was something special in her voice for me, something like concern, but then I told myself it was just my imagination.

I sat up on the edge of the bed. "I'm all right."

"You hardly ate anything tonight."

"I wasn't very hungry."

"Could I make something for you?"

"I'm all right. You needn't bother."

"I'd like to fix you something."

To change the subject I said, "How about the carbine? Did you try it today? It would be just right for you, a light gun like that."

She shuddered. "I tried. I tried real hard, Sam. I actually picked it up once but that's all. I put it down right away. Guns make my skin crawl. They always have. I don't think I could ever force myself to shoot one."

"There's really nothing to it," I said. "I don't know why you should be so afraid."

"But I *am*," she said, and shuddered again and hugged herself with her arms. Her eyes widened and stared off into that secret, sad somewhere that only she could see. "Call it a phobia. Maybe something that happened when I was a child and which I can't remember." She uttered a small, nervous laugh, her lips twitching stiffly. "Maybe I should go see a psychiatrist. Are you sure you don't want me to fix you something?"

"I'm very sure. Thanks anyway."

"Well, good night, Sam."

"Good night, Mrs. Endicott . . ."

There was something about those tracks that disturbed me from the moment I saw them but I had no idea what it was. My mind was too full of other things, of hopelessness and frustration and disgust with myself and that fear of the ugly evil I had not known I possessed.

I left Endicott in a clearing while I made a circle around through the woods to see if I could scare up something to drive past him but there was no deer sign today. Only the wilderness was there, green and somber and patient, full of awesome silence, full of lonesome brooding.

I doubled back finally and started up that hill, remembering yesterday and the dark impulse and the rifle at my shoulder and the sights staring at Endicott's back; and in the midst of all this frightening remembrance I noticed the tracks. They paralleled mine except that they went up the hill whereas mine had gone down. I noticed where, just before reaching the crest, they veered off to the left and seemed to have headed for the timber.

He was seated on the same stump below with his rifle across his knees, smoking a cigarette. I forced myself to continue without breaking stride or pausing. That could have been yesterday's mistake, the stopping and the thinking and then seeing her in my mind.

I made enough noise so that he heard me coming. He rose to wait for me. I could feel his eyes examining me. Did he know? Did he suspect about yesterday?

He glanced at his wrist watch. "You've been gone a long time," he said, and the concern in his voice sounded genuine. "I'd begun to worry about you."

"What's there to worry about?"

He gave me that peering look again. "I don't know. You just don't seem to be yourself the last couple of days. If you don't feel so hot we could knock off hunting for a day or two."

I began to breathe easier. It wasn't what I had thought it was. "I'm okay."

"So I don't get my buck. I can come back next year, can't I? Stay in, tomorrow at least. I can hunt close to the cottage and along the roads. I won't get lost. Don't knock yourself out just because I hired you. You'll get paid anyway."

I almost screamed at him. Why do you have to be such a right guy? Aloud I said, "I never felt better in all my life. Come on, let's get back and have a drink."

She sat between us, slouched a little with her thighs together and her hands clasped in her lap. Her face looked pale in the glow from the dashboard light, paler than I remembered. The shadows caressed her features and I envied them for I dared not touch her.

"Turn left up ahead," I said. These were the first words I had spoken since we had left the cottage.

Endicott braked the car and turned off the road. There were several cars parked in front of the tavern and as I got out I could hear the juke box going and the sound of voices. I hung back, letting her and Endicott enter first. There was a small vestibule just inside the entrance and we hung our jackets there. I still remember what the juke box was playing because it fitted in with the way I felt inside:

Got you on my mind,
Feeling kind of sad and low . . .

We went up to the bar and Endicott laid a twenty down for the first round. I ordered whiskey and drank it in one gulp and then ordered a round myself right away. I saw both Endicott and Rosemary glance at me because they had not touched their drinks yet. I sat and listened to that song.

Tears begin to fall
Every time I hear your name . . .

It was a hunter's crowd, loud and jovial. The talk was almost all of hunting, of the deer they'd killed, the ones they'd wounded, the big ones they'd missed, good-natured ribbing and joking, everyone roughly dressed in heavy woolen shirts and red trousers, even the women; the men were unshaven and smelling of the woods, of spruce and pine needles and resin, and all of them talking loudly so as to be heard above each other, and in the background the juke box blaring.

No matter how I try
My heart keeps telling me that I
Can't forget you . . .

It was not long before Endicott became one of them, engaged with two other hunters in a discussion of the best rifle for deer. I'd had three more whiskeys, quick ones, and the liquor was working in me, mellowing me. Some of the gloom lifted from my mind and I would have been glad except that I knew it would return once the effect wore off.

A couple of times I caught her eyes in the bar mirror and it was always me who broke the glance. Finally I turned and looked directly at her.

At the moment she was toying with her shot glass, drawing moist circles with it on the bar and studying the pattern with a withdrawn preoccupation. After a while she looked up and around at me and our eyes locked and I thought I read a message for me in hers.

"Would you like to dance?" I asked.

She fitted nicely into my arms and I realized that this, too, had been a mistake.

"What's the matter, Sam?" she asked as we circled the floor. "I thought going out might cheer you up. In fact, I was the one who suggested it to Elroy. What's the matter? Won't you tell me?"

The record ended and we came to a stop. When the next one began she seemed to have read my mind for she made no move to resume dancing.

"It's stuffy in here," she said. "I think I'll get some air."

The cars were all frosted over from the cool, damp air coming off the lake. She stood there with her back to me like she was lost in those deep thoughts of hers again and at first I fought it; then I thought what the hell this might be all the chance I'll ever have and it was a mixture of desire and frustration. I turned her around by the shoulders and took her in my arms.

I guess she struggled at first. Anyway, it felt like that but she was so slim and frail to begin with and I was so angry and bitter that I didn't think about maybe being too rough. Her lips were cool and indifferent at first and then they moistened and warmed and I knew I had not been mistaken after all.

It was the sudden blast of sound as someone opened the door that brought us out of it. She noticed it even before I did and pushed away. I spun around, thinking it was Endicott, but it was just another couple. They passed us by and got into a car.

We went back inside.

The day was gray, as gray as my thoughts. The clouds hung low in dark swells and billows, the air had a damp, bitter feel, the smell of an impending snowfall lay over the wilderness.

I stood outside, waiting for Endicott to take his leave of her. They were always reluctant partings for him. He'd stand on the steps with her in the open doorway, hesitating like a high school kid saying good night to his first crush. It made me grit my teeth, this time, because I was remembering the night before with her in my arms.

"Didn't you hear her, Ludlow?"

That brought me out of it. I turned away from my study of the lake and looked at them.

"She asked you if you think it'll snow today?"

I caught her eyes but read nothing in them. She was too far away for that anyway. "I'm pretty sure it will."

"Very much?" he asked.

"Could be," I said.

He kissed her then, long and hard. "So long, hon," he said.

"Be careful, dear."

I started up the road.

"Good-by, Sam."

For the briefest moment my step faltered but I didn't

stop or even look around. "Be seeing you," I called to her.

He made no attempt to talk as we walked along and neither did I. The only sound was the soft scuffing of our boots in the snow.

Where the road divided I came to a halt and he stopped beside me. "Let's do it different today," I said. "Let's both strike out on our own. You know the country fairly well now and you won't get lost as long as you follow this railroad bed. It eventually crosses the fire lane again and you can come back that way or double back on this. I'll scout the timber. Maybe I can knock something over. Okay?"

He looked at me without answering. Does he know? I thought. Does he understand the real reason behind this? Does he guess that I'm scared of myself, scared of what I might do?

A couple of vagrant snowflakes fell, drifting slowly between us, and then he said, "Okay, Ludlow."

"You needn't wait for me," I told him. "Just return to the cottage when you're tired of hunting. Only don't go off into the woods. This is big country and you might never find your way out if the snow covers your tracks."

He nodded and started off.

I took the spur that wound and twisted its way up and over the hills. In the old days it had been the geared Shay engines that had clattered and squealed their slow, tortuous way up and down these steep grades. Now they were only memories, eventually to be forgotten like I wished all my memories could be forgotten.

I picked up the deer tracks heading south. They looked fresh and so I turned off the logging spur into the timber. The snow was building up, the flakes were thicker. It would not be long before it was snowing full force.

It was not long before the deer tracks crossed the old main line. I could see the trail made by Endicott where he had passed earlier. When I saw the second pair of tracks following his I pulled up sharply. They were the same tracks I had noticed the day before and as I stared at them I realized with a sick feeling what it was about them that had disturbed me.

They were small—tracks made by a boy, or a woman. I followed them . . .

She was crouched behind a large stump, the remnant of what had once been a giant Norway pine, and she was so intent on aiming that she was not aware of my coming up quietly behind her. He had stopped some distance up the road to light a cigarette and his back made a nice red target.

In the vast stillness of the forest the click as she cocked the carbine was a distinct sound. She had taken the mitten off her trigger hand. I still wore mine. I clamped down on the action just in time. Startlement made her pull the trigger but my thumb was there and the hammer snapped down and caught some of my glove between it and the firing pin and that was what kept the carbine from going off. Surprise so unsettled her that I easily tore the carbine out of her grasp.

She huddled there in the snow, pressed up hard against the stump, her balled right fist against her mouth. She had uttered a sharp, short gasp. That had been her only sound.

He never knew what happened behind him. When I glanced his way he was moving on, rifle cradled in the crook of his arm. He never once looked back. Soon he was out of sight.

I had known pain of mind and heart before but it was nothing compared to what I experienced now. Now it was the deep anguish of final disillusionment.

I looked down at her. There was hurt in me, lots of hurt, the kind of hurt that fades but never dies, yet there was no hate and I was surprised at that. Even now when I finally knew her for what she really was I still couldn't hate her. What I had felt for her had been too real, too deep to be replaced by hate.

"So you don't know how to shoot," I said, "and guns scare you and you'd get lost if you wandered more than ten feet from the cottage." It was snowing steadily now and a wind had begun to blow. The tracks we'd made were filling in. "You wanted to make sure you'd never be suspected, didn't you? That's why you didn't try it yesterday, why you waited until today; today the snow would cover your tracks. And in case you were suspected you prepared for that, too. My carbine. If they dug the bullet out of him and had a ballistics done on it, it would be me, wouldn't it, since you don't know how to shoot?"

Two tears welled up in her eyes, trembled a moment on the lashes, then trickled down her cheeks. She shook her head mutely from side to side. Another time this might have touched me and moved me but I was suddenly old now and wise.

"Even last night," I went on, "when you let me kiss you and be seen kissing you . . . it was all to set me up, wasn't it? A motive for killing him. What would be a better one than his wife. Are you alone in this?"

She spoke now, her lips moving stiffly. They had lost their rose color, they were almost as pale as the snow that passed in front of her face. "I love you, Sam; I love you."

"Do you? Or is it someone back home? Is that why you tried it? Or is he too old for you and you want to be free of him but you want his money, too?"

"I love you, Sam. I do. Please believe me."

She saw it was no use. "What're you going to do?"

"I won't tell a soul, Rosemary. I won't ever tell anyone. Who would believe me against you anyway? Let's go."

"Go? Where?"

"Back to camp . . ."

It would be my word against hers. Remembering how Endicott doted on her, I realized it would be useless to tell him anything. She would twist it around in her favor somehow. She would turn those big, sad, lost eyes on him and look frail and weak and persecuted and he would believe her rather than me.

And she would try it again. Not any more this way, perhaps, but some other way, some other time. I couldn't tell him—he loved her too much.

I turned off the fire lane into the timber. She stopped and hesitated. "That isn't the way back," she said.

"Short cut," I said.

Still she hesitated.

"Can't you see how it's storming? I want to get back as soon as I can. You coming?"

She followed. The timber closed about us. The wind moaned in the tree tops but down on the ground we hardly felt it. This was another world down here, a primeval world, a baffling world of trees and more trees, all of them alike, every direction alike, not even the sun to tell which way was which, nor the sky, for the snow swirled so thick and fast you could not see above the tree tops.

I quickened my pace.

"Sam," she called, "please slow down, Sam. I can't keep up with you." Each word was a gasp.

I moved still faster.

"Sam," she screamed finally, and began to run after me.

I broke into a run. "Sam, Sam, Sam," and then she tripped and went sprawling and I kept on, running, running.

"Sam, Sam, Sam . . ."

Running, running, tripping, swiping my face against a low limb and behind me the shrill, terrified shrieking.

"Sam, Sam, Sam . . ."

Fainter and fainter until I knew it was only in my mind.

I was with the search party that found her and so was he. The storm had let up after two days and we found her huddled behind a windfall, all curled up on her side with one cheek pillowed on her folded hands. The sheriff brushed the snow gently from her face and she seemed to be asleep with her eyes closed and her lips a thin, sad line and that melancholy look on her features. I turned away and almost wept but no one thought anything of it because they all felt the same way.

"Why?" he cried, tears streaming down his cheeks. "Why did she wander away? *Why*, when she was so scared of the woods? Will somebody tell me why?"

THE CURIOUS FACTS PRECEDING MY EXECUTION

•

Richard Stark

Life in the suburbs, from all reports, is one gay round after another. Week ends are sunny. Commuting is a conversation piece. And among the premiums offered for a book or two of green stamps is tranquillity.

I'm not sure when it was, exactly, that I knew I must murder Janice. Oh, I'd been thinking of it, wistfully, for months, but I don't know precisely at what moment my idle daydreams metamorphosed into a cold and determined plan.

Perhaps it was the day the mailman brought the bill for Janice's mink coat, a coat I had not even heard of until then. And when I asked her if I could at least *see* this coat for which I was expected to pay almost two thousand dollars, a fifth of a year's wages, she informed me, off-handedly, that she had lost the dear thing on the train, coming home from the city after an exhausting and nerve-racking day spent shopping along Fifth Avenue.

Or perhaps it was before that, the evening I returned to our midtown apartment, wearied from my labors in the advertising vineyard, and learned that in my absence Janice had managed to buy a house in Connecticut. No more were we to be pallid cliff-dwellers in Manhattan. The invigorating air of the ranch style developments for us. It would be good for my health, too, for me to arise an hour earlier each morning and sprint for the train.

Or perhaps it was that evening, out in our little bit of suburbia, when I was poring over our household financial records and discovered that, in the last six months, we had spent more in bank-fines resulting from overdrawn checks than we had spent on food. Janice's rejoinder, when calmly I shrieked this news at her, was that it was obviously my fault, since I didn't put enough money into the bank to cover the money she wanted to take back out.

Or perhaps it wasn't even Janice at all. Perhaps the catalyst was Karen.

Karen, ah Karen! I had finally received the promotion which made it at least possible for me to feel optimistic about catching up with Janice's spending, and with the promotion had come my own office and my own secretary, and Karen was that secretary.

It was the old story. At home, a wife who was a constant source of frustration and annoyance. At the office, a charming and intelligent—not to say lovely—secretary, with whom I felt I could talk, with whom I could relax. I took to spending evenings in town, telling Janice I was working late at the office, and the inevitable happened. Karen and I were in love.

But ours could not be a dark and furtive office romance. Karen was too honest, too gentle, too *good* for such a relationship. I knew I had to free myself of Janice and marry Karen. And I knew that, if I were free, Karen would have me.

I considered divorce. I had no doubt that Janice

would grant me one, since divorce is quite fashionable in our circle, and Janice wished always to be in fashion. But then I remembered alimony. In any divorce action, I would be the plaintiff, and Janice the defendant. And that meant alimony. And I knew only too well Janice's insatiable need for money. It was impossible as it was for me to support both Janice and myself. Add Karen, and I would be in debtor's prison within six months.

No, divorce was out, and for a while the spot I was in seemed hopeless. Then Janice bought one of those little foreign cars, and I waited hopefully for her to demolish both the auto and herself on the Merritt Parkway, but nothing ever came of it. Those cars are mawkishly ugly, but they are also exasperatingly safe.

Our home was brick outside, plaster and linoleum and plastic inside. Not much likelihood of a good flash fire. The commuter trains had their derailments and so on from time to time, but the accidents were almost invariably minor and never on Ladies' Day.

Finally, I had to admit to myself that it was up to me. If Janice were to make way for Karen's and my happiness, it would have to be at my instigation.

This conviction grew in me, becoming stronger and stronger until at last I dared broach the subject to Karen. She was, at first, shocked and appalled at my suggestion. But I talked to her, reasoning with her, explaining why it would never be possible for us to wed while Janice still lived, and slowly she too accepted the inevitability of it.

Once decided, the only questions left to answer were when and how. I had four types of murder from which to choose: murder made to look like an accident, murder made to look like suicide, murder made to look like natural death, and murder made to look like murder.

I ruled out accident at once. I had daydreamed for months of possible accidents for Janice, and had finally come to realize that they were all unlikely. If they were unlikely to me, who passionately desired that Janice should have an accident, how much more unlikely would they surely be to the police?

As for suicide, there were far too many of Janice's suburban friends who would be delighted to volunteer the information that Janice was happy as a lark—and about as bright—and that she had absolutely no reason in the world to want to kill herself.

As for natural causes, I knew far too little about medicine to want to try to outwit a coroner at his own game.

Which left murder. Murder made to look like murder. And I planned accordingly.

My opportunity came on a Wednesday late in May. On the Thursday and Friday of that week, there was to be an important meeting in Chicago, concerning a new ad campaign for one of our most important accounts, and I was scheduled to attend. All I had to do was arrange for Karen to accompany me, an easy matter to justify, and then my plan went into action.

Here was the plan: I had two tickets on the three p.m. train Wednesday for Chicago, due to arrive in that city at eight-forty the following morning. Karen was to take this train, carrying both tickets. We would leave the ad agency together at noon, ostensibly headed for Grand Central, lunch and the train. But while Karen went to Grand Central, I would hurry uptown, to the 125th Street station, where there was a twelve fifty-five train for my portion of Connecticut. I would arrive at my station at two-ten, wearing false mustache, horn-rimmed glasses, and the kind of hat and topcoat I never wear. Our mortgaged paradise was a good twenty blocks from the station. I would walk this distance, shoot Janice with the .32 revolver I had picked up second-hand on the lower East Side two weeks before, ransack the house, take the five-oh-two back to the city, go to a movie, take the twelve forty-five plane for Chicago, arriving at three-forty a.m., and be at the railroad station when Karen's train arrived at eight-forty. We would immediately turn in our return trip tickets, claiming we had decided to go back to

New York by plane. This would necessitate my filling out and signing a railroad company form. It was fool-proof. And, after a decent period of mourning, I would marry Karen and live happily and solvently ever after.

The day arrived. I told Janice I would see her on the following Monday, and I brought my suitcase with me to the office. Karen and I left at twelve, and I headed immediately uptown, stopping off only to buy a hat and topcoat. I checked my suitcase in a locker at the 125th Street station, and in the men's room on the train, donned the horn-rimmed glasses and the mustache.

At two-fifteen, I was stepping from the train at my station, which was virtually deserted at this time of day. I saw no one I knew in the twenty block walk to the house. I let myself in the front door with my key, the pistol an unaccustomed weight in my pocket.

Janice was seated in the living room, on the unpaid-for new sofa, reading a slick women's magazine and being instructed, no doubt, in some new way to spend my hard-earned money.

At first, she didn't recognize me. Then I removed the hat and glasses, and she exclaimed, "Why, Freddie! I thought you were going to Chicago!"

"And so I am," I told her. I redonned hat and mustache, and moved forward to close the picture window drapes.

She said, "Whatever are you doing with that mustache? You look terrible with a mustache."

I turned to face her and withdrew the pistol from my pocket. "Walk out to the kitchen, Janice," I said. I planned to make it look as though the burglar had come in the back way, Janice had heard him and gone to investigate, and he had shot her.

She blinked at the gun, then stared wide-eyed at my face. "Freddie, what on earth—"

"Walk out to the kitchen, Janice," I repeated.

"Freddie," she said petulantly, "if this is your idea of a joke—"

"I'm not joking, Janice," I said fiercely.

All at once, her eyes lit up, and she clapped her hands together childishly, as she always did when charging something we couldn't afford. "You old dear!" she cried.

"You did buy me that new washer-dryer after all!" And she leaped to her feet and virtually ran out to the kitchen, her high heels going clack-clack on the linoleum. Even then, in the last moments of her life, all she could think of was that she was going to add yet another possession to the mound of goodies she had already bled from me.

I followed her to the kitchen, where she turned, puzzled, to say, "There isn't any washer-dryer—"

I shot from the hip. Naturally, I missed, and the bullet perforated a dirty pot on the stove. I abandoned cowboy style forthwith, aimed more carefully, and the second shot cut her down in mid-scream.

Three seconds of silence. And they were followed by the sudden *brrrinnnng* of the front doorbell, the clapper of which was on the kitchen wall three feet from my head.

I froze, not knowing what to do. My first thought was to stay frozen and wait for whoever it was to go away. But then I remembered the little foreign car, sitting in the driveway, advertising Janice's presence at home. If there were no answer, the visitor might get alarmed, might call for help from the neighbors or the police, and I would never manage to get away on foot.

So I had to go to the door. With the horn-rimmed glasses and the mustache, and a voice disguised by making it hoarser and deeper than usual, I should be able to avoid recognition. I would say I was the family doctor, that Janice was sick in bed and could see no one.

The bell rang again while I was still thinking this through, and the second ringing unfroze me. Putting the gun back in my pocket, I hurried through the living room and stopped at the front door. I took a deep breath, steeled myself, and eased the door open an inch. Peering through this opening, I saw what was obviously a door-to-door salesman. He carried a tan briefcase. He wore a slender gray suit, a white shirt, a blue tie and a smile containing sixty-four gleaming teeth. He said, "*Good* afternoon, sir. Is the lady of the house at home?"

"She's sick," I said remembering to be hoarse.

"Well, sir," he bubbled, "perhaps I could talk to *you* for just a moment or two, if you have the time."

"Not interested," I told him. "Sorry."

"Oh, but I'm sure you will be interested, sir. My company has something of interest to every parent—"

"I am not a parent."

"Oh." His smile faltered, but came back with redoubled fury. "But my company isn't of interest only to parents, of course. Briefly, I represent the Encyclopedia Universicana, and I'm not actually a salesman. We are making a preliminary campaign in this area—"

"I'm sorry," I said firmly. "I'm not interested."

"But you haven't heard the best part," he said urgently.

"No," I said, and I slammed the door, reflecting that Janice would have bought the Encyclopedia Universicana, and that I had dispatched her just in time.

But I had to get on with the plan. I would now ransack the house, emptying bureau drawers onto the floor, hurling clothing around in closets and so forth. Then, when it was time, I would leave for my train.

I turned toward the bedrooms, and the phone rang.

Once again, I froze. To answer, or not to answer? Once again, as with the doorbell, and for much the same reasons, I decided to answer, and to be, again, the family doctor.

I picked up the phone therefore, said hello, and a falsely hearty woman's voice chirped, "Magill Communications Survey calling. Is your television set on, sir?"

I stood there, with the phone to my ear.

"Sir?"

"No," I said, and I hung up.

Doggedly, I turned again toward the bedrooms. And

this time, I got there. Opening a bureau drawer, I tossed its entire contents on the floor. I didn't have to worry about fingerprints. My fingerprints were quite naturally all over everything anyway. The police would simply assume that the burglar, being a professional, had known enough to wear gloves.

I was working on the third drawer, having pocketed three pairs of earrings and an old watch, for realism's sake, when the doorbell rang.

I sighed, plodded wearily to the living room, and opened the door perhaps an inch.

A short stout woman, smiling like an idiot, said "*Hel*-lo, there! I'm Mrs. Turner from over on Marigold Lane, and I'm selling chances for our new car raffle at the United Protestant Church."

"I don't want any raffles," I said.

"New *car* raffle," she said.

"I don't want any cars," I said. I closed the door. Then I quickly opened it again. "I have a car," I said. And I closed the door again.

On the way back to the bedroom, the echo of that conversation returned to me. I hadn't been very coherent. Could it be that I was more nervous than I thought?

No matter. In little more than an hour, I would leave here and catch my train for New York.

I lit two cigarettes, stubbed one out in annoyance, and went back to work. I finished the bureau and the one drawer in the vanity table, and was about to start with the closet when the phone rang.

I had never before realized just how shrill, just how *grating*, that telephone bell actually was. And how long each ring was. And what a little space of time there was between rings. Why, it rang three times before I even took a step, and it managed to get in one more jarring ring for good measure as I was on my way down the hall to the living room.

I picked up the phone and a male voice said in my ear, "Hello, Andy?"

"Andy?"

He said it again, "Hello, Andy?"

Something was wrong. Something was terribly wrong. I said, "Who?"

He said, "Andy."

"Wrong number," I said and hung up.

The doorbell clanged.

I jumped, knocking the phone off its stand onto the floor. I scooped it up, fumbling, and the doorbell sounded again.

I raced across the room and, forgetting caution, hurled the door open wide.

The man outside the door was gray-haired, portly and quite dignified. He wore a conservative suit and carried a black briefcase. He smiled upon me and said, "Has Mister Wheet been by yet?"

"Who?"

"Mister Wheet," he said. "Hasn't he been here?"

"No one by that name here," I said. "Wrong number."

"Well, then," said the portly man, "I suppose I'll just have to talk to you myself." And, before I knew what was going on, he had slipped past me and was standing in the living room, looking around with a great show of admiration and saying, "Lovely. A really lovely living room."

"Now, see here—" I began.

"Sampson," said the portly man, extending a firm plump hand. "Encyclopedia Universicana. Little woman at home?"

"I'm afraid she's sick," I said. "I was just fixing some broth for her. Chicken—broth. Perhaps some other—"

"I see," said the portly man. He frowned as though thinking things over, and then smiled and said, "Well, sir, you go right ahead. That'll give me a chance to get the presentation set up."

And all at once he was sitting on the sofa. I opened my mouth, but he opened the briefcase faster, dove in, and emerged with a double handful of paper. Sheets and sheets of paper, all standard typewriter size, all gaily-colored in red and green and blue, prominently

featuring photographs of receding rows of books.
SAVE! roared some of the sheets of paper, in black
block print. FREE! screamed others, in red. TRIAL
OFFER! shrieked still more, in rainbow hues.

Portly Mister Sampson leaned far forward, puffing
a bit, and began to arrange his papers in rows upon
the rug, just in front of his pointed-toe, highly polished
black shoes. "Our program," he explained to me, smiling, and lowered his head to distribute more sheets of
paper over the floor.

I stared at him. Not five feet from where he was sitting, my late wife Janice lay sprawled upon the kitchen
floor. In the bedroom, chaos was the order of the day.
In just about an hour, I would leave here and catch
the train back to the city. I would leave the .32 in a
litter basket, knowing full well some enterprising soul
would shortly pick it out again and that by the time
the police got hold of it, if they ever did, it would have
committed any number of crimes past this current one.
And then I would fly to Chicago and see Karen. Lovely
Karen. Dear, darling Karen.

And this miserable man was trying to sell me ency-
clopedias!

I opened my mouth. Quite calmly, I said, "Get out."

He looked up at me, smiling. "Eh?"

"Get out," I said.

The smile flickered, "But—you haven't seen—"

"Get out!" I said, this time a bit louder. I pointed
at the door, upsetting a table lamp. "Get out! Just—
just—just get out!"

The miserable creature began to splutter. "Well,
but—see here—"

"GET OUT!!"

I dashed forward and grabbed all his papers, crumpling them this way and that, gathering them in my
arms, and bore them to the front door. In turning
the knob, I dropped half of them. The remaining
half I hurled outward, and they fluttered to the lawn.
I kicked at those remaining, and turned to glare at
Mister Sampson as he scuttled from the house, wanting

to bluster but a bit too afraid of me to say anything.

I slammed the door after him and took a deep breath, forcing myself to be calm. I lit a cigarette. I lit another cigarette. Irritably, I stubbed the first one in a handy ash tray, and lit a third. "Tcha!" I cried, and mashed them all out, and stormed back to the bedroom, where I tore into the closet with genuine pleasure. Once the closet was a hopeless wreck, I ripped the covers from the bed and dumped the mattress on the floor. Then I surveyed my handiwork.

And the doorbell rang.

"If that is Mister Sampson," I muttered to myself, "by Heaven I'll—"

It rang again. We had an incredibly loud doorbell in that house. Odd I'd never noticed it before.

It rang again as I was on my way to answer, and I almost shouted at it to shut up. But I managed to bring myself under control by the time I reached the door, and to remember to open it not more than an inch.

A tiny girl in a green uniform stood looking up at me; she was bearing a box of cookies.

Life, I reflected at that moment, is unkind and cruel. I said, "We already bought some, little girl," and I softly closed the door.

And the telephone screamed.

I leaned against the door and let my nerves do whatever they wanted. But I knew I couldn't stay there. The telephone would only make that noise again. And again and again and again, until finally I gave up and answered it. The thing to do, I told myself calmly, was to answer it now. Then it couldn't make that noise any more.

A good plan. I was full of good plans. I went over and picked up the phone.

"Hiya, neighbor!" shouted a male voice. "This is Dan O'Toole, of WDEW. Can you Top That Mop?"

"What?"

"This is the grand new radio game everybody's talking about, neighbor. If you can Top That—"

I suppose he kept on talking. I don't know. I hung up.

I caught myself about to light a cigarette, and made myself stop. I also forced myself to be calm, think rationally, consider the circumstances. The house, except for my own ragged breathing, was silent.

With waning fervor, I studied once more the tableau I was leaving for the police. The dead woman in the kitchen, the ransacked house. All that remained was to fix the back door to make it look as though the burglar had forced his way in.

It seemed as though my plan should work perfectly well. It really seemed that way.

Slowly, I trudged out to the kitchen. For some reason, I suddenly no longer believed in my plan. All of life was involved in a great conspiracy against me. And it occurred to me that I hadn't known until today what Janice's existence at home had been like, and that her reckless spending might simply have been a form of escape.

At the back door, I paused, listening for doorbells and phone bells and church bells and jingle bells, but there was only silence. So I opened the door, and a short round woman was standing there, our next-door neighbor, wearing dress and apron and holding an empty cup.

I stared at her. She looked at me with puzzled surprise, and then her gaze moved beyond me and came to rest on something behind me, at floor level. Her eyes widened. Then she screamed and let go of the cup and went dashing away.

With the scream, I went rigid. I stared at the cup. It seemed to hang there in mid-air for the longest while, and then, very slowly at first, it started to fall. It fell faster and faster and finally splattered with a terrible crash on the patio cement.

And when the cup splattered, so did I. I went all limp and sat down with a bump on the kitchen floor.

And there I sat, waiting. I sat waiting, waiting for the census taker and the mailman with a Special Delivery letter, for the laundry man and the Railway Express driver, for the man from the cleaners, a horde of Boy Scouts on a paper drive, a political candidate, five wrong numbers, the paper boy, the police, a lady collecting for a worthy charity, the milkman, a call from the tax assessor's office, a young man working his way through college selling magazines ...

YOUR WITNESS

●

Helen Nielsen

With a degree of bitterness, a lawyer has been defined as one who can make black appear white or white appear black. Our detestable, forensic hero is singular only in that he proved a red traffic light green.

It was murder, although slaughter was a better term for it—or even assassination. Naomi Shawn settled on murder because it was a word that felt strangely at home in her mind. The crime, by any name, was happening to a bewildered citizen, one Henry Babcock, whose place of execution was the witness stand in Judge Dutton's court. Henry Babcock was in a somewhat similar circumstance to the late Agnes Thompson, housewife, who had been struck down by a Mercedes-Benz and subsequently buried. Henry was being buried, too; but he had the uncomfortable disadvantage of not being dead.

From her seat among the courtroom spectators, Naomi watched the scene with fascinated eyes. Arnold Shawn was a man of electrifying virility, persuasive charm, and intellectual dexterity. He was a dramatist, a strategist, a psychologist, and could, if need be, display the touch of the poet. He was more handsome at fifty than he'd been at twenty-five, more confident, more successful, more feared and much more hated. He was a lawyer who selected his clients with scrupulous care, basing his decision solely on ability to pay. But once a retainer was given, the accused could sit back with whatever ease an accused can muster and know that his fate was in the hands of as shrewd a legal talent as money could buy.

And the biggest heel.

Naomi Shawn's vocabulary wasn't as extensive as her husband's. He would have found a more distinctive way of describing his own character. In fact, he had done that very thing only a few hours earlier.

"I'm not cruel, Naomi; I'm honest. I could lie to you. It would be easy, easier than you know, my dear. I could prove to you, beyond your innermost feminine doubt, that I am an innocent, loyal, devoted husband who is passionately in love with you, and everything you think you've learned to the contrary is pure illusion. But I won't lie. There is another woman."

Naomi tried not to listen to echoes. Arnold was speaking, and Arnold commanded attention when he spoke.

"Now, Mr. Babcock," he was saying, "you have testified that you saw my client's automobile run a red light, strike the deceased, Agnes Thompson, drive on for a space of some fifty yards, stop, back up to a spot parallel with the body, and then drive on again without my client, Mr. Jerome, so much as alighting from the vehicle . . ."

Mr. Jerome. He was nineteen. A slight nineteen, with an almost childlike face and guilty blue eyes that stared disconsolately at his uncalloused hands laced together on the table before him. His blond hair was combed back neatly, and he wore a conservative tie, white shirt and dark suit, as per Arnold's instructions. Kenneth Jerome looked more like an honor Bible student than a cold-blooded hit and run killer. And he was that; Naomi was the one spectator in the court-room who knew. She had gone to Arnold's office one morning. He hadn't been home all night, a situation that was becoming alarmingly frequent. It was time to have a showdown. But young Jerome and his father had come to the office that day, and she was shunted off to another room. She heard the story. Kenneth Jerome couldn't deny hitting his victim; the police had already traced his car to the garage where it was being repaired.

"I didn't know I'd hit a woman," Kenneth Jerome explained. "I didn't see anyone. I thought I felt a thud, but it's open country out near the airport. Sometimes you hit a rabbit or even a cat late at night. And it was late. Somewhere near three-thirty, I think. Anyway, I thought that's what happened when I got home and saw my right front fender. I thought I'd hit a rabbit or a cat."

And Arnold's voice had queried him from across the desk.

"Is that what you told the police?"

"Sure, it is. What else could I tell them?"

"Is there a traffic signal at that intersection?"

"There is—but there wasn't another car in sight."

"Was the signal with you, or against you?"

"It was with me. It was green."

"Is that what you told the police?"

"Sure, it is. I said the woman must have tried to cross against the light. I didn't see her at all."

And then Arnold had smiled. From the next room, Naomi couldn't see the smile; but she could hear it in his words.

"Very good, Mr. Jerome. Now, unless you want me to throw this case back in your teeth, tell me what really happened last night. I don't deal with clients who aren't honest with me . . ."

Honest was one of Arnold's favorite words. It had an exceptional meaning to him.

"To be perfectly honest with you, Naomi, I never

did love you. Not the way a man wants to love a woman. Your father had influence and I needed a start. It was that simple."

Echoes. She pushed them from her mind. She had come to watch Henry Babcock take his punishment for being a good citizen.

Arnold's voice came again. "You were standing on the sidewalk near the intersection at the time of the accident, is that right?"

Henry Babcock was merely nervous at this stage of the cross-examination. He was a rather slight man, balding, had a clean shaven face and wore thick lensed glasses that magnified his eyes owlishly. He might have been Arnold's age, Naomi realized with a sense of incredulity. There was no other similarity. Henry Babcock looked shabby and servile. There was a natural elite, Arnold had always maintained, that was predestined to govern any society. At the moment, the validity of his theory seemed self-evident.

"Not exactly," Henry Babcock answered. "I was sitting on a bench at the bus stop, waiting for a bus."

"And how far was the bench from the intersection, Mr. Babcock?"

Henry Babcock hesitated. "I don't know as I could say, exactly. Not very far."

"Not very far." Arnold smiled. He was always dangerous when he smiled. "That doesn't help the jury much, does it, Mr. Babcock? Can't you be more specific? Was it as far"—he turned slowly, his eyes sweeping the courtroom and finally coming to rest—"as from where you're sitting to where the defendant is sitting?"

"Well, now, I don't know—"

"Yes or no, Mr. Babcock?"

The question was like a whip. Henry Babcock straightened his glasses and sat at attention.

"Well, yes," he said.

"The bench was the same distance from the intersection as you are from Mr. Jerome at this moment?"

"Yes, sir."

"Very good. Now please continue and tell the jury just what happened . . ."

What had happened? Naomi's mind would wander, no matter how she tried to keep it in line. Was it really as simple as Arnold had said—merely a marriage of convenience? It was difficult to believe. She knew why she'd married Arnold. She had loved him; she still loved him, in spite of what he'd become. Was she somehow responsible for that? She'd tried to be a good wife and mother; she tried to keep up with Arnold's dazzling success . . .

"Mr. Babcock"—Arnold's voice intruded on the memories again—"I want you to clarify one detail. You say that you didn't see Agnes Thompson prior to the accident. You were sitting on the bench waiting for a bus. Mrs. Thompson approached the intersection from the east—"

Someone had set up a blackboard in view of the judge and the jury. On it was drawn the intersection with crosses indicating the location of the bench and Henry Babcock, the spot where the accident occurred, and now, at Arnold's instruction, another cross for Mrs. Thompson approaching the intersection.

"We know that she came from the east," Arnold continued, "because we know that she had been visiting a sick grandchild and was returning to her own home, six blocks distant, only after the grandchild had shown signs of recovery and gone to sleep. Presumably, Mrs. Thompson was weary after the strain of her vigil; presumably, she walked with a heavy tread—she was a rather heavy woman. How do you account for not hearing Mrs. Thompson approach the intersection, Mr. Babcock?"

Henry Babcock appeared puzzled. He rubbed his jaw thoughtfully with one hand, and the light glinted off the lens of his eyeglasses. The staring eyes of the jury and the courtroom seemed to bother him. The question bothered him, too.

"I didn't say that I didn't *hear* her," he answered.

"Then you did hear her."

"I didn't say that, either. Maybe I heard her. I don't remember. I was tired, too. I'd just come from work."

"At the Century Club?"

"Yes sir. I clean up there after the place closes at two o'clock."

"Two a.m., that is."

"Yes, sir."

Two a.m. It was difficult to find an accident witness in broad daylight; but when, a few days after taking the case, Arnold had received an urgent telephone call from Jerome Sr. at a similar hour of a different morning, he knew there was work ahead. It was in the downstairs hall. Arnold had just come in. He still wore his black Homburg and black topcoat over his tuxedo. Naomi had descended most of the way down the stairs, having started when she heard him come in. He took the call in silence, concluding it with a curt assurance that he would handle everything. He'd dropped the telephone back into the cradle for a moment; then took it up again and dialed.

"Fran? Arnold here. Sorry to call you now, but something's come up. The Jerome case—a witness. Yes, the police are keeping him under wraps; but old man Jerome just got wind of it at a cocktail party and passed the word along. Now, here's what I want you to do. Get the wheels rolling. Get everything you can on Henry Babcock. That's right. Babcock. He's a ja... or porter, or some such thing at the Century Clu... was waiting for a bus to go home after work wh... accident happened. I want him tabbed from the ... One. You know how."

Arnold had dropped the telephone back into the cradle and turned around. Naomi was at the bottom of the stairs by that time. He stared at her without seeming to see her at all.

"Is that who she is?" Naomi had asked. "Is it Fran, your secretary?"

Arnold's eyebrows had a way of knitting together when he was annoyed. At that moment she hadn't been sure whether he was more annoyed with her question or with Jerome's call; but it was probably the latter. She didn't even possess nuisance value any more.

"Is that who *who* is?" he'd asked.

"The woman you've been with tonight."

She'd reached out and straightened his tie. Old-fashioned as it was, and Arnold did hate being old-fashioned about anything.

"You're talking nonsense, Naomi. Go to bed."

It was the way to dismiss a child. He'd stalked upstairs, his mind busy with the problem of Henry Babcock, good citizen, bent on the folly of doing his duty...

And so they were in the courtroom, and Arnold was solving his problem.

". . . so, at approximately half-past three, having finished your work at the Century Club, you were sitting on a bench at the bus stop waiting for transportation to take you home. Where do you live, Mr. Babcock?"

It was an innocent question. Henry Babcock answered without hesitation.

"In Inglewood," he said. "I've got a three-room apartment."

"And do you live alone?"

"Yes, sir. Since my wife died three years ago."

"Since your wife died," Arnold repeated. "My sympathies, Mr. Babcock. It must be lonely, coming home to an empty apartment."

The prosecutor stirred uneasily. He seemed to sense some ulterior motivation behind the question. Before he could object, Henry Babcock, who sensed nothing but the discomfort of the witness box, had answered.

"Yes, sir, it is," he said.

"But you do have friends."

"Friends?"

"At your place of employment. I believe the Century Club employs entertainers, including several very attractive young ladies. I understand that you do little favors for them, such as bringing coffee to the dressing rooms—"

The prosecutor leaped to his feet.

"Your Honor, I object to this line of questioning. We aren't here to ascertain the witness's sociability, or to delve into his personal life."

Arnold turned toward him, smiling.

"And why aren't we?" he asked. "The witness has testified in direct contradiction to the sworn statement of my client. Obviously, one of these two men is either mistaken or an outright liar. I see nothing objectionable, in attempting to establish the character of the witness. For that matter, I see nothing objectionable —although the learned prosecutor seems to differ with me on this point—in a lonely widower bringing coffee to a ladies' dressing room."

There was something diabolical about Arnold in action. Naomi was beginning to realize that. In a few words, he'd turned the prosecutor into an unwitting counsel for the defense. The man sat down, chastened and confused.

Arnold turned back to Henry Babcock.

"Agnes Thompson approached the intersection from the east," he resumed. "That means that she came from behind you, doesn't it?"

"Yes, sir," Babcock answered.

"Yes, because you sat on a bench parallel to a street running north and south. The bench"—Arnold referred to the blackboard again—"is on the southeast corner of the intersection. The signal, which you have testified was red when my client's automobile struck Mrs. Thompson, is approximately ten feet north of the bench, which would have been to your right as you sat facing the street. Correct?"

Henry Babcock adjusted his glasses and leaned forward to follow Arnold's indications on the blackboard map.

"Yes, that's correct," he agreed.

"And so, you were sitting on the bench, tired after the night's work."

"Yes, sir."

"And alone?"

"Yes, sir."

"Waiting for a bus to take you home to your apartment where you live alone."

Babcock's forehead had corrugated into a puzzled frown, but he answered.

"Yes, sir."

"You looked at the signal, and saw that it was red."

"Yes, sir."

"And before it changed to green, my client's automobile raced past the intersection, striking down Mrs. Thompson, whom you hadn't noticed prior to the accident—" Arnold paused, as if only at that instant discovering a flaw in the testimony. "Now, that does seem strange," he mused aloud. "You turned your head to the right and saw that the signal was red. Why didn't you also see Mrs. Thompson preparing to step down into the cross-walk?"

There was a slight murmur in the courtroom. Arnold's strategy was beginning to take hold.

"I don't know," Babcock answered. "I guess she wasn't there yet when I looked."

"Then you must have looked away from the light for a time."

Babcock hesitated, sensing a trap.

"The light was red!" he insisted.

"But you didn't see Mrs. Thompson."

"It was dark."

"Isn't there a street lamp at that intersection? Think, Mr. Babcock."

"There's a street lamp, but it only shines so far. After that, it's dark."

"And yet Mrs. Thompson would have had to come into that arc of light, wouldn't she?"

"Maybe she came too fast for me to see her. Maybe she was running."

"Running?" Arnold caught up the word and dangled it before the ears of the court. "Now, why would she have been running, Mr. Babcock? Haven't we already established that it was late, very late, and that she must have been weary from sitting up with a sick grandchild?"

Henry Babcock was an uncomplicated man who, very likely, had never sat in a witness box before in his life. He'd come to do his duty, and yet, by answering extemporaneously a few minor questions he hadn't thought through, he'd gotten himself into trouble. He glanced pleadingly at the prosecutor, who was helpless at the moment, and then got himself into worse trouble.

"Maybe she was afraid."

"But why should she have been afraid?" Arnold demanded.

"Because it was so late. It's not safe for a woman out alone at that hour. Things happen. You read about it in the paper all the time."

Arnold listened carefully to Henry Babcock, so carefully that he caught up the entire courtroom in his attitude and everyone listened, carefully.

"I read about it?" he echoed. "What do *I* read about?"

The accentuated pronoun forced Henry Babcock to a correction.

"I mean, people do," he explained. "Anybody."

"I think what you mean," Arnold interpolated, "is that *you* read about it all the time. Now, just what do *you* read?"

Henry Babcock was perspiring freely. He didn't bother to wipe his brow.

"Things that happen," he said. "Robberies, attacks—"

"And you always read about these things, is that right, Mr. Babcock? When you're all finished bringing coffee to the ladies' dressing room, and cleaning up the deserted club, you go home to your apartment, alone, and read about terrible things that happen to women who go out on the streets at night—"

Arnold's voice was an instrument played with professional skill. It was impossible not to be drawn along

© Lorillard 1975

C'mon

Come for the filter. ## You'll stay for the taste.

19 mg. "tar," 1.2 mg. nicotine av. per cigarette, FTC Report Apr.'75.

Warning: The Surgeon General Has Determined That Cigarette Smoking Is Dangerous to Your Health.

I'd heard enough to make me decide one of two things: quit or smoke True.

I smoke True.
The low tar, low nicotine cigarette.
Think about it.

King Regular: 11 mg. "tar", 0.6 mg. nicotine,
King Menthol: 12 mg. "tar", 0.7 mg. nicotine, 100's
Regular: 13 mg. "tar", 0.7 mg. nicotine, 100's Menthol: 13 mg.
"tar", 0.8 mg. nicotine, av. per cigarette, FTC Report April '75.

Warning: The Surgeon General Has Determined
That Cigarette Smoking Is Dangerous to Your Health.

with it. But he got no farther before the prosecutor was on his feet shouting an objection. Arnold smiled at him with an expression of tolerant patience, and only Naomi understood what was happening. The innocent must always be made to appear guilty. This was Arnold's secret of success.

". . . I don't want a scene, Naomi. This woman need never have come between us if you hadn't insisted on a showdown. I'm not planning to divorce you, or to allow you to divorce me. I can't afford a scandal, and you have the children to consider even if my career means nothing to you . . ."

The innocent must always be made to appear guilty.

"Your Honor," Arnold continued, with mock humility, "I'm deeply sorry if my remarks have caused prejudice in the minds of the jury. It wasn't my intention to infer that the witness has socially undesirable tendencies. Nevertheless, I'm still curious as to how he could have turned his head to observe the traffic signal and not have seen a woman about to step out into the crosswalk. If he was tired, he might have been dozing; but then, he wouldn't have seen the signal. If, however, he was alert enough to notice the signal, why didn't he see Mrs. Thompson?"

With these words, Arnold swung back to Henry Babcock.

"Or did you see her, Mr. Babcock?"

Henry Babcock drew back in the box.

"No," he said.

"Are you sure, Mr. Babcock? A few moments ago you were positive that you didn't see her; a few moments later you thought that you might have heard her. Now you can't seem to explain why you didn't see her. Isn't it possible that you did see her? That perhaps you spoke to her?"

"No—"

"That you approached her?"

"No! I never left the bench!"

"You never left the bench, and yet, with an automobile approaching, and surely Mrs. Thompson could have seen the headlights, the victim stepped off the curb and into its path. Why did she do that, Mr. Babcock, unless, as you have suggested, she was startled out of her wits? Was there anyone else in the vicinity at the time?"

Babcock was no longer bewildered; he was furious. "No!" he shouted.

"Then no one could have startled Mrs. Thompson unless it was yourself."

"I didn't say she was startled."

"But you suggested it. You suggested that she might have been running. These are interesting suggestions, in view of the fact that you knew no one other than yourself was in the vicinity. Since you've volunteered this much light on the mystery of what happened at that intersection the night Mrs. Thompson died, perhaps, remembering that you're under oath, you would like to tell the whole truth."

Arnold waited for an answer, and the court waited with him.

"I told the truth!" Babcock insisted. "The whole truth!"

"Thank you, Mr. Babcock."

Arnold stepped back. He seemed ready to release the witness; only Naomi knew it was a feint. There had been another telephone call only this morning. She'd overheard enough to know Henry Babcock wasn't going to get off so easily.

". . . Yes, Fran, he's going to be tough to crack—too clean. Nothing on him unless I can color up that job of his. What? Do you have proof? Good girl! Of course, it's enough. I'll make it enough."

And then he'd looked up to find Naomi staring at him accusingly.

"What are you going to do to that poor man?" she had asked.

"I'm going to win my case," he had answered.

"Your client is guilty."

"Not until the jury brings in a verdict. Don't look so shocked, Naomi. You can't be that naïve! A courtroom is just like a battlefield. When a soldier's ordered to take an objective, he can't consider if innocent people will be hurt. There are no innocent people; there are only the quick and the dead. I'm one of the quick. Because of that, you live in a beautiful home, wear lovely clothes, drive an expensive sedan—"

"Who is the woman, Arnold?"

And that was when he had stopped evading her.

"I'm not cruel, Naomi; I'm honest. I could lie to you. It would be easy, easier than you know . . ."

Sitting among the spectators in the courtroom, Naomi learned how easy it was.

"Mr. Babcock—" Arnold swung back to face the witness, his sudden movement and the sound of his voice magnetizing attention. "How long have you been employed at the Century Club?"

The change of tactic puzzled Babcock.

"Ten months," he said.

"I don't suppose your salary is anything remarkable."

"I don't need much."

"Still, it's not comparable to—let us say, an instructor of mathematics and mechanical drawing at Freeman High School, which position you held for fourteen years prior to your employment at the Century Club. Tell me, Mr. Babcock, why does a man of your background work as a porter in a cheap night club? Why are you reduced to pushing a broom and running errands for showgirls? Or does this explain better?"

No one was prepared for Arnold's next move, least of all Henry Babcock. When Arnold reached out and snatched the glasses from his eyes, Babcock rose from the chair, grasped at empty air, and barely steadied himself against the side of the bench short of falling.

"My glasses—" he gasped.

"Your *eyes*, Mr. Babcock!" Arnold corrected. "Isn't it true that you relinquished your profession because you were going blind?"

"No! I had cataracts—"

"Because your vision was eighty-five per cent im-

paired when you underwent surgery eight months ago?
Because you were totally *color* blind?"

Arnold had won his case. Naomi could sense the
feeling of the court even before her ears picked up the
murmur. By that time, Henry Babcock was trying to
explain that an operation had restored vision to one
eye and he was awaiting the required full year before
a second operation that would restore the other; but
few people heard.

"I'll be good as new!" he insisted. "I'll get my teaching job back—"

"But you weren't 'good as new' the night you claim
to have seen my client go through a red light!"

"With my glasses, I can see color!"

"Out of which eye?"

"The left eye. The one that had the operation."

"But the signal is to your right."

"I turned my head."

"But you didn't see Mrs. Thompson."

"I couldn't. I can't see out of the sides—only straight
ahead."

"Only straight ahead!" Arnold pounced on the
phrase, as if he had been waiting for it all this time.
"And how far straight ahead, Mr. Babcock? As far as
from where you are sitting to the defendant—that's
what you said, didn't you?"

Henry Babcock leaned forward, a grotesque figure of
a man trying to peer through a fog.

"With my glasses—" he began.

"Your Honor," Arnold announced, "I move that the
testimony of the witness be stricken from the record.
It's obvious to everyone in this courtroom that he is
not capable of giving reliable information on anything
of a visual nature. The distance from the witness stand
to the defendant, which Mr. Babcock has, under oath,
declared to be the same as the distance from the bench
on which he was seated at the time of the accident to
the point at which the accident occurred, can't possibly
measure in excess of thirty feet. I invite the prosecution to check me on this." There was no need to

check. Naomi, remembering, realized when Arnold had
set his trap. He was always dangerous when he smiled.
"I have already checked the distance between the
bench and the place of the accident," he added, "and
it is, ladies and gentlemen of the jury, exactly sixty-
two feet! Not only is the witness color blind, not only
is he incapable of seeing out of the sides of his eyes;
he is also completely unable to estimate simple dis-
tances. Unless he's deliberately lying about everything,
unless he did leave the bench and does know some
reason why Mrs. Thompson stepped out in front of
a fast moving automobile, the most charitable conclu-
sion can reach is that this poor man's mind has
been feebled by the double tragedy of losing his wife
and almost losing his sight, and is incompetent to
testify in a court of law!"

The prosecution roared a protest. Arnold turned
toward him with a gesture of contemptuous dismissal.

"Your witness!" he said.

The jury was out fifteen minutes. After the acquit-
tal, Arnold received congratulations with his cus-
tomary indifference. The courtroom emptied. Naomi
watched a defeated little man make his way toward
the corridor: Henry Babcock, ex-good citizen. She
caught his eyes, magnified by the lenses of the glasses,
as he went by. It had been murder. He went out and
she waited alone for Arnold.

"So that's how you take an objective," she said. "Did
you have to destroy his character as well as his testimony? Do you think he'll ever get that teaching job
back now?"

"If he's man enough," Arnold said. "That's his
problem, not mine."

"Your problem is only how to get rid of a bother-
some wife, isn't it?"

Arnold didn't seem to consider the question worth
answering. They went out together. The sidewalk was
deserted now except for a dejected man waiting at the
bus stop, a man for whom Arnold didn't have so much
as a glance. At the entrance to the parking lot, he

looked up and frowned at the sky. It was starting to rain lightly.

"I'm glad you decided to visit court today, Naomi," he said. "I've got a five o'clock appointment and it's the very devil to catch a cab in bad weather."

"Five o'clock?" Naomi echoed. "That gives you time to pick up flowers. Shall I stop at a florist?"

"No, thank you, Naomi. Just get your car, please. I'll wait."

And Arnold waited. He stood at the edge of the parking lot driveway, so supremely confident that he didn't so much as step back when Naomi brought the sedan around. He didn't even have time to change his self-satisfied expression to surprise when she suddenly cut the wheels and slammed her foot on the accelerator and

After the police officer had extracted Arnold's lifeless from under the wheels, Naomi tried to explain.

"It was a mistake!" she sobbed. "I meant to put my foot on the brake, not the accelerator! It was a terrible mistake!"

A small crowd had gathered, but there was only one eye-witness. The officer turned to him, and for a moment Naomi caught a glimpse of the man's eyes. The sympathy she'd given him in the courtroom was in them.

"If this woman is the victim's wife, surely she's telling the truth," he said. "Anyway, what I might have seen couldn't contradict her." Henry Babcock removed his glasses and blinked at the blur which was the policeman. "It's a legal fact," he said, "that I'm not a reliable witness."

BLACKOUT

•

Richard Deming

One should make a confession of murder properly. As is the case at all social functions, suitable attire is most important. When admitting to first-degree murder, a dark, conservative business suit—in keeping with premeditation—is beyond reproach. Shun the hand-painted tie, the light-colored sock, and the electrified bow tie.

The man came into the homicide squadroom about nine a.m. He was about forty-five, well-dressed and freshly shaven. His suit had been so recently pressed, it looked as though he hadn't even sat down in it since it left the ironing board. His whole appearance was neat, except that his necktie was slightly off-center and his hair was sloppily combed.

He gave the impression that he had been busily trying to sober up after an all-night binge by having a cold shower and a lot of black coffee. He'd also made himself presentable. The sobering-up process had, obviously, not been completely successful.

I said, "Yes, sir?"

Leaning his hands on the edge of the table where I was sitting, he carefully looked me up and down. "You a policeman?"

"Uh-huh," I said. "Sergeant Sod Harris."

"You're not wearing a policeman's suit," he said owlishly.

"In the detective bureau we don't wear policemen's suits," I said. "Believe me, I'm a policeman."

He let go of the table edge, straightened up and swayed slightly. "All right. If you're a policeman, lock me up."

I looked him over thoughtfully. Sam Wiggens, who was checking a case in one of the filing cabinets, put the folder back, and came over to stand alongside of me.

I said, "You done something to be locked up?"

The man gave his head an impatient shake. "Just want to be locked up."

"Why?"

"You need a reason?"

Sam Wiggens said, "There has to be a charge, mister. We're not running a boarding house."

The man turned his gaze to Sam. It took him time to focus his eyes. "Is drunk good enough?" he inquired.

Sam looked him up and down. "Might be."

"Well, you ever see anybody drunker?"

Sam looked at me and I looked at him. Turning back to the drunk, I asked, "How'd you happen to come here?"

"What?"

"To this office. Know where you are?"

He considered this before saying brightly, "Sign on the door said Homicide."

"Yeah," I said. "You wanted to turn in drunk, why didn't you just go to the Central District desk downstairs?"

This presented him with a problem. He had to consider some more before saying, "Just came in the first door I saw."

"On the third floor?" Sam inquired. "You didn't notice any doors on the way up?"

The drunk looked from Sam to me and back again. He couldn't seem to think of any answer.

I said, "Want to tell us your name, mister?"

He shook his head. "I don't see that that's necessary. Look, gentlemen, I came in here voluntarily. I wasn't arrested and dragged in. There's no reason to treat me like a criminal."

Sam said, "Nobody's treating you like a criminal. We just want to know who you are."

"Mind if I sit down and explain things?" he said.

"Go ahead," I told him.

The man carefully seated himself across from me, fumbled out a package of cigarettes and gave me an inquiring look. I pushed an ash tray toward him and held a lighted match to his cigarette.

"Thanks," he said, inhaling.

He offered the pack to us, and we both shook our heads.

"About this explanation—" I prodded.

"Well, first you must understand that I have a rather prominent social position."

"Uh-huh."

"I wouldn't want it in the papers that I'd been booked as a common drunk. Even though I am a common drunk."

Sam said, "You going to get to the point, mister?"

"I'm getting there. You see I'm an alcoholic."

"No!" I said.

"Fact. A periodic. Sometimes I go for months without a drink. Doesn't bother me a bit. Go to cocktail parties, watch everybody else slugging it down, don't have the least desire to touch it myself. Then, for no reason, I decide to try a single sip. And bingo."

Neither Sam nor I said anything.

"Don't know why I do it," he went on. "Same thing always happens."

"What's that?" I inquired.

"I get drunk and stay that way for days."

Sam asked, "How long's it been this time?"

"Three and a half days," he said promptly. Someone must have told him, because he couldn't have been keeping track of time. "After eighteen months without a drink."

I said, "You still haven't said why you came here."

"Well, sir, I decided the only way to stop was to get myself locked up. No way I could get hold of it in jail, you see."

I grunted and Sam said, "You always sober up this way?"

"Sir?"

"Ever turned yourself in before?"

He shook his head. "First time I've tried it."

"What made you decide this time?"

He shrugged. "Just seemed like a good idea."

I said, "Want to tell us your name now?"

He shook his head again. "I explained why I can't do that."

After looking him over for a moment, I said, "Mind emptying your pockets?"

Agreeably, he began removing items from his pockets and laying them on the table. There was a handkerchief, a pack of cigarettes, a book of matches, a key ring with some door keys on it, some change and a money clip containing a few bills.

I said, "No wallet?"

He smiled. "I anticipated this. I left all identification at home."

Sam and I exchanged glances. Sam asked, "You ever been arrested?"

"No, sir," he said with an emphatic headshake.

Picking up the key ring, I handed it to Sam. "Take this up to the lab, Sam, and run them all through the key machine."

The man straightened in his chair. "What's the key machine?" he asked suspiciously.

"A machine that identifies locks," I told him. "We'll have your home address in fifteen minutes."

He looked at me uncertainly. "I didn't know you could do that."

"You know it now. Go ahead, Sam."

Sam was moving toward the door when the man said, "Wait a minute."

Sam halted to look at him. We both waited.

The man said, "I wouldn't want my wife to know about this."

We continued to wait.

"All right," he said with an air of resignation. "My name's George Cooper."

I asked, "Where do you live?"

He gave me an address on Lindell Boulevard. While I was writing it down, Sam tossed the key ring back on the table and returned to his previous spot.

I said, "Now let's get back to the important question. Why'd you come to Homicide?"

"I told you," Cooper said. "It was the first door I saw."

The phone rang and Sam answered it. "Homicide. Wiggens."

After listening a moment, he said, "Yeah, he made it. Thanks for checking."

He hung up, glanced at Cooper, then at me. "Information desk downstairs," he said. "Just checking up."

"On what?" I asked.

"Fellow asked where to find Homicide. They wondered if he ever got there. They thought he might have been too drunk to find his way."

We both looked at George Cooper, who tapped ashes from his cigarette in an elaborate pretense that **he didn't know** what Sam was talking about.

I said to Sam, "See if he has a record."

Sam went over to pick up the phone. I gazed at George Cooper steadily while Sam was giving his name and description to Records. Avoiding my eyes, the man butted his cigarette.

While waiting for Records to phone back, we continued to question Cooper, but he still refused to say why he had turned himself into Homicide instead of downstairs. When Records finally phoned back that there was no package on the man, we gave up. We decided to take him down to Central District and book him.

Rising, I said, "Okay, Cooper. Let's go."

"Where?" he inquired.

"Downstairs. You wanted jail, didn't you?"

Getting to his feet, Cooper began putting his possessions back in his pockets. "Well, finally," he said. "It's certainly hard to get arrested around here." Then he paused with his key ring in his hands. "It's all right to take my things back, isn't it?"

"For now," Sam said. "They'll check them for you downstairs."

Cooper returned the rest of the items to his pockets. He emitted a relieved sigh.

"Now I won't have to worry any more," he said.

"About what?" I asked.

"Getting in trouble."

"What kind of trouble?"

"You know," he said vaguely. "I forget things when I black out. Later people tell me I've done things I shouldn't."

"Like what?" I asked.

"Oh, different things. Get belligerent, maybe. Start a fight."

"You have a fight somewhere?"

"No, no," he said quickly. "I was just giving an example."

I said, "You turned in here to keep from getting in a fight?"

He pursed his lips. "Well, you might say that."

"With who?"

"A friend of mine," he said reluctantly.

"He got a name?"

"Henry Marks," he said even more reluctantly. "My next-door neighbor."

Sam asked, "You have some trouble with this Marks?"

"Not trouble," Cooper said with a shake of his head. "He's been hanging around my wife, is all. I just told him to stay away."

Sam looked at me. "That name ring a bell, Sod?"

I shook my head. "Not to me."

Sam puzzled over it for a moment then walked over to the bulletin board. After glancing it over, he nodded with satisfaction.

"Thought I'd seen it," he announced. "On the M.P.

bulletin. Henry Marks has been missing since last Friday."

We both stared at George Cooper, who suddenly looked uncomfortable.

"You better sit back down again, Mr. Cooper," I said. "We've got a lot more talking to do."

It took us another half hour to get about half a story out of Cooper. At first he insisted he knew nothing of Henry Marks's whereabouts. But eventually he began to change his story. He admitted having a fight with Henry Marks when he discovered him in his home. But he insisted that it hadn't been much of a fight and that the missing man was all right when he left Cooper's home immediately after the fight. He further insisted that the fight had taken place only the previous night. According to the M.P. report, at that time Marks had been missing three days.

I said, "Last night was Monday. You sure this fight didn't take place Friday?"

"Of course I'm sure," he said in a sullen voice.

"Maybe you had one of your blackouts," Sam suggested. "Maybe you lost a couple of days."

Cooper said, "Listen, it was last night. I *was* blacked out, but the fight sobered me up. When I saw what I'd done—"

He stopped abruptly and stared from one to the other of us, appalled at his slip of the tongue.

"Go on," I said quietly.

"I mean—you see, I don't remember the fight at all. Don't remember coming home—anything about it. My wife had to tell me."

"Tell you what?" I asked.

Cooper looked from me to Sam with a trapped expression on his face. He opened and closed his mouth twice before he finally got anything out.

"I may as well tell you," he finally managed. "I meant to when I came in."

"Go ahead," I told him.

"I got cold feet. I meant to tell the whole thing when I came here. Then I got scared."

Sam and I waited.

After a long pause, he said in a bare whisper, "I killed him."

The man dropped his face in his hands. We sat watching him and after a moment he listlessly dropped his hands to his sides and sat in a dejected attitude, his head down.

"Want to tell us about it?" I inquired.

He told us then. Once he had brought himself to admit the crime, he answered everything we asked willingly, but without spirit. He said he had left his home in a mildly intoxicated condition about 8:00 p.m. the previous Friday. After a round of taverns and night clubs, he had checked into a hotel and continued drinking in his room. Saturday, Sunday and Monday were largely blank. Except for brief periods he recalled nothing until he was awakened on his front-room couch by his wife shaking him. Henry Marks lay on the floor dead, his skull crushed by a pair of fire tongs.

I said, "You remember nothing at all about the fight?"

"Just what Helen told me," he said dully. "She saw it."

"What's her story?"

"I came staggering in, found Henry there and accused him of chasing Helen. One thing led to another, and finally he hit me." He felt of his jaw. "Ought to remember that. Still hurts. But I don't."

"Then what happened?" I asked.

"Helen says I fell near the fireplace. When I got up, I had the tongs in my hand. I swung them and George dropped." His voice grew tired. "That's all there is to it."

"Not quite," I said. "There's still one small item you haven't covered. What did you do with the body?"

"Oh, that," he said almost with indifference. "I buried him in the back yard." After a pause, he offered, "I'll show you right where, if you'd like."

We told him we'd like. Booking him on suspicion

of homicide, we had him checked out in our custody. Before leaving headquarters, we called the lab and asked for a technician to meet us at Cooper's home. We suggested he bring along a pair of strong-backed rookies with shovels. Then we drove out to Cooper's home on Lindell Boulevard.

Cooper lived right across from Forest Park, in one of the richest sections in St. Louis. He, therefore, might very well have been as socially prominent as he had claimed. His home, a two-story affair of tan brick, was set fifty feet back from the street and had about a hundred feet between it and the houses either side.

Sam turned the car into the driveway and parked alongside the house. We all got out and walked around to the back. Leading us to the rear of the yard, Cooper dully nodded toward a freshly-spaded section of garden.

"Right there," he said in a low voice.

Sam said, "It's a neat job. Smoothed off nice and even. What'd you do with the extra dirt?"

"Dumped it out back in a ditch."

"How'd you manage such a clean job, as drunk as you were?" Sam asked. "And how come the neighbors didn't see you?"

"Helen helped me. And it was dark last night. We didn't use a light except to check up on how it looked afterward."

The back door opened and a slim, rather pretty woman of about forty came outside. She wore a concerned expression on her face and her eyes widened when she got close enough to see Cooper's handcuffs.

"What is it?" she asked on a high note. "Are you men police officers?"

I said, "Yes, ma'am. I'm Sergeant Sod Harris of Homicide. This is Officer Sam Wiggens."

"Homicide?" she said. "Why is my husband handcuffed? George, what is it?"

In a low voice Cooper said, "I told them about it."

"About what?" She looked at me. "What's he done?"

"We understood you knew, lady," I said.

She looked frightenedly from me to Sam and then at her husband. "Knew what?"

"It's no use, Helen," Cooper said in a weary tone. "I told them everything."

Her nervous gaze made another circuit of all three of us. She took a deep breath and said rapidly, "I didn't have anything to do with it."

I said, "Afraid it's not that easy. Your husband says you helped him conceal the body."

Glancing at Cooper, she nervously worked her hands together.

Sam said, "Makes you an accessory, lady."

"You can't blame me for not reporting it," she said. "He's my husband. A wife doesn't have to testify against her own husband. Right?"

"Sure," Sam said dryly. "But she doesn't have to help him bury bodies either."

Art Ward from the lab came around the corner of the house carrying a lab kit and a camera. He had two uniformed cops with him carrying shovels. Mrs. Cooper stared at the shovels as if she'd never seen one before.

"Hi, Sod, Sam," Ward said. "What's the scoop?" He gave Cooper and Mrs. Cooper a curious glance.

I pointed to the spaded area. "Right there, Art. Should be a body." I turned to the woman. "Maybe we'd better go inside while they're digging, Mrs. Cooper."

She nodded and then led the way toward the house, with her husband following and Sam and me bringing up the rear. One of the policemen sank his shovel into the ground as we walked away.

She only took us as far as the kitchen. Offering us seats at the kitchen table, she said in a flustered voice, "You'll have to excuse the house. The servants have been gone several days. I—I always let them have off when George . . ." She let her voice trail off.

Cooper said glumly, "She means she gives them a vacation when I fall off the wagon. She doesn't want them to know how I am."

I glanced around. The place looked clean enough to me.

I said, "Now, Mrs. Cooper, you want to tell us about last night?"

She was standing by the window over the sink, her attention divided between us and what was going on outside. "What is there to tell?" she asked. "George said he told you all about it."

"We'd like your version," I said. "Incidentally, we came inside so you wouldn't have to watch what was going on out there. Don't you think it would be better if you came away from the window?"

Flushing, she came over to the table and sank into a chair. "What do you want me to tell you, Sergeant? George came home drunk and found Mr. Marks here. They had a fight and George hit him with the fire tongs. That's all there is to it."

"How did Marks happen to be here?" I asked.

"He came to the door about fifteen minutes before George got home. He'd been drinking too, but I didn't realize that until after I'd let him in. He—he tried to get fresh with me. I ordered him out of the house, but he wouldn't go. Then George staggered in and the argument started. It would never have happened if George had been home where he belonged instead of out getting drunk. Drink was the cause of the whole thing. How many times I've warned my husband. George, haven't I done everything possible to make you stop?"

"I guess," Cooper said in a low voice.

There was a knock at the back door. Mrs. Cooper started to get up, but I waved her back to her seat and answered it myself. Art Ward was standing on the back porch. Stepping out, I closed the door behind me.

"It was there all right, Sod," he said. "Got a bashed-in skull. He was only buried about a foot down."

I walked back to the grave with him to look at the

body. It had been lifted out alongside of the hole. It was still all covered with dirt.

"How long do you figure?" I asked Ward.

He shrugged. "No bloating. I'd guess under twenty-four hours. You'll have to wait for the coroner's physician to make a post mortem if you want it pinpointed."

I said, "Our information is he died last night."

"I'd figure about that," he agreed. "In this weather it doesn't take long for them to begin to swell. And he hasn't started yet."

I sent one of the uniformed policemen over next door to break the news to the victim's wife and bring her over to identify the body. She was a mousy little woman of middle age and she went all to pieces when she saw what was left of her husband. She managed to identify him, but she was too upset right then to question. I sent her back home accompanied by the same officer who had brought her over. I told him to phone her family doctor to come over and see if he could quiet her down. Then I went back inside.

I took Art Ward back inside with me, having him bring his lab kit. Mrs. Cooper took us into the front room and pointed out the fire tongs, which still lay next to the fireplace with dried blood on them. I told Ward to check them for prints, then take them back to the lab.

There wasn't much more we could do at the scene. Sam called City Hospital for an ambulance to take the body to the morgue, while I went next door to see how Mrs. Marks was doing. Her family doctor had arrived and had put her under a sedative. I left word with a servant for Mrs. Marks to drop down to headquarters the next day if she felt better, or to phone me if she wasn't up to it.

We took both Mr. and Mrs. Cooper back downtown. Cooper had already been booked, so we just turned him over to Central District and had him put in a cell. Pending further investigation, we booked Mrs. Cooper on suspicion of being an accessory to homicide and held her overnight.

The next morning, Wednesday, Mrs. Marks's maid phoned that her mistress was feeling better and would be down to see us about ten a.m., if that was suitable. I said it was fine.

A few minutes later Art Ward phoned from the lab.

"Fingerprints all over those fire tongs," he said. "Mr. Cooper's, Mrs. Cooper's, some other people who will probably turn out to be servants. Everybody who ever fixed the fire last winter, I guess."

"Any superimposed over the others, to show who handled them last?"

He snorted. "That's for the movies. We're not that brilliant."

Mousy little Mrs. Marks came into the squadroom just as I hung up. She hadn't met Sam yesterday because he had been inside with the Coopers. After introducing him, I asked the woman to have a seat.

"We're sorry to impose on you so soon after your loss, Mrs. Marks," I said. "But it has to be done."

"It's all right," she said listlessly.

I said, "We'll make this as short as possible. We know it's painful for you."

"I have plenty of time," she said drearily. "Time is all I have left. But I suppose I shouldn't complain. I've spent most of my life waiting anyway."

"How's that?" I inquired.

"For him. If I had back all the hours I've waited up, wondering where he was . . ."

When her voice trailed off, I said, "Your husband?"

She nodded. "I never really blamed him for it. He *was* awfully handsome, you know. And I'm so plain. I suppose I was lucky to have Henry at all, even to share with other women."

It seemed like a peculiar philosophy, but I wasn't going to argue with her. I said, "There's some question about the date of your husband's disappearance, Mrs. Marks. It may help to backtrack his movements. Now the M.P. report says you first missed him about nine Friday evening."

"Oh, no," she said. "I didn't miss him until eight

Saturday morning. Nine Friday evening was just the last I saw him."

I said, "I don't think I follow."

"He went out about nine Friday night," she explained. "I was upset when he didn't come home, but not worried. About anything having happened to him, I mean. It wasn't the first time he'd stayed out all night. I didn't really begin to worry until about seven-thirty the next morning. By eight I knew something had happened."

Sam asked, "How was that?"

"He always came home to shave and shower before going to work. He owned Marks's Department Store, you know, and he never missed being there at opening time. He always said if the boss couldn't get to work on time, he couldn't expect the help to. He never came in later than seven-thirty unless it was a Sunday."

I asked, "Any idea where he went when he left the house Friday evening?"

"I thought I had. But I decided I was wrong when I saw her go off shopping Saturday morning."

"Who?" I inquired.

"Mrs. Cooper, next door. She always goes downtown shopping Saturday morning. Get's all dressed up and leaves about eleven. When I saw her leave at her usual time, I figured I was wrong. She'd hardly have left him alone over there."

Sam said, "You mean you thought your husband might have spent the night at the Cooper home?"

"Naturally," she said. "Helen Cooper was his latest interest. Everybody in the neighborhood knew that."

"Oh?" I said. "Including Mr. Cooper?"

"Well, maybe not him. But everybody else did. It was common gossip."

I asked her to be a little more specific and she gave us the names of two neighbor friends whom she said would confirm what she had said about her husband and Helen Cooper. We also questioned her about her husband's last movements, but she wasn't very helpful on that point. She said she had watched him walk up the street in the direction of King's Highway and go right past the Cooper home. If he had later doubled back, she hadn't observed it.

We thanked her for her co-operation and let her go home.

"Let's check with those neighbor women now," I said to Sam Wiggens.

It was noon when we finished this chore. Both neighbors whose names Mrs. Marks had given us verified her contention. They said Marks had often been seen going into the Cooper home, when George Cooper wasn't there.

We caught some lunch before driving back downtown. Instead of immediately returning to headquarters, we stopped by the morgue, which is just down the street from police headquarters.

Dr. Allan Swartz was the coroner's physician who had performed the post mortem. We found him in his office.

"You want medical terms or lay terms?" he inquired.

"Keep it simple," I said. "Sam didn't have much education."

Sam looked at me. "Sure," he said. "Sod went all the way through grade school with honors."

"He had his skull crushed by a blunt instrument," Dr. Swartz told us. "That good enough?"

"Fine," I said. "Were you able to fix a time of death?"

"You couldn't even fix a date of death in a case like this. Unless you can tell me when he had stuffed peppers for dinner."

"What do you mean?" I inquired.

"The body's been under some kind of refrigeration. He could have been dead a week."

Sam and I looked at each other. Sam said, "What's the least amount of time he could have been dead?"

The doctor shrugged. "A few days. Last Friday night, Saturday morning, maybe."

We thanked him and returned to headquarters. Stopping by Central District, we checked George and Helen Cooper out of their cells and took them upstairs for further questioning. Cooper was sober now and had an obvious hangover. It left him in a less co-operative mood than he had been in yesterday. When his wife took a seat, he refused one, preferring to stand and stare from me to Sam and back again with a truculent expression on his face.

"Well?" he asked. "Have you officers completed your investigation?"

"Just about," I said. "Except for a few questions."

"Just how thorough an investigation did you make?"

His tone caused me to examine him curiously. "What do you mean, Mr. Cooper?"

"I just wondered how you cops worked. When somebody confesses to a crime, do you let it go at that, or do you go out and do a little digging?"

"We do a little digging," I assured him.

He opened his mouth to say something more, then winced and felt his head. "Wow! You got any aspirin?"

Sam said, "In my locker. Over here."

He led Cooper across the room to his locker, then over to the water cooler for a glass of water to chase the aspirin.

I said to the woman, "Couple of things came up since we talked to you yesterday, Mrs. Cooper."

"What things?"

"You forgot to mention how friendly you were with Henry Marks."

Her face stiffened. "What do you mean by that?"

"Seems to be common knowledge in the neighborhood that he—"

"Gossip!" she interrupted indignantly. "Is that the way you policemen work? Go around listening to gossip?"

"One way."

"Well, it isn't true. I bet I know who started that rumor."

"Yeah? Who?"

ded slowly, quietly, emotionlessly at his image in the mirror, then there might be a chance. But tonight all the world was burning down into ruin. There was no green of spring, none of the freshness, none of the promise.

There was a soft running in the hall. "That's Marion," he told himself. "My little one. All eight quiet years of her. Never a word. Just her luminous gray eyes and her wondering little mouth." His daughter had been in and out all evening, trying on various masks, asking him which was most terrifying, most horrible. They had both finally decided on the skeleton mask. It was "just awful!" It would "scare the beans" from people!

Again he caught the long look of thought and deliberation he gave himself in the mirror. He had never liked October. Ever since he first lay in the autumn leaves before his grandmother's house many years ago and heard the wind and saw the empty trees. It had made him cry, without a reason. And a little of that sadness returned each year to him. It always went away with spring.

But it was different tonight. There was a feeling of autumn coming to last a million years.

There would be no spring.

He had been crying quietly all evening. It did not show, not a vestige of it, on his face. It was all somewhere hidden, but it wouldn't stop.

A rich syrupy smell of candy filled the bustling house. Louise had laid out apples in new skins of caramel, there were vast bowls of punch fresh mixed, stringed apples in each door, scooped, vented pumpkins peering triangularly from each cold window. There was a waiting water tub in the center of the living room, waiting, with a sack of apples nearby, for bobbing to begin. All that was needed was the catalyst, the inpouring of children, to start the apples bobbing, the stringed apples to penduluming in the crowded doors, the candy to vanish, the halls to echo with fright or delight, it was all the same.

Now, the house was silent with preparation. And just a little more than that.

Louise had managed to be in every other room save the room he was in today. It was her very fine way of intimating, Oh look, Mich, see how busy I am! So busy that when you walk into a room *I'm* in there's always something I need to do in *another* room! Just see how I dash about!

For a while he had played a little game with her, a nasty childish game. When she was in the kitchen then he came to the kitchen, saying, "I need a glass of water." After a moment, he standing, drinking water, she like a crystal witch over the caramel brew bubbling like a prehistoric mudpot on the stove, she said, "Oh, I must light the window pumpkins!" and she rushed to the living room to make the pumpkins smile with light. He came after her, smiling, "I must get my pipe." "Oh, the cider!" she had cried, running to the dining room. "I'll check the cider," he had said. But when he tried following she ran to the bathroom and locked the door.

He stood outside the bath door, laughing strangely and senselessly, his pipe gone cold in his mouth, and then, tired of the game, but stubborn, he waited another five minutes. There was not a sound from the bath. And lest she enjoy in any way knowing that he waited outside, irritated, he suddenly jerked about and walked upstairs, whistling merrily.

At the top of the stairs he had waited. Finally he had heard the bath door unlatch and she had come out and life below stairs had resumed, as life in a jungle must resume once a terror has passed on away and the antelope return to their spring.

Now, as he finished his bow-tie and put on his dark coat there was a mouse-rustle in the hall. Marion appeared in the door, all skeletonous in her disguise.

"How do I look, Papa?"

"Fine!"

From under the mask, blond hair showed. From the

skull sockets, small blue eyes smiled. He sighed. Marion and Louise, the two silent denouncers of his virility, his dark power. What alchemy had there been in Louise that took the dark of a dark man and bleached and bleached the dark brown eyes and black black hair and washed and bleached the ingrown baby all during the period before birth until the child was born, Marion, blond, blue-eyed, ruddy-cheeked? Sometimes he suspected that Louise had conceived the child as an idea, completely asexual, an immaculate conception of contemptuous mind and cell. As a firm rebuke to him she had produced a child in her *own* image, and, to top it, she had somehow *fixed* the doctor so he shook his head and said, "Sorry, Mr. Wilder, your wife will never have another child. This is the *last* one."

"And I wanted a boy," Mich had said, eight years ago.

He almost bent to take hold of Marion now, in her skull mask. He felt an inexplicable rush of pity for her, because she had never had a father's love, only the crushing, holding love of a loveless mother. But most of all he pitied himself, that somehow he had not made the most of a bad birth, enjoyed his daughter for herself, regardless of her not being dark and a son and like himself. Somewhere he had missed out. Other things being equal, he would have loved the child. But Louise hadn't wanted a child, anyway, in the first place. She had been frightened of the idea of birth. He had forced the child on her, and from that night, all through the year until the agony of the birth itself, Louise had lived in another part of the house. She had expected to die with the forced child. It had been very easy for Louise to hate this husband who so wanted a son that he gave his only wife over to the mortuary.

But—Louise had lived. And in triumph! Her eyes the day he came to the hospital were cold. I'm alive, they said. And I have a *blond* daughter! Just look! And when he had put out a hand to touch, the mother had turned away to conspire with her new pink daughter-child—away from that dark forcing murderer. It had all been so beautifully ironic. His selfishness deserved it.

But now it was October again. There had been other Octobers and when he thought of the long winter he had been filled with horror year after year to think of the endless months mortared into the house by an insane fall of snow, trapped with a woman and a child, neither of whom loved him, for months on end. During the eight years there had been respites. In spring and summer you got out, walked, picnicked; these were desperate solutions to the desperate problem of a hated man.

But, in winter, the hikes and picnics and escapes fell away with the leaves. Life, like a tree, stood empty, the fruit picked, the sap run to earth. Yes, you invited people in, but people were hard to get in winter with blizzards and all. Once he had been clever enough to save for a Florida trip. They had gone south. He had walked in the open.

But now, the eighth winter coming, he knew things were finally at an end. He simply could not wear this one through. There was an acid walled off in him that slowly had eaten through tissue and tissue over the years, and now, tonight, it would reach the wild explosive in him and all would be over!

There was a mad ringing of the bell below. In the hall, Louise went to see. Marion, without a word, ran down to greet the first arrivals. There were shouts and hilarity.

He walked to the top of the stairs.

Louise was below, taking wraps. She was tall and slender and blond to the point of whiteness, laughing down upon the new children.

He hesitated. What was all this? The years? The boredom of living? Where had it gone wrong? Certainly not with the birth of the child alone. But it had been a symbol of all their tensions, he imagined. His jealousies and his business failures and all the rotten rest of it. Why didn't he just turn, pack a suitcase and leave? No. Not without hurting Louise as much as she had hurt him. It was simple as that. Divorce wouldn't hurt her at all. It would simply be an end to numb indecision. If he thought divorce would give her pleasure in any way he would stay married the rest of his life to her, for damned spite. No, he must hurt her. Figure some way, perhaps, to take Marion away from her, legally. Yes. That was it. That would hurt most of all. To take Marion away.

"Hello down there!" He descended the stairs, beaming.

Louise didn't look up.

"Hi, Mr. Wilder!"

The children shouted, waved as he came down.

By ten o'clock the doorbell had stopped ringing, the apples were bitten from stringed doors, the pink child faces were wiped dry from the apple bobbing, napkins were smeared with caramel and punch, and he, the husband, with pleasant efficiency had taken over. He took the party right out of Louise's hands. He ran about talking to the twenty children and the twelve parents who had come and were happy with the special spiked cider he had fixed them. He supervised PIN THE TAIL ON THE DONKEY, SPIN THE BOTTLE, MUSICAL CHAIRS and all the rest, midst fits of shouting laughter. Then, in the triangular-eyed pumpkin shine, all house lights out, he cried, "Hush! Follow me!" he said, tiptoeing toward the cellar.

The parents, on the outer periphery of the costumed riot, commented to each other, nodding at the clever husband, speaking to the lucky wife. How *well* he got on with children, they said.

The children crowded after the husband, squealing.

"The cellar!" he cried. "The tomb of the witch!"

More squealing. He made a mock shiver. "Abandon hope all ye who enter here!"

The parents chuckled.

One by one the children slid down a slide which

Mich had fixed up from lengths of table-section, into
the dark cellar. He hissed and shouted ghastly utter-
ances after them. A wonderful wailing filled the dark
pumpkin-lighted house. Everybody talked at once.
Everybody but Marion. She had gone through all the
party with a minimum of sound or talk; it was all inside her, all the excitement and joy. What a little troll,
he thought. With a shut mouth and shiny eyes she had
watched her own party, like so many serpentines,
thrown before her.

Now, the parents. With laughing reluctance they
slid down the short incline, uproarious, while little
Marion stood by, always wanting to see it all, to be
last. Louise went down without his help. He moved
to aid her, but she was gone even before he bent.

The upper house was empty and silent in the can-
dleshine.

Marion stood by the slide. "Here we go," he said,
and picked her up.

They sat in a vast circle in the cellar. Warmth came
from the distant bulk of the furnace. The chairs stood
on a long line down each wall, twenty squealing children, twelve rustling relatives, alternately spaced, with
Louise down at the far end. Mich up at this end, near
the stairs. He peered but saw nothing. They had all
groped to their chairs, catch-as-you-can in the blackness. The entire program from here on was to be en-
acted in the dark, he as Mr. Interlocutor. There was a
child scampering, a smell of damp cement, and the
sound of the wind out in the October stars.

"Now!" cried the husband in the dark cellar.
"Quiet!"

Everybody settled.

The room was black black. Not a light, not a shine,
not a glint of an eye.

A scraping of crockery, a metal rattle.

"The witch is dead," intoned the husband.

"Eeeeeeeeeeeee," said the children.

"The witch is dead, she has been killed, and here is
the knife she was killed with."

He handed over the knife. It was passed from hand to hand, down and around the circle, with chuckles and little odd cries and comments from the adults.

"The witch is dead, and this is her head," whispered the husband, and handed an item to the nearest person.

"Oh, I know how this game is played," some child cried, happily, in the dark. "He gets some old chicken innards from the icebox and hands them around and says, 'These are her innards!' And he makes a clay head and passes it for her head, and passes a soupbone for her arm. And he takes a marble and says, 'This is her eye!' And he takes some corn and says, 'This is her teeth!' And he takes a sack of plum pudding and gives that and says, 'This is her stomach!' I know how *this* is played!"

"Hush, you'll spoil everything," some girl said.

"The witch came to harm, and this is her arm," said Mich.

"Eeeee!"

The items were passed and passed, like hot potatoes, around the circle. Some children screamed, wouldn't touch them. Some ran from their chairs to stand in the center of the cellar until the grisly items had passed by them and on to the next child.

"Aw, it's only chicken insides," scoffed a boy. "Come back, Helen!"

Shot from hand to hand, with small scream after scream, the items went down the line, down, down, to be followed by another and another.

"The witch cut apart, and this is her heart," said the husband.

Six or seven items moving at once through the laughing, trembling dark.

Louise spoke up. "Marion, don't be afraid; it's only play."

Marion didn't say anything.

"Marion?" asked Louise. "Are you afraid?"

Marion didn't speak.

"She's all right," said the husband. "She's not afraid."

On and on the passing, the screams, the hilarity.

The autumn wind sighed about the house. And he, the husband, stood at the head of the dark cellar, intoning the words, handing out the items.

"Marion?" asked Louise again, from far across the cellar.

Everybody was talking.

"Marion?" called Louise.

Everybody quieted.

"Marion, answer me, are you afraid?"

Marion didn't answer.

The husband stood there, at the bottom of the cellar steps.

Louise called, "Marion, are you there?"

No answer. The room was silent.

"Where's Marion?" called Louise.

"She was here," said a boy.

"Maybe she's upstairs."

"Marion!"

No answer. It was quiet.

Louise cried out, "Marion, Marion!"

"Turn on the lights," said one of the adults.

The items stopped passing. The children and adults sat with the witch's items in their hands.

"No." Louise gasped. There was a scraping of her chair, wildly, in the dark. "No. Don't turn on the lights, don't turn on the lights, oh, God, God, God, don't turn them on, please, please *don't* turn on the lights, *don't!*" Louise was shrieking now. The entire cellar froze with the scream.

Nobody moved.

Everyone sat in the dark cellar, suspended in the suddenly frozen task of this October game; the wind blew outside, banging the house, the smell of pumpkins and apples filled the room with the smell of the objects in their fingers while one boy cried, "I'll go upstairs and look!" and he ran upstairs hopefully and out around the house, four times around the house, calling, "Marion, Marion, Marion!" over and over and at last coming slowly down the stairs into the waiting, breathing cellar and saying to the darkness, "I can't find her."

Then . . . some idiot turned on the lights.

STOP CALLING ME "MISTER"

●

Jonathan Craig

An occasional reminder about good manners can be helpful to all. I thus offer this chilling little study wherein a man's insistence that formality be dropped led to the most dire consequences.

Harvey Wilson was trying his best to be a proper host, but it was difficult to restrict his thoughts to the present, to keep them from exploring the possibilities of the hours ahead. Tonight might very well be *the* night, he knew. And again, it might not; it might be just like any one of the previous nights when there'd been a fatal hitch at the last moment. All he could do was wait and see—and that was the worst part of all, the waiting.

Harvey's guest took another sip of his drink and glanced about the tiny living room appreciatively. "Nice place you got here, Harve," he said. "You say you built it all by yourself? Everything?" He had been drinking steadily ever since he arrived, and his voice was a little blurred.

Harvey nodded. "All except the plumbing, Mr. Lambert. I figured I'd better leave that to an expert." He smiled at his wife, who sat on the sofa beside Calvin

Lambert. "And Doris did some of the inside painting. Picked it up in no time at all."

Doris crossed her legs and frowned at the wall above Harvey's head. She was in her late twenties, a doll-faced woman with shoulder-length black hair, exquisite legs, and a lush, provocative body that in another year or two would be overripe. She, too, showed the effects of drinking a great deal, and the dark eyes behind their incredibly long lashes were very bright.

"I only did it because Harvey kept after me so," she said defensively. "I'm really not the kind of woman who enjoys wielding a paint brush, Mr. Lambert." She looked at her glass, then held it out toward her husband. "Refill, Harvey. And this time, for God's sake, put some whiskey in it."

Harvey rose, took the glass, and glanced at Lambert. "How about you, sir?" he asked. "You about ready for another?"

"Good thought, Harve," Lambert said. He handed his glass to Harvey and nodded solemnly. "When a night's as cold as this one, a man needs a little extra anti-freeze."

"That's right," Harvey said, smiling. Lambert was probably a much better looking man at forty than he had been at twenty, Harvey reflected; two decades had touched his temples with just the right amount of gray and had erased all but a few of the acne scars.

"We must apologize for its being so chilly in here," Doris said. "Everything about this house is too small, even the furnace." She grimaced at the portable gas heater in the middle of the floor. "We've had to help the furnace along with that ever since the cold spell started."

"Me, I'm quite comfortable," Lambert said.

Doris would be too, Harvey thought, if she'd only wear something under her dress. But she never did. She never wore anything at all, winter or summer, but dresses and rolled stockings and high-heeled pumps.

"Two drinks coming right up," Harvey said. "You want yours the same way, Mr. Lambert?"

"Yes," Lambert said. "And listen here, Harve. I wish you'd call me Cal. It feels pretty awkward to drink a man's liquor and enjoy his hospitality, and have him call you Mr. Lambert that way." He turned to smile at Doris. "Why don't you both call me Cal? Then it'll be just Cal and Harve and Doris. Okay?"

Doris recrossed her legs—carelessly, the way she always did it. "That'll be fine," she said.

"Darn right," Lambert said. "I don't hold with that old theory that a man has to call another man 'mister' and say 'sir' to him and all that, just because the other man happens to be his boss. Isn't that the way you look at it—Doris?"

"Yes," Doris said. She glanced up at her husband. "You'll never get those drinks made standing there like that."

Harvey turned, pushed open the kitchen door and let it swing shut behind him. He heard the muted creak of a spring in the sofa, and a repressed giggle from Doris, and then nothing at all. He moved to the drainboard, where the whiskey and mixer were laid out.

The clock above the sink said twenty minutes past nine. Harvey was due on his job at midnight, and from then until his mid-morning lunch hour at four, he would have nothing to do but take an occasional look at the dials and gauges on the control panel in the sub-basement of Cal Lambert's sheet-plastics factory just this side of town. He didn't like the job, but it gave him time to study, and the pay was as good as a man with his lack of training could make anywhere else. Tonight, he looked forward to the cozy warmth of his personal cubbyhole and his stack of technical magazines.

And after all, tonight might be the night it happened.

He took his time making the drinks, humming softly to himself as he worked. When he finished with them, he took one in each hand and walked to the window that looked across the dark lot separating his house from Cal Lambert's. Lambert, a bachelor, had moved in only three weeks ago; before that the big house had stood vacant for almost half a year. These were the only two homes in the area, because most people preferred to live either in Lairdsville, where the Lambert factory was, or out in the country proper. Harvey studied the dark outline of Lambert's house for a long moment; then he walked back to the swinging door, pushed it open with his shoulder, and stepped into the living room.

Doris was sitting very close to Lambert now and the hem of her skirt was up above her knees. She brushed the skirt down casually and held out her hand for her drink.

"Harvey," she said, "I thought you'd decided to distill the stuff yourself." There was a deep flush in her cheeks and her full lips had the pouty, slightly swollen look they'd had when she and Harvey were first married and made love so violently.

Harvey handed her one of the glasses and gave the other to Lambert. "I might have to distill some, at that," he said. "We're running pretty low."

"I thought I told you to bring a couple of bottles home with you this morning," Doris said.

"You did," Harvey said. "I forgot. Just didn't think about it."

"Naturally," Doris said.

"I didn't know we were going to have company," Harvey said, smiling apologetically at Lambert. "I'll take a quick run into town and pick some up."

Lambert's face was almost expressionless. "I'd go over to my place for some," he said. "But I'm fresh out. A bottle or so of beer, maybe, and that's all."

"It'll only take a few minutes," Doris said. "Harvey doesn't mind at all."

Lambert made a move to rise, with obviously no intention of completing it. "I'll go with you, Harve," he said.

"Stay where you are, Mr. Lambert," Harvey said. "I—"

"Cal," Lambert said. "Call me Cal, doggonit, Harve."

"Sure, Cal. Now you stay put. It doesn't take two full-grown men to carry a couple of little bottles."

"Well," Doris said, "I hope you two boys can come to some kind of an agreement. We're going to be ready for another one pretty soon."

Harvey laughed. "You folks listen to some records or something. I'll be right back." He walked to the hat tree beside the front door and took down his overcoat. There was a mirror behind the hat tree, and as Harvey buttoned up his coat he could see Cal Lambert turn to smile broadly at Doris and then look away again, lips pursed, as if he were about to whistle.

The drive to Lairdsville took less than ten minutes. Harvey parked in front of Teddy's Taproom and went inside. There were only two men at the bar, Bill Wirt and Gus Bialis, and both of them insulted Harvey loudly and affectionately as he approached them. They were both lifelong friends of his, and, before his marriage to Doris four years ago, his constant drinking companions. At a table near the front end of the bar sat George Helm, another of Harvey's friends, but one who didn't drink at all.

"I'll need a couple fifths of the usual, Ted," Harvey said to the bartender. "And you'd better give me a couple bottles of soda to help out with the weight."

"Check," the bartender said, moving toward the shelves where he kept his package goods. "If you want to spoil good liquor with soda, Harvey, it's no skin off mine."

"Well, what do you know," Bill Wirt said. "You and the missus must be figuring on throwing a real one, Harvey. Something special happen?"

"No," Harvey said. "Cal Lambert dropped over. Just a neighborly visit, I guess you'd say."

Bill looked knowingly at Gus Bialis and then back at Harvey. "You mean to say, Harvey, you left your wife there with Lambert while you traipsed off down here for liquor? Is that what you done?" He shook his head wonderingly. "Man, you sure got a world of trust in human nature. Don't it worry you—them two being out there all alone like that?"

Harvey smiled. "Not so you could notice it, Bill."

"Well, like I said, you sure got a lot of trust in human nature."

"Yes," Gus Bialis said. "He sure'n hell has, hasn't he? Of course, that little lady of his is straighter'n a string, and we all know it—but what's the use of tempting fate, I always say."

"Right, Gus!" Bill said. "You said it right, by God!"

Harvey grinned, paid for his whiskey and mixer, and went back outside. George Helm was waiting for him just outside the doorway.

"I didn't see you step out," Harvey said. "How've you been, George?"

"All right," George shrugged, not meeting Harvey's eyes. He was somewhere in his early fifties, a short, heavy-set, balding man who made a living buying and selling second-hand farm equipment. "I kind of wanted to talk to you private, Harvey," he said.

Harvey shifted the bottles to his other arm and nodded. "What is it, George?"

George slapped his mittened hands together and hunched his shoulders against the bitter slice of the wind. "Cold, ain't it?"

"Sure is," Harvey said. "What was it you wanted, George?"

"Well," George said hesitantly, "I guess it really ain't none of my business, when you get right down to it . . ." He paused. "I guess you know I get around these parts a good bit, Harvey. My type business keeps a man on the move all the time. He has to talk with a lot of people, and sometimes he hears a thing or two. You know how it is. Like maybe he hears that some man's wife is sort of playing around with somebody else. You know what I mean, Harvey?"

"Sure, George," Harvey said a little impatiently. "But—"

"Now listen a minute. This here's a kind of ticklish

thing I want to say, Harvey. But supposing you was to find out something like I just said? Would you tell the woman's husband what she was up to? I mean, don't you think a man in that position should know what's going on?"

Harvey frowned. "Well . . . Well, hell, George, it's hard to say."

"Yes, but put yourself in his place. If you was him, wouldn't you want to know?"

Harvey took a tentative step toward his automobile, then paused. "I guess so, George," he said. "But no two men feel the same way. Some of them would be better off if they never found out."

"Yes," George persisted, "but don't you think a man like me, when he knows something's going on, has a duty?"

Harvey sighed and took another step towards his automobile. "That's something you'll have to decide for yourself, George. With things like that, nobody else can make up your mind for you."

George had moved along with him, and now he studied Harvey's face carefully. "Supposing you put yourself in this man's position for a minute, Harvey," he said. "Just say you was him. If you found out your wife had been fooling around, what would you do?"

Harvey opened the car door slowly, put the bottles on the back seat, and got behind the wheel. He started to close the door, but George caught it and held it open.

"Well?" George said. "You ain't answered my question, Harvey. If you was this husband, and knew your wife was fooling around, what would you do?"

Harvey took a deep breath. "I'd try to find out what was to blame, George," he said. "That's the first thing I'd do. Chances are, it'd turn out to be me."

George's mouth sagged open. "You?"

"That's right," Harvey said. "It's always easy to blame the woman in a case like that, George. Me, I'd ask myself what I might have done to make her do what she did. I'd figure there must be something wrong with me—some lack, maybe, or something I was doing wrong that I didn't know about." He turned on the motor and sat listening to it, his eyes thoughtful. "And then I guess I'd sit down with her and have a long talk, George. I'd try to find out how I was failing her, and then I'd do my damnedest to make it up to her."

George swallowed twice and shook his head incredulously. "You—you wouldn't *do* anything to her? You wouldn't take a whip to her or anything like that? You wouldn't even do anything to the man?"

"No, George," Harvey said quietly. "I'd know it was my fault to begin with. Why should I try to punish someone else for something I'd caused myself?"

"Lord," George whispered. "I can't hardly believe what I hear. I'll just be goddamned."

Harvey smiled. "Got to be getting home, George," he said and shut the door.

Doris and Cal Lambert were dancing to the record player when Harvey came in with the whiskey and mixer. Both of them had obviously been at the last of the liquor Harvey had left in the kitchen, and they were dancing close together in a way that required them to move their feet scarcely at all.

Doris stopped dancing, took the bottles from Harvey's arms, and lurched into the kitchen without a word. Her black hair was a little disheveled, Harvey noticed, and there were a number of long, horizontal wrinkles in her skirt. Cal Lambert had a self-satisfied look on his face, and the collar of his white shirt was wilted, as if he had been sweating profusely.

"Harve!" he said. "We thought you'd forgotten your way back home, boy!"

"I got tied up for a few minutes," Harvey said, smiling.

Lambert grinned, glanced warily toward the kitchen door, and winked knowingly. "You didn't just happen to run into something distracting, did you, Harve? Something about five-two and oh boy, maybe?"

Lambert was very drunk, Harvey saw; the heavy, rapid drinking had finally caught up with him. He wasn't quite so drunk as Doris, of course, but it wouldn't be long.

"I thought maybe you came across a little fluffy something on a bar stool. You know, Harve?"

Harvey laughed. "Nothing like that, Mr. Lambert."

"Cal."

"Yes, Cal. No, it wasn't anything like that."

Lambert shook his head sadly. "Too bad, Harve, old man. Maybe better luck next time."

Doris returned with drinks for herself and Lambert and a glass of ginger ale for Harvey. "You have to be at work soon, Harvey," she said thickly. "I didn't think you'd want anything more to drink."

"No," Harvey said. "I don't think I'd better."

"Drink all you want," Lambert said. "Hell, I'm the boss of that place. If you want to drink, Harve, by God, you drink!"

Harvey smiled. "The ginger ale'll be fine, Cal. Just fine."

Doris raised her glass and, watching Harvey unblinkingly over the rim, drank steadily until the glass was empty. "There," she said. "I guess you saw that, didn't you, Harvey? That's the way it's supposed to be done." She turned to smile at Lambert. "Show him, Cal."

Lambert hesitated for a moment, then shrugged and emptied his glass. There were tears in his eyes when he finished, and he laughed as he wiped them away with the back of his hand. "Boy," he said. "I haven't done anything like that since I was in high school."

"I could never do it, even then," Harvey said.

"Oh, be quiet, Harvey," Doris said. "You'd better think about getting to work."

Harvey glanced at his wrist watch. It was much later than he'd thought, almost a quarter past eleven. "I guess you're right," he said.

Doris smiled at Lambert and took the empty glasses back into the kitchen.

"A shame you have to leave, Harve," Lambert said.

Harvey smiled and shrugged.

Lambert went on about what a shame it was until Doris came back with fresh drinks. She staggered over to the sofa, sat down heavily, and crossed her legs—apparently oblivious of the skirt that settled a good four inches above the taut round garters that encircled her white thighs.

"Come sit over here, Cal," she said.

Lambert stared at her for a moment, then moistened his lips and looked along his eyes at Harvey. "I think I'd better be going, Harve," he said.

"Don't be ridiculous," Harvey said. "No use breaking up the party just because I have to go to work."

Lambert smiled uncertainly, trying hard to keep his gaze away from Doris. "Well . . . if you're sure, Harve. I mean, I wouldn't want to—"

Harvey laughed. "Don't give it another thought, Cal. I know my wife—and I know you. Why it'd be one hell of a world if a man couldn't even trust his own wife and his own boss together."

Grinning, Lambert slapped Harvey on the shoulder. "By gosh, that's right, Harve. It'd sure be some world, wouldn't it?"

"Yes," Harvey said, smiling. "It sure would." He looked at his watch again. "Damn, it's almost eleven-thirty. I'd better be getting along." He moved toward the front door. Doris glanced up at him sullenly, then shrugged one shoulder and took a long pull at her drink.

Harvey opened the door and stood for a moment with his hand on the knob. "Well, good night," he said. "Sorry I can't stay and—"

"For God's sake," Doris said. "Either come in or out. This place is cold enough without your letting all that air in here."

Harvey went out, quickly, not saying a word.

At exactly four a.m., Harvey made a last-minute check of the control panel in the sub-basement of Cal Lambert's factory, took his coat from the hook near the door, and walked rapidly along the dimly lighted passageway that led to the parking area at the rear of the building.

This looked like the night, he reflected. If he could have that short stretch of road between the factory and his house all to himself, just this once, it *would* be the night. This was his fourth try; he had a feeling it would be the last.

Harvey had not parked his car in the parking area, but at the end of the long drive at the rear of it. He knew the drive had sufficient incline to permit him to start his car by coasting it—which meant that the elderly nightwatchman in the upper part of the factory would not be able to hear the motor start. And there was no chance of his seeing Harvey drive off, either, for the rear wall of the factory had no windows at all.

No, the nightwatchman wasn't a problem; the only problem was that short stretch of road. At four o'clock in the morning, you wouldn't think that there'd be any traffic at all along it, especially on a winter night as cold as this one. But there had been on the other nights. There'd been someone on the road on each of Harvey's three previous tries. He'd recognized neither the vehicles nor the drivers, but he had preferred three consecutive postponements to taking the smallest unnecessary risk. After all, what real difference did a day or a week make? Or even a month? There was no real hurry. If things went wrong again tonight, there'd be another night, and another.

But that feeling was there. It was going to be tonight; Harvey was almost certain of it.

He got into his car, switched on the ignition, and released the brake. The car began to inch forward, then to pick up momentum. Harvey waited until it reached the end of the incline, and then eased it into gear and listened to the tiny flutter of the motor as it caught hold and drew the car ahead. There had been hardly any sound at all.

There had been no other vehicles on the road when Harvey had driven along it a little over four hours ago, and there were none now. There might be one or more on his return trip, though, and that was what concerned him most. It would mean that he would have to go back to his house and undo what he had done.

He pulled off the road, drove along the driveway that led to the rear of his house, and parked the car. The house was dark and silent, and Harvey smiled grimly. Everything was as it should be. He got out of the car, crossed silently to the back door, and inserted his key in the lock.

He walked noiselessly through the kitchen, avoiding the creaking board midway across the floor, and opened the door to the living room. There was no one there—and that, too, was as it should be. He moved down the short corridor to the bedroom and slowly nudged the door open with his fingertips.

They were there. Just as he had expected them to be. Just as he had found them three times before. The moonlight slanted through the window. Lying there beside Cal Lambert, Doris looked even smaller than she actually was, almost childlike. Both she and Lambert were breathing very slowly, very deeply, sleeping the trancelike sleep of alcohol and exhaustion. Harvey didn't have to look at the alarm clock on the chair beside the bed to know that it would be set for eight a.m., just as it had been on all the other mornings. He could picture how it had been on those other mornings—Lambert waking and dressing hurriedly and cutting across the lot to his own house, and Doris getting into her house dress and busying herself in the kitchen preparing breakfast for the husband who would be home in less than twenty minutes.

Harvey stepped close to the bed and looked down at Doris for a full minute while his eyes grew more accustomed to the dark. She was still wearing her pumps and stockings, he noticed now. He bent down and trailed his fingertips from garter to hip, and then suddenly took the tiny fold of flesh at her waist between his thumb and forefinger and pinched it as viciously as he could.

She didn't stir. Harvey put the palm of his right hand flat against Lambert's nose and pushed hard. Lambert turned his head slightly, but that was all.

Harvey sighed thankfully. He didn't have to worry about either of them waking up too soon; that was for sure.

Harvey stepped back from the bed and glanced about the small, low-ceilinged room. In every way, things were exactly as they should be. He turned and went into the living room and returned with the portable gas heater. He set it down midway between the bed and the window, lighted it, and then checked the window to make sure it was tightly closed. There was only one window and one door, and when closed, neither of them admitted any air whatever.

Harvey took one last look at Doris; then he closed the door behind him and left the house by the same way he had entered.

He met no other vehicles on his short drive back to the factory, and he saw no one when he parked his car behind the building and walked along the passageway to his engine room. He checked his control panel and then sat down in his chair and looked at his watch.

He had been gone exactly thirty-four minutes.

It had taken just thirty-four minutes to rectify the mistake he had made in marrying Doris and to open the door on an entirely new life for himself. Or rather, to recover the life he had given up when he married. He could go back to school now, and in two years' time he would have the training he needed to be more than just another boiler-watcher. It was too bad he couldn't merely have divorced Doris, but that had been impossible. She would have imprisoned him in an alimony trap. Vengefully, she would have kept him in it and that would have made it impossible for him to go back to school, that would have kept him a nothing man in a nothing job.

But now, with Doris dead, he could go back to school. The policy on Doris' life, taken out when they were first married, was for only two thousand dollars, but there would be the money he'd get for his house and lot—say thirteen thousand—and another thousand or fifteen hundred for his car. Pretty nearly fifteen thousand dollars. Enough. He'd be able to live well during the two years of his schooling. He thought of Cal Lambert and smiled. There'd even be enough for that occasional bit of fluff on a bar stool that Cal had joked about. It was funny, he reflected, but by killing Lambert along with Doris he had probably knocked himself out of a job. Not that it mattered; he would have quit soon anyway.

At eight o'clock the next morning, Harvey initialed the control sheet, said good morning to his relief, and went upstairs to the factory cafeteria to have breakfast.

"You and your old lady feuding?" the cashier laughed, totaling up Harvey's check on her register.

Harvey smiled. "What makes you ask that?"

The cashier winked. "Lots of men have their breakfast in here for that very reason, Harvey. You'd be surprised."

"No feuding," Harvey said, letting his smile widen. "We had a little party last night. I figured I'd let her sleep."

The cashier looked at him admiringly. "More men should be that thoughtful," she said.

Harvey paid his check and took his tray to a table in the front of the room, pretending not to notice George Helm seated alone at a table near the wall. George made good money with his speculations in used farm equipment, but he lived in a cheap room in a rooming house and never failed to take his meals in the factory cafeteria. He always said it was because the cafeteria was a good place to make business contacts, but Harvey knew very well that George ate there solely because of the very low prices.

Harvey had decided to let George discover the bodies. It would be better that way. He had computed his time very carefully. He had known exactly how long the two people and the gas heater would take to exhaust the oxygen in the small bedroom—at which time, of course, the flame would have gone out and the heater would have filled the room with gas.

Harvey was glad to see George Helm sitting there. If George, however, had missed breakfast this morning, or had come in later, Harvey could have called on any of several others.

"Harvey!" George called to him. "Over here. What're you trying to do, give me the high-hat?"

Harvey smiled, checked his course, and went over to George's table. "Glad to see you, George," he said as he sat down. "In fact, I was coming over to your office right after I had breakfast."

George hunched his short, heavy body a little closer to Harvey and looked at him expectantly. "You mean about what we was discussing last night, Harvey?"

Harvey smiled. "No, George. I was wondering if you were interested in second-hand furniture."

"Yours?"

"Yes. I've been thinking about outfitting the house with new stuff, from top to bottom. You interested?"

George nodded. "Sure. What're you asking?"

Harvey took a forkful of his eggs. "Suppose you take a look at it," he said. "I know you'll do right by me, George."

"Sure," George said. "That's one thing you can count on, Harvey. When'd you want me to look at it?"

"This morning okay?"

"Couldn't be better. You got some nice things out there, Harvey."

"I was thinking I might look around the stores this morning," Harvey said. "Why don't you just drive on out there, George? Doris'll be glad to show you around." He paused. "One thing, though. She might be sleeping a little late. If she doesn't answer the bell, go around to the bedroom window and knock on it with your car keys or something. That'll raise her."

"Sure," George said, getting to his feet. "I think we'll be able to make a good deal, Harvey."

"I'll be seeing you," George said, and turned toward the door.

"You haven't finished your breakfast," Harvey said.

"Business first," George called back over his shoulder as he walked rapidly toward the door.

Harvey ate slowly, enjoying his food for the first time in months. He wouldn't have long to wait, he knew. It was only a matter of minutes. George Helm was probably rapping on the bedroom window at this very moment—rapping and then, naturally, looking inside at the man and woman on the bed. Maybe he had already discovered them and was on his way back to town. Much better having George the first person on the scene. And George would have to come back to town, for Harvey had no phone, and Cal Lambert wouldn't be available to loan George his. All George could do was bring the bad news back to town with him.

Harvey finished eating, went back to the service counter for a second cup of coffee, and lighted a cigarette. He had no intention of going over to Franklin's to price new furniture. George would look for him in the cafeteria first anyhow.

He sipped at his coffee, savoring it, making it last through these final few minutes. It was strange, he thought, but Doris was already beginning to lose reality for him. And as for Cal Lambert . . . Lambert had been just a prop, just a thing to explain why Doris had gone to sleep with the heater on and the window shut and the door closed.

Harvey mashed out his cigarette carefully, rose, and walked outside. It would be better to receive the news on the street, he decided. Besides, there was just a chance that George Helm might waste time by going over to Franklin's after all. He crossed the street and paused in front of the bank, as if waiting for it to open; and then, as he leaned back against the wall to light another cigarette, he saw George's ancient car careening down the street toward him and he smiled.

George braked the car to a shuddering stop, leaped out, and ran over to Harvey. His face was a sickly white and his eyes seemed ready to burst from his head.

"Harvey!" he said hoarsely. "Harvey! Oh, my God!"

Harvey looked at him questioningly. "You look like you'd seen a ghost, George. What's wrong?"

"Harvey," George said. "They're out there."

"They?" Harvey asked. "What do you mean?"

"I saw them in there," George said, glancing about him wildly. "On the bed. I knew something was mighty wrong, and I busted the glass out, and then all that gas hit me in the face and I—"

"George!" Harvey said sharply. "Get hold of yourself. What are you talking about?"

"My God," George said. "I don't hardly know how to tell you, Harvey. It—it was your wife—her and Cal Lambert."

"What!" Harvey exclaimed.

"Jesus, I hate saying this, Harvey. They was on the bed, see, and they'd left the gas heater on, and it must have gone out during the night. They—they're dead, Harvey—both of them. The gas killed 'em both."

Harvey clutched George by both shoulders and shook him. "Killed them? What the hell are you saying, George?"

"They was on the bed," George said raggedly. "Laying there naked as they could get. There was a bottle on the floor beside the bed. I guess they must have passed out or something."

"You're lying!" Harvey shouted. "Damn you, George! You're lying to me!"

"No," George said, almost sobbing. "No, I ain't, Harvey. You can still smell the gas on me. It almost got me, too, when I busted in there. It—it's just plain hell out there, Harvey."

Harvey stared at George for a long moment; then he turned, walked to George's car, and sank down on the running board and covered his face with his hands.

It's all over now but the acting, he thought. Everything came off exactly the way I wanted it to. I'm set for life, really set . . .

George Helm walked over slowly and put his hand on Harvey's shoulder very gently. "You poor guy," he said. "I wish there was something I could do for you."

THE LAST ESCAPE
●
Jay Street

The worker of magic draws your attention to one hand, so he can do his foul trickery with the other. This, technically, is known as misdirection and is the greatest thing from a magician's standpoint since the invention of the rabbit.

They lashed the heavy braided cord about Ferlini's wrists and knotted it tightly. Of the two men the smaller was the most belligerent; he yanked and tugged until the cord seemed to bite through flesh. Grunting, they put the leg irons on his ankles, slamming the thick metal locks shut and testing their security. Finally, panting with their exertions, they stood over their victim and seemed smugly satisfied with his helplessness.

Then the woman was putting the screen in front of Ferlini's bound body. In less than a minute, it was thrown aside by Ferlini himself, the cord and the irons upraised triumphantly in his outstretched hands.

The audience of the small supper club gasped, and then exploded into tumultuous applause. Ferlini glowed at the sound of it. He was fair-skinned, almost albino, even the desert sunshine failed to alter his color, but an audience's approbation could tint his cheeks with the red flush of gratified vanity.

The two volunteers from the audience, shaking their heads and grinning sheepishly, returned to their tables and their jeering companions and the six-piece band swung into a traveling theme. Wanda, Ferlini's wife and professional partner, moved mechanically across the floor to pick up the screen and carry it backstage. There were some catcalls and a smattering of light applause, but she knew it was only in appreciation of her bare-legged costume. She was over forty, and her face was dependent on increasing layers of theatrical makeup for its passable beauty, but her legs were still long, lithe, and without blemish.

On her way to the dressing room, Baggett stepped in front of her and displayed his soulful eyes. "Let me help," he said, putting his hand on the screen.

"It's all right," Wanda whispered. "You better not, Tommy."

"They liked him tonight, didn't they?"

She frowned, putting cracks in the thick makeup. "It's that kind of crowd." She shrugged. "They'll like you, too."

"Thanks," Baggett, an aging crooner, said dryly.

"No, I didn't mean it that way." She placed the screen against a concrete wall and swayed toward him, her eyes dreamy. "You know what I think of you, Tommy. Your singing, I mean."

"Is that all you mean?"

"I better go," Wanda said.

When she entered the dressing room, she found her husband in a good mood, and it was the mood she liked least. He was staring into the mirror and rubbing his shoulders vigorously with a towel, his face split into a wide smile that showed every one of his large, strong teeth. "Yeah, it was good tonight, it was good," he said happily. "I could have gotten out of steel boxes tonight, that's how I felt. You see that little guy?" He guffawed and slammed the dressing table with his palm. "Little fella thought he was gonna fix me. You see how tight he worked the rope? I tell you, the little guys, they're the worst. It's a pleasure to fool 'em."

He swung around and looked at his wife, who was staring at nothing. He made fists of his big hands and flexed his exaggerated muscles, swelling out his chest to display the incredible expansion that was so important to his art. "Look at that, hah, will you look at that? You think anybody ever take me for forty-six? What do you say?"

"You're a Greek god," Wanda said bitterly. "Only speaking of Greeks, we're invited out to dinner tonight. Roscoe's treat."

"Ah, that Phil, he spoils my appetite," Ferlini said, still with a grin. "You hear him talk, the escape business is dead. He should have seen that crowd tonight, that's all I say. He'd know different."

"He booked you in this job, didn't he? He ought to know if it's dead or not." She yawned, and began to change into street clothes. Then she remembered something, and came to her husband's dressing table, wiping at her makeup. "Listen, when we see Phil tonight, don't start up again about that water business, huh? I'm sick of hearing about that."

"Aah," Ferlini said, waving his hand. "You're gettin' old, Wanda, that's your trouble."

"Look who's talking! You're no chicken either, Joe, and don't forget it!"

He turned to look at her, grinning shrewdly. "I count ten new wrinkles on you since last week, sugar. You take a good look at yourself? Go on, take a look, you got a mirror."

"Aw, go to hell."

"Go on, look!" Ferlini shouted suddenly. Then his muscular arm whipped out and caught her wrist. He bent her down toward the lighted mirror on his table, forcing her to face it. She looked up at her reflection, at the streaked orange makeup on her forehead and chin, at the age lines around her mouth, the puffy flesh beneath her eyes. She turned her head aside, and Ferlini's grip tightened cruelly.

"Stop it, Joe! For God's sake!"

"Who you callin' an old man, hah? I'm younger'n you, understand, on account of I keep in shape! Don't call me no old man, you hear me?"

"All right, all right!"

He released her, with a growl of disgust. His good mood was dissipated. Wanda, tears blurring her sight, went to the other side of the room and completed dressing.

"Not everybody thinks I'm so old," she whispered. "Not everybody, Joe."

"Shut up and get dressed. We're supposed to go to dinner, let's go to dinner. Besides," he said, standing up and slapping his flat stomach, "I want to talk to Roscoe about something. About the water trick."

Wanda said nothing.

The restaurant Roscoe had picked was just like Phil Roscoe himself: past its prime, seedy, congenial, and well-lit. Roscoe held Wanda's chair gallantly for her, but Ferlini dropped heavily into a chair, reached for a roll and tore it in half. With his mouth stuffed, he said, "Hey, you should have seen me tonight, Phil, I was the best. You tell him, Wanda, ain't it true?"

Wanda smiled weakly. "It was a good crowd."

"Good? I had three curtain calls!" Ferlini said, forgetful that he worked without curtains, and without encores. "I'm tellin' you, Phil, the escape business is comin' back with a bang. And I'm gonna be right on top when it does. Especially after we do that water routine—"

"What, again?" Phil groaned. "Look, we haven't even had a drink, and you're talking about water."

Ferlini roared with laughter, and shouted for the waiter.

For Wanda, the meal was tiresome from first course to last. Ferlini and his manager did the talking, and she had heard it all before.

"Look, Joe," Roscoe said, "You know as well as me that times are different. Few years ago, a good press agent could ballyhoo an escape guy right onto the front page. Only Houdini's dead, Joe, don't forget it."

"Sure, Houdini's dead. Only I'm alive!" He thumped his chest. "Me, Joe Ferlini!"

"That's one thing about you, Joe, you never had any trouble with false modesty."

"Listen," Ferlini grated, "what could Houdini do I can't? I work with ropes, chains, irons. I can get out of bags, boxes, hampers, chests. I can do handcuff routines. That bolted-to-a-plank stuff. I can do that Ten Ichi Thumb Tie. I can do the straitjacket. I can do escape tricks Houdini never even *thought* of. Besides, you know he used a lot of phony trick stuff—"

"And I suppose you don't?" Wanda snorted.

"Sure, sometimes. I mean, I got my skeleton keys and my phony bolts and that other junk. But you know me, Phil, I do my best tricks with muscle. Am I right?"

"Sure, sure," the manager said wearily. "You're the greatest, Joe."

"I keep in shape, you ask Wanda here. One hour a day, I'm with the barbells. I still got a terrific chest expansion. I can do this water thing, Phil. It'll be great!"

"But it's been *done*, Joe, that's what I'm trying to tell you. People don't get excited about it no more."

Ferlini made a noise of contempt. "You drink too much, Phil; your brain's soft. Sure, it's been done, only how many years ago? There's a whole new generation now. Right? And the way you handle things, it could be a real big deal. What do you say?"

Roscoe sighed, and it was a sigh of surrender.

"Okay, Joe, if you really want it. How do you want to work the act?"

Ferlini beamed. "I figure I'll do it up good. First I'll let 'em handcuff me. Then the rope around my body, about fifty feet, and the leg-irons. Then they put me in a sack and tie it up good. Then they put the whole business in a big iron chest and dump me into Lake Truscan. How does that sound?"

"Like sudden death. How much is trick and how much is muscle?"

"The rope is muscle; I'll just give 'em the chest expansion routine and the whole thing'll slip right off me. I'll have a skeleton key to the handcuffs in a double-hemmed trouser cuff. Once I get them off, I'll take a razor and slit the bag open. The chest'll have a phony bottom; I push it open and swim to the surface; the whole works sink and I come up smelling like a rose." He gave Phil his victory grin.

"How good a swimmer are you?"

"The best. Don't worry about that part. When I was a kid, I wanted to go over and swim the Channel, that's how good I was."

"We could drop you by motor boat, and pick you up the same way. That'll lessen the risk."

"Sure, it's a cinch. I knew you'd see it, Phil."

"I see it," the manager said, "but I still don't like it. Hey, waiter! Where's that bourbon?"

From their apartment hotel room on the third floor, Wanda could look out of the window and see her husband stroking rapidly across the outdoor pool in the courtyard. He moved like a shark through the water, his graying hair slicked back and crinkling at the edges, the thick muscles in his back and shoulders rippling with every smooth motion of his arms. Once, fifteen years ago, she would have been rapt with admiration. Now she knew better. The great Ferlini needed only one admirer, and he saw him in the shaving mirror every day.

With a sigh, she came back into the room, sat down, and listlessly turned the pages of *Variety*. There was a timid knock on the door a few moments later, and she called out permission to enter. When she saw Baggett in the doorway, she caught her breath in surprise and guilt.

"Tommy! What are you doing here?"

"I had to see you, Wanda. I knew Joe was in the pool, so I thought it would be a good time. Looks like he'll be there the rest of the day—"

"You're probably right."

She was flustered, but tried not to show it. She offered him a drink, but he said no. She tried to make small talk, but he wasn't interested. In the next minute, she was in his arms. But she was uncomfortable there, and soon broke from him and started to talk about her husband.

"You just don't know what he's like. Every year he gets worse, every day. All he thinks about is the act, night and day it's escape, escape, escape. Sometimes I think I'll go crazy, Tommy, I mean it. When we were in Louisville, last year, I actually went to a head-shrinker for a while, did you know that? For three months I went, and then he got the job in Las Vegas, so that ended that."

"If you ask me," Baggett growled, "he's the one that's crazy, treating you the way he does."

"You know he even escapes in his sleep sometimes? No kidding. He wakes up in the middle of the night, throws off the covers, and takes a bow." She laughed without a change of expression, and then the tears flowed. Baggett surrounded her in his arms again. "Sometimes I wish he'd get tied up where he *can't* escape. Not ever—"

"What do you mean?"

She looked up at him.

"You know the water trick, where he gets thrown in a lake? He's going to do it in a couple of weeks. You know what I've been thinking about, ever since he decided on it?"

She went to the window, looking down at the pool where Ferlini was still stubbornly plowing the water.

"I was thinking that maybe something would go wrong. He's good; I know that. He can escape from almost anything. But if one little piece of the act doesn't work right—he'd drown. Do you think I'm terrible, having a thought like that?"

"I don't blame you for a minute!" Baggett said loyally.

Moving slowly, Wanda went to the bureau and opened the second drawer. From a welter of paraphernalia, she removed a pair of steel handcuffs and two small metal objects.

She brought the handcuffs to Baggett, and said, "Do me a favor, Tommy? Put these on?"

He blinked. "You mean it?"

"Please."

He held out his wrists willingly, and she clamped them around them, pushing the lock into place.

"Now try and get out," she said.

Baggett, a thin, romantic type, strained mightily, until the blood rushed up in a crimson column on his neck.

"I can't do it!" he panted.

"Of course you can't. Nobody could, not even Ferlini, unless he happened to have this on him somewhere." She held up a small key, and handed it over. "Now try it," she said.

Twisting his fingers, his tongue tucked into the corner of his mouth, Baggett managed to insert the tiny key into the hole. He turned it, but nothing happened.

"It's not working," he said. "The key doesn't turn."

"No," Wanda said dreamily. "It doesn't, does it?"

"But why not? What's wrong?" There was a hint of panic in Baggett's voice.

"It's the wrong key," Wanda said. "That's the problem. This is the right one." She held up a second key, then came over and inserted it herself. The lock sprung free, and the handcuffs came off. Baggett, rubbing his wrists, looked at her questioningly.

"I think you better go now," Wanda said.

Phil Roscoe was pleased with the results of his publicity campaign. Four local newspapers in the Denver area were touting the event, and one major news service had put it on the wire. But the great Ferlini wasn't so easily pleased; his visions had been of television coverage, national magazines, and Hollywood offers, but these were sugarplums that Roscoe had been unable to obtain.

"For the love of mike," Roscoe told him, "don't expect the moon out of this. It's not big news anymore, not since Houdini did it. Be satisfied with what you got."

Ferlini grumbled, but was satisfied.

On the day of the event, Wanda Ferlini woke up looking older and more haggard than ever before. It had been a bad night; her husband had twice startled her out of sleep with his wild dreams of incredible escapes. But it wasn't only sleeplessness which dulled her eyes and slowed her responses. It was anticipation, the dread of something going wrong.

Roscoe had hired a chauffeur-driven, open-top Cadillac for the occasion; they drove up to the site of Ferlini's adventure in style. Wanda, sitting beside Roscoe in the back seat of the car, wore her best dress and never looked worse. Roscoe, flushed with excitement and bourbon, held tightly to her hand. Ferlini, riding the high seat of the Cadillac, waving his arms to the crowd, wore a full dress suit with a white tie, his muscular shoulders stretching the glossy fabric almost to the point of bursting seams.

If Ferlini had any further complaints about Roscoe's publicity build-up, they were forgotten now. The crowd on the edge of Lake Truscan numbered in the hundreds. Roscoe's efforts to enlist the mayor in the program had failed, but there was a city councilman, the chief of police, the assistant fire commissioner, and two of the town's leading businessmen in attendance. The supper club had supplied the affair with its full six-piece orchestra, and their ragtime marches made the occasion seem more festive and significant than it really was. Best of all, there were a dozen newsmen and photographers.

Roscoe had planned it all well, but there were still some disappointments. The public address system developed a high-pitched squeal that made its use impossible; so there were no introductory speeches. The weather had seemed ideal in the early morning, but by one-thirty, a black trimmed cloud had moved overhead. Wanda Ferlini shivered when she saw it. Roscoe, moving busily among the officials, tried to speed up the program before rain made Ferlini's escape attempt even more difficult.

They were ready to go at two.

The handcuffs were snapped on first, by the police chief; it seemed appropriate. The chief, a bluff man with a forced smile, examined the handcuffs carefully before placing them on Ferlini's wrists, and pronounced them thoroughly genuine.

The two businessmen were selected to wind the thick rope about Ferlini's body. He stripped off his coat jacket, his white tie, and his formal shirt, and then kicked off his shoes. In the T-shirt, his muscular chest drew admiring exclamations from the crowd's female element. The businessmen were both short and pudgy, and they were puffing by the time they had the fifty-foot rope coiled around Ferlini's body.

"Knot it, knot it!" Ferlini urged them, exposing the teeth made strong and sharp by years of tearing and biting at ropes. They knotted it, in odd, lumpy knots that accented the coil from head to foot. They were so busy that neither they nor the spectators were aware that Ferlini was pumping his lungs full of air, increasing the circumference of his chest by almost seven inches. He smiled complacently when they were through, confident that he could wriggle free of his bonds in only a few seconds.

The assistant fire commissioner was given the task of assisting Ferlini into the cloth sack. He rested it on the ground, and Ferlini was lifted up over it; then the official lifted up the cloth until it covered the escape artist completely. The crowd murmured when the cloth was securely fastened over Ferlini's head.

But it was the sight of the huge iron chest that brought the sharpest reaction from the spectators. Somewhere in the throng, a woman screamed, and Roscoe grinned with pleasure. It was great showmanship. He sought Wanda's eyes to share the moment, but he found her face pale and drawn, her own eyes closed and her lips moving soundlessly.

Then Ferlini was deposited inside the chest, and the chest was locked and bolted by the city councilman. The committee examined it, declared it escape proof, and then stood back as a quartet of hired musclemen lifted the chest from the ground and deposited it in the stern of the motor boat that was moored to the dock.

The supper club orchestra struck up the funeral march, swinging the mournful melody. Roscoe stepped into the boat first, and then helped Wanda—who looked like a bereaved widow—aboard. The pilot of the craft, a jaunty crew-cut young man, waved at the crowd and unfastened the line. He started the engine, and moved the boat slowly out towards the deep of the lake.

"You all right?" Roscoe asked the woman.

Wanda murmured something, and reached for his hand.

When they were five hundred yards off shore, the pilot cut the engine.

"This okay, Mr. Roscoe?"

"This'll do fine." Roscoe trained binoculars on the edge of the lake, to see what the newsmen were up to. They were watching him just as eagerly; the photographers, some with telescopic lenses on their cameras, were hard at work.

"Let 'er go," Roscoe said.

Wanda cried out feebly, and the pilot grinned, put his hands against the iron chest, and tipped it over the side. It fell into the water with a splash that sprayed them all, and then vanished from sight, spreading a huge ripple all the way back to the shore.

Then they waited.

Roscoe looked at his watch. When thirty seconds went by, he looked at Wanda and smiled reassuringly. Then they waited some more.

At the end of the first minute, the pilot's grin faded, and he began to whistle off-key. Wanda shrieked at him to be quiet, and he stopped.

At the end of the second minute, Roscoe could no longer look at the terrible chalk-whiteness of Wanda's face, so he lifted his binoculars again and studied the shore-line. The crowd had pressed forward to the water's edge by now, moving like some dark, undulating animal.

"My God," the pilot said. "He's not coming up, Mr. Roscoe!"

"He's got to come up! He's got to!"

Three minutes passed, but there was no sign of the great Ferlini.

At the end of six minutes, Wanda Ferlini moaned, swayed, and fainted. Roscoe caught her falling body before it struck the floor of the boat. Five minutes later he ordered the pilot to head back for shore.

They recovered Ferlini's handcuffed body late that night.

Baggett tried to see Wanda on the day of the funeral but it was Phil Roscoe who refused him admittance. Phil didn't care about Wanda's love life; he had too many problems of his own. But he was still a businessman, and Wanda was still a client, even without her famous husband. It just didn't seem smart to have Wanda appear as anything more than a tragic widow.

Wanda was playing the role well. By some strange cosmetic alchemy, her sorrow made her look younger. Her white-powdered face and pale lipstick contrasted well with her black mourning attire.

Roscoe had made the funeral arrangements, and they were almost as spectacular as the water escape itself. The turnout was large and well-covered by the press; a horde of show people, not averse to being seen themselves, were on hand to mourn the passing of the great escape artist. The funeral procession wound slowly through the streets of the town, requiring a full half-hour to pass any one city block, but by the time Ferlini's coffin had reached the point of no return the crowd had thinned out considerably. Only a handful watched the final ceremonies in the graveyard.

Wanda sobbed against Roscoe's shoulder, and he patted her consolingly.

"It's the way he wanted it," he said inanely.

"I know, I know," Wanda said.

The eulogy, delivered by the town's most prominent clergyman, was brief. He spoke of Ferlini's courage, of his devotion to his art, of the pleasure he had given so many people in his lifetime. As he spoke, Wanda's eyes glazed oddly, and for a moment, Roscoe was fearful that she might swoon again.

They brought the coffin to the edge of the grave. The bearer in front, a waiter in the supper club, seemed puzzled by something, and murmured to the man beside him. Roscoe stepped forward, spoke briefly to them, and then conferred hastily with the minister. The conference piqued the curiosity of the solitary newsman on the scene, who came out of the sidelines to ask what was happening.

"I dunno," Roscoe said, scratching his head. "Freddy here thinks something is wrong. Says the coffin feels strange."

"How do you mean, strange?"

The waiter shrugged. "Light is what I mean. It feels too light."

"Really," the minister whispered. "I hardly think—"

"No, he's right," another bearer said. "Hardly weighs anything at all. And you know Ferlini, he was a big, hefty guy."

They looked at the coffin, waiting for someone to make a suggestion. It was Roscoe, finally.

"I hate to do this," he said softly. "But I think we'd better open it."

The minister protested, but they were already working on the lid.

"What's happening?" Wanda said. "What's going on, Phil?"

"Keep back," he pleaded. "I don't want you to see this, Wanda—"

But there was no way for her to avoid it. The lid was opened, and the truth was revealed to the sight of all. It sent a shock through the crowd as tangible as a blow.

The coffin was empty, and Wanda Ferlini was screaming like a high wind among the treetops.

Dr. Rushfield rolled a pencil along the blotter of the desk, and said, "Go on, Mr. Roscoe, I want to hear it all."

Phil Roscoe licked his dry mouth and wished he had a drink.

"You've got to understand how it is in my business, Doctor. Everything is showmanship, everything. That's why Ferlini made this deal with me, maybe ten, twelve years ago."

"And just what was this deal?"

"Nobody else knew about it, just him and me. It was crazy, I told him that. But you don't know how stubborn a guy like that can be. He made me promise that if anything ever happened to him, I mean if he died, that I would arrange for one last trick—something that would make him remembered even longer than Houdini. That's what it was, Doc."

"A trick?"

"A real easy one. I just slipped the undertaker fifty bucks, and he arranged to have Ferlini buried some place in secret. Then he put an empty coffin in the hearse, and that was that. You see what I mean, don't you? Honest-to-goodness showmanship."

"I see," Rushfield said, frowning. "But I'm afraid that it had quite an effect on Mrs. Ferlini. I gather that she wasn't too well-balanced before this happened, and now . . ." He sighed, and stood up. "All right, Mr. Roscoe. I can let you have one look at her, but I can't let you talk to her. I'm sorry."

Roscoe followed the doctor down the hall. They stopped at a door with a small barred window, and Roscoe looked inside. He drew back, appalled, at the sight of Wanda, her eyes round and unseeing, her arms straining uselessly to escape from the tight, unrelenting grip of the straitjacket.

NOT A LAUGHING MATTER
●
Evan Hunter

Don't laugh—or smile ambiguously—when a sensitive person is present. He may very well be a paranoiac. Perchance he may even be given to homicide—a homicide that may be your very own.

He hated the manager most.

Last night he had come to that realization. This morning, as he entered the department store with the Luger tucked into the waistband of his trousers, he allowed his hatred for the manager to swell up blackly until it smothered all the other hatreds he felt. The manager knew; of that he was certain. And it was his knowledge, this smirking sneering patronizing knowledge which fed the hatred, nurtured it, caused it to rise like dark yeast, bubbling, boiling.

The Luger was a firm metal reassurance against his belly.

The gun had been given to him in the good days, in Vienna, by an admirer. In the good days, there had been many admirers, and many gifts. He could remember the good days. The good days would sometimes

come back to him with fiercely sweet nostalgia, en-
gulfing him in waves and waves of painful memories.
He could remember the lights, and the applause,
and . . .

"Good morning, Nick."

The voice, the hated voice.

He stopped abruptly. "Good morning, Mr. Atkins,"
he said.

Atkins was smiling. The smile was a thin curl on his
narrow face, a thin bloodless curl beneath the ridicu-
lously tenuous mustache on the cleaving edge of the
hatchet face. The manager's hair was black, artfully
combed to conceal a balding patch. He wore a gray
pin-stripe suit. Like a caricature of all store managers
everywhere, he wore a carnation in his buttonhole. He
continued smiling. The smile was infuriating.

"Ready for the last act?" he asked.

"Yes, Mr. Atkins."

"It *is* the last act, isn't it, Nick?" Atkins asked, smiling. "Final curtain comes down today, doesn't it? All
over after today. Everything reverts back to normal
after today."

"Yes, Mr. Atkins," he said. "Today is the last act."

"But no curtain calls, eh, Nick?"

His name was not Nick. His name was Randolph
Blair, a name that had blazed across the theater mar-
quees of four continents. Atkins knew this, and had
probably known it the day he'd hired him. He knew it,
and so the "Nick" was an additional barb, a reminder
of his current status, a sledgehammer subtlety that
shouted, "Lo, how the mighty have fallen!"

"My name is not Nick," he said flatly.

Atkins snapped his fingers. "That's right, isn't it? I
keep forgetting. What is it again? Randolph Something? Clair? Flair? Shmair? What *is* your name, Nick?"

"My name is Randolph Blair," he said. He fancied
he said it with great dignity. He fancied he said it the
way Hamlet would have announced that he was Prince
of Denmark. He could remember the good days when
the name Randolph Blair was the magic key to a

thousand cities. He could remember hotel clerks with fluttering hands, maître d's hovering, young girls pulling at his clothing, even telephone operators suddenly growing respectful when they heard the name. Randolph Blair. In his mind, the name was spelled in lights. Randolph Blair. The lights suddenly flickered, and then dimmed. He felt the steel outline of the Luger against his belly. He smiled thinly.

"You know my name, don't you, Mr. Atkins?"

"Yes," Atkins said. "I know your name. I hear it sometimes."

His interest was suddenly piqued. "Do you?" he asked.

"Yes. I hear people ask, every now and then, 'Say, whatever happened to Randolph Blair?' I know your name."

He felt Atkins' dart pierce his throat, felt the poison spread into his bloodstream. *Whatever happened to Randolph Blair?* A comedian had used the line on television not two weeks before, bringing down the house. Randolph Blair, the ever-popular Randolph Blair. A nothing now, a nobody, a joke for a television comic. A forgotten name, a forgotten face. But Atkins would remember. For eternity he would remember Randolph Blair's name and the face and terrible power.

"Don't ..." he started, and then stopped abruptly.

"Don't what?"

"Don't ... don't push me too far, Mr. Atkins."

"Push you, Nick?" Atkins asked innocently.

"Stop that 'Nick' business!"

"Excuse *me,* Mr. Blair," Atkins said. "Excuse *me.* I forgot who I was talking to. I thought I was talking to an old drunk who'd managed to land himself a temporary job ..."

"Stop it!"

"... for a few weeks. I forgot I was talking to Randolph Blair, *the* Randolph Blair, *the* biggest lush in ..."

"I'm not a drunk!" he shouted.

"You're a drunk, all right," Atkins said. "Don't tell me about drunks. My father was one. A falling-down drunk. A screaming, hysterical drunk. I grew up with it, Nick. I watched the old man fight his imaginary monsters, killing my mother inch by inch. So don't tell me about drunks. Even if the newspapers hadn't announced your drunkenness to the world, I'd have spotted you as being a lush."

"Why'd you hire me?" he asked.

"There was a job to be filled, and I thought you could fill it."

"You hired me so you could needle me."

"Don't be ridiculous," Atkins said.

"You made a mistake. You're needling the wrong person."

"Am I?" Atkins asked blandly. "Are you one of these tough drunks? Aggressive? My father was a tough drunk in the beginning. He could lick any man in the house. The only thing he couldn't lick was the bottle. When things began crawling out of the walls, he wasn't so tough. He was a screaming, crying baby then, running to my mother's arms. Are you a tough drunk, Nick? Are you?"

"I'm not a drunk!" he said. "I haven't touched a drop since I got this job. You know that!"

"Why? Afraid it would hurt your performance?" Atkins laughed harshly. "That never seemed to bother you in the old days."

"Things are different," he said. "I want . . . I want to make a comeback. I . . . I took this job because . . . I wanted the feel again, the feel of working. You shouldn't needle me. You don't know what you're doing."

"Me? Needle you? Now, Nick, Nick, don't be silly. *I* gave you the job, didn't I? Out of all the other applicants, I chose you. So why should I needle you? That's silly, Nick."

"I've done a good job," he said, hoping Atkins would say the right thing, the right word, wanting him to say the words that would crush the hatred. "You know I've done a good job."

"Have you?" Atkins asked. "I think you've done a lousy job, Nick. As a matter of fact, I think you *always* did a lousy job. I think you were one of the worst actors who ever crossed a stage."

And in that moment, Atkins signed his own death warrant.

All that day, as he listened to stupid requests and questions, as he sat in his chair and the countless faces pressed toward him, he thought of killing Atkins. He did his job automatically, presenting his smiling face to the public, but his mind was concerned only with the mechanics of killing Atkins.

It was something like learning a part.

Over and over again, he rehearsed each step in his mind. The store would close at five tonight. The employees would be anxious to get home to their families. This had been a trying, harrowing few weeks, and tonight it would be over, and the employees would rush into the streets and into the subways and home to waiting loved ones. A desperate wave of rushing self-pity flooded over him. *Who are my loved ones?* he asked silently. *Who is waiting for me tonight?*

Someone was talking to him. He looked down, nodding.

"Yes, yes," he said mechanically. "And what else?"

The person kept talking. He half-listened, nodding all the while, smiling, smiling.

There had been many loved ones in the good days. Women, more women than he could count. Rich women, and young women, and jaded women, and fresh young girls. Where had he been ten years ago at this time? California? Yes, of course, the picture deal. How strange it had seemed to be in a land of sunshine at that time of the year. And he had blown the picture. He had not wanted to, he had not wanted to at all. But he'd been hopelessly drunk for . . . how

many days? And you can't shoot a picture when the
star doesn't come to the set.

The star.

Randolph Blair.

Tonight, he would be a star again. Tonight, he
would accomplish the murder of Atkins with style and
grace. When they closed the doors of the store, when
the shoppers left, when the endless questions, the endless requests stopped, he would go to Atkins' office. He
would not even change his clothes. He would go
straight to Atkins' office and he would collect his pay
envelope and he would shoot him. He would run into
the streets then. In the streets, he would be safe. In the
streets, Randolph Blair—the man whose face was once
known to millions—would be anonymously safe. The
concept was ironical. It appealed to a vestige of humor
somewhere deep within him. Randolph Blair would
tonight play the most important role of his career, and
he would play it anonymously.

Smiling, chuckling, he listened to the requests.

The crowd began thinning out at about four-thirty.
He was exhausted by that time. The only thing that
kept him going was the knowledge that he would soon
kill Mr. Atkins.

At four forty-five, he answered his last request. Sitting alone then, a corpulent unsmiling man, he
watched the clock on the wall. Four fifty. Four fifty-
two. Four fifty-seven. Four fifty-nine.

He got off the chair and waddled to the elevator
banks. The other employees were tallying the cash register receipts, anxious to get out of the store. He buzzed
for the elevator and waited.

The door slid open. The elevator operator smiled
automatically.

"All over, huh?" he asked.

"Yes, it's all over," Blair said.

"Going to pick up your envelope? Cashier's office?"

"Mr. Atkins pays me personally," he said.

"Yeah? How come?"

"He wanted it that way," he answered.

"Maybe he's hoping you'll be good to him, huh?" the operator said, and he burst out laughing.

He did not laugh with the operator. He knew very well why Atkins paid him personally. He did it so that he would have the pleasure each week of handing Randolph Blair—a man who had once earned $5,000 in a single week—a pay envelope containing forty-nine dollars and thirty-two cents.

"Ground floor then?" the operator asked.

"Yes. Ground floor."

When the elevator stopped, he got out of it quickly. He walked directly to Atkins' office. The secretary-receptionist was already gone. He smiled grimly, went to Atkins' door, and knocked on it.

"Who is it?" Atkins asked.

"Me," he said. "Blair."

"Oh, Nick. Come in, come in," Atkins said.

He opened the door and entered the office.

"Come for your pay?" Atkins asked.

"Yes."

He wanted to pull the Luger now and begin firing. He waited. Tensely, he waited.

"Little drink, first, Nick?" Atkins asked.

"No," he said.

"Come on, come on. Little drink never hurt anybody."

"I don't drink," he said.

"My father used to say that."

"I'm not your father."

"I know," Atkins said. "Come on, have a drink. It won't hurt you. Your job's over now. Your *performance* is over." He underlined the word smirkingly. "You can have a drink. Everyone'll be taking a little drink tonight."

"No."

"Why not? I'm trying to be friendly. I'm trying to . . ."

Atkins stopped. His eyes widened slightly. The Luger had come out from beneath Blair's coat with considerable ease. He stared at the gun.

"Wh . . . what's that?" he said.

"It's a gun," Blair answered coldly. "Give me my pay."

Atkins opened the drawer quickly. "Certainly. Certainly. You didn't think I was . . . was going to cheat you, did you? You . . ."

"Give me my pay."

Atkins put the envelope on the desk. Blair picked it up.

"And here's yours," he said, and he fired three times, watching Atkins collapse on the desk.

The enormity of the act rattled him. The door. The door. He had to get to it. The wastepaper basket tripped him up, sent him lunging forward, but his flailing arms gave him a measure of balance and kept him from going down.

He checked his flight before he had gone very far into the store. Poise, he told himself. Control. Remember you're Randolph Blair.

The counters were already protectively concealed by dust-sheets.

They reminded him of a body, covered, dead. Atkins.

Though he bolted again, he had enough presence of mind this time to duck into a rest room.

He was unaware of how long he had remained there, but when he emerged it was evident he had completely collected himself. His walk suggested the regal, or the confident calm of an actor sure of his part. And as he walked, he upbraided himself for having behaved like a juvenile suddenly overwhelmed by stage fright.

Randolph Blair pushed through the revolving doors. There was a sharp bite to the air, the promise of snow. He took a deep breath, calmly surveyed the people hurrying along, their arms loaded with packages.

And suddenly he heard laughter, a child's thin, piercing laugh. It cut into him like a knife. He turned and saw the laughing boy, tethered by one hand to the woman beside him, the boy's pale face, his arm and forefinger pointing upwards, pointing derisively.

More laughter arose. The laughter of men, of

women. A festive carousel, in the show window to one side of him, started up. Its music blared. It joined in the laughter, underscoring, counterpointing the laughter.

Blair felt caught in a punishing whirlpool. There seemed no way he could stop the sound, movement, everything that conspired to batter him.

Then the sight of policemen coming out of the store was completely unnerving. They appeared to be advancing toward him. And as he pulled the Luger on them, and even as he was overpowered and disarmed, a part of his mind felt that this was all unreal, all part of the dramatic role which he was playing.

But it was not a proper part for one wearing the red coat and trousers, the black belt and boots of a department store Santa Claus, the same clothes three thousand other men in the city were wearing. To blend into their anonymity, he lacked only a white beard, and he had lost his in the frantic exit he had made from Atkins' office.

And of course to a child—and even to some adults—a Santa Claus minus a beard might be a laughing matter.

MOST AGREEABLY POISONED

Fletcher Flora

Here we have an attempt to solve a marital problem somewhat differently, by means of poison—as sophisticated and swift a solution, incidentally, as any that has been put forward up to this time. Of course, a question arises: Who shall take the poison? The interesting thing is it doesn't much matter—just as long as somebody does.

"Darling," Sherry said, "I'm so glad you're behaving like a civilized being."

"Oh, I'm a great believer in civilized beings," I said. "In my opinion, they are essential to civilization."

"Nevertheless," she said, "it is absolutely exceptional of you to suggest that the three of us get together and talk things out quietly and courteously. Not," she added, "that it will change anything in the end."

"What do you mean, not that it will change anything?"

"I mean that I am quite determined to leave you, of course. Surely you understand that."

"I understand that it's your intention, but I am hoping to change your mind."

"Well, it's only fair to give you a chance, which I am willing to do, but I assure you that it's impossible. I am in love with Dennis and am going to marry him, and that's all there is to it. I'm truly sorry, darling, but it's necessary to my happiness."

"This means, I take it, that you are consequently no longer in love with *me*. Is that true?"

"Not at all. Please don't be absurd. I love you very much, as you very well know, but in a less exciting way. I am *madly* and *deliriously* and *irresistibly* in love with Dennis."

"Once you were madly and deliriously and irresistibly in love with me. At least you said you were."

"So I was, but now the way I am in love with you is unfortunately changed. It's sad, isn't it, the way things change?"

I looked at her with a great aching in my heart, for however sadly and unfortunately her way of loving me had changed, my way of loving her had not changed at all. So bright and fair and incredibly lovely, I also saw that she was wearing a soft white gown that achieved a perfect balance of exposure and suggestion.

"Will you have a martini?" I said.

"When Dennis gets here, we will have one together. It will make everyone feel relaxed and comfortable, don't you think? Martinis are quite good for that."

"I thought we might just have one beforehand. We can have another later, of course."

"Well, I'm not averse to that, but there's the doorbell now, if I'm not mistaken, and it's surely Dennis."

She was right about its being the doorbell. She was almost certainly right, too, about its being Dennis. I was compelled to accept this reluctantly.

"You had better let him in," I said.

She went out into the hall and opened the front door, and it was Dennis outside. He came into the hall, and Sherry put her arms around his neck and kissed him. It was nothing new for her to kiss various men, but this kiss was different and plainly special. It was ardent, to say the least, and it lasted for quite a long time. From my position in the living room, I could see it clearly, but I quit looking at it before it was finished, and started mixing martinis, and I was still mixing the martinis when Sherry and Dennis came in.

"Well, you two," Sherry said, "here we are."

"That's true," I said. "We're here, all right."

"This is Dennis, Sherm," Sherry said. "Dennis, this is Sherm."

"Glad to meet you, Sherm," Dennis said.

He was not as tall as I, nor quite so heavy, but I had to admit that he looked like he was probably in better condition. He had short blond hair and a face like the guy who plays juvenile leads until he's thirty, and he apparently felt that he was playing the lead in this particular turkey. Which he was, even though I didn't like to admit it. I put down the shaker of martinis and shook his hand.

"His name is actually Sherman," Sherry said, "but I call him Sherm."

"Sometimes we got real intimate," I said.

"This is exceedingly decent of you, Sherm," Dennis said.

"Civilized," I said. "I'm being civilized, which makes everything much more comfortable for everyone. Will you have a martini?"

"Thanks. I don't mind if I do."

I poured the martinis, and they sat on the sofa and held hands. When I served the martinis, he took his in his left hand, and she took hers in her right hand, and this made it possible for her left hand and his right hand to go on holding each other. As for me, I was in a position to hold my martini in either hand or both, as the notion struck me.

"I suppose," I said, "that we might as well get it over with."

"Sorry, Sherm," Dennis said, "but I suppose we had." He looked at me with a man-to-man expression.

"Well," I said, "as I understand it, you want something of mine, and I naturally want to keep what I have, and this poses a problem."

"Problem?" he said. "I don't see that there's any particular problem."

"Neither do I," Sherry said. "No problem at all. You and I will simply get divorced, Sherm, and you and I will simply get married, Dennis, and that's all there is to it."

"As I see it," Dennis said, "that's all."

"As I see it," I said, "not quite. I'm willing to be civilized and congenial, which is one thing, but I'm not willing to surrender supinely, which is another. I must insist on a fair chance in this affair, but at the same time I want to be agreeable, which is evident, and so I have thought of a way in which everything can be settled amicably. Would you like to hear it?"

"I don't think so," Dennis said. "I don't think I care to hear it at all."

"Oh, let's hear it, Dennis," Sherry said. "It can't do any harm to hear it."

"All right," Dennis said. "I suppose it's only fair."

"Good," I said. "You two just continue to sit here and hold hands for a minute, and I'll be right back."

Crossing the room to a liquor cabinet, I got three small bottles filled with red port and returned. I lined the bottles up on the coffee table in front of the sofa.

"Whatever are they?" Sherry said.

"Little bottles of port wine," I said. "I prepared them myself earlier today."

"It seems perfectly ridiculous to me. Whatever for?"

"Well, they are part of my plan to settle our problem amicably. One of these bottles is slightly different from the other two, you see. Two of them are filled with plain port, as I said, but the other one contains also enough poison to curl your toes in a minute. It's my plan that one of us shall drink the poisoned port and curl his toes and cease forthwith to be a problem to the other two."

"Sherm," Sherry said, "you've always had a perverted sense of humor, and it's obviously time you were told about it."

"It's a reasonable chance for everyone to get everything or nothing," I said. "It's civilized, that's what it is. Besides being civilized, it's sophisticated. It's quite appropriate and acceptable for three civilized sophisticates like us."

"Now that you've explained it," Sherry said, "I believe you're right. It's certainly about as civilized and sophisticated as it could possibly be."

For the first time since sitting down, she disengaged her held hand and put her chin in it. Before putting her chin in the hand, she put her elbow on her knee. She sat staring at the little bottles of port, plainly intrigued by the prospect of two amicable men risking having their toes curled on the alternate chance of possessing her if the port didn't happen to be spiked.

"Look here," Dennis said. "There are *three* bottles there. Do you seriously expect Sherry to participate in this fantastic business?"

"It's necessary," I said, "in order to give all alternatives a chance. If I get the poisoned port, you get Sherry. If you get the poisoned port, I get Sherry. If she gets the poisoned port, neither of us gets her. This thing must be done properly and thoroughly, if at all, and I'm sure Sherry will agree."

"I do agree," Sherry said. "It's only fair that I participate."

"I absolutely forbid it," Dennis said.

"Don't be presumptuous, darling," Sherry said. "You are hardly in a position to forbid anything."

"You'll have to concede that, Dennis," I said. "None of us is presently qualified to dictate to either of the others. The most you can do is to decline to participate yourself."

Sherry turned her head and looked at Dennis with wide eyes. It was apparent that such a reluctance on the part of Dennis had not seriously occurred to her before.

"Yes, Dennis," she said, "if you don't feel like taking a simple chance for my sake, you are certainly under no compulsion."

"It's not merely the chance," Dennis said. "Think of the complications. Suppose we all take a bottle and gulp it down. One of us gets the poison and dies. You can surely see that the other two would be all mucked up with the police over it."

"That's true," I said. "I've anticipated that, and have thought of a way to avoid it. We do not drink the port here. Each of us takes a bottle when we separate. Each drinks the port when he is alone, and the two survivors meet tomorrow afternoon at, say, three o'clock in the cocktail lounge of the Café Picardy. This, to my way of thinking, besides solving the problem of the police, introduces an appealing element of romance, to say nothing of suspense. Who will be the two? Who will meet at the Picardy tomorrow?"

Dennis looked at me bitterly. "I hope to hell it isn't you and I," he said bitterly.

"Does that mean you agree to do it?"

"I suppose so. I can see that Sherry is all for it."

"I am," Sherry said. "I surely am. Sherm, this last part is absolute genius. Although I was inclined at one time to exaggerate your virtues, I see now that in certain respects I didn't give you the credit you deserved. In this matter, I can think of only one thing you neglected to do which is rather disappointing."

"Yes? What's that?"

"You should have used sherry instead of port."

"Oh. Sherry for Sherry. I did miss a nice touch there, didn't I? I'm afraid, however, that it's too late now to change."

"Yes. Disappointing as it is, we'll have to go along with port."

"Wait a minute," Dennis said. "Do you know which bottle has the poison?"

"No," I said. "The bottles are identical, and I messed them around with my eyes closd. At any rate, you and Sherry may choose the bottles you want, and I'll take the one that's left. Is that acceptable?"

"It's perfectly acceptable," Sherry said, "and I don't think it was quite nice of you, Dennis, to imply that Sherm might cheat in an affair of honor of this sort. I suggest now that we all have another martini and be compatible."

We had the martinis compatibly, and afterward I went downtown to a hotel and took a room. In the room, after putting on a pair of pajamas I was willing to be caught dead in, I drank the port and lay down on the bed.

I was sitting at the bar drinking an ambrosia highball when Sherry came in. It was not the cocktail lounge of the Café Picardy by any means, but it was a pleasant place, and there was a talented and pretty girl who sat on a little dais and played pretty tunes on a concert harp. Sherry was certainly astonished to see me, and apparently uncertain whether to be happy or otherwise. Anyhow, she sat on a stool beside me.

"What on earth are *you* doing here?" she said.

"Hello, Sherry," I said. "It's odd that you should use that expression."

"What expression?"

"On earth."

"Oh." She stared at me and frowned and tapped on the bar rapidly with the nail of the index finger of her right hand, which was a sign that she was angry. "Well, never mind being evasive with me, for I understand everything clearly now. Sherm, you so and so, you put poison in *two* of those little bottles, and then you contrived somehow to have them chosen by you and me, and it was nothing but a damn dirty trick to get me permanently away from Dennis. There is simply no limit to your duplicity."

"You do me an injustice to accuse me of playing a dirty trick like that," I said. "It's true that things were not quite as I said, but I certainly didn't discriminate against anyone. We all had exactly the same chance."

"Explain yourself, if you don't mind."

"The truth is, I put poison in *all three* of the bottles."

"In that case, where's Dennis?"

"Yes, indeed," I said. "Where is he?"

"I haven't seen him around anywhere."

"Neither have I. Nor will we. Not for a long time."

"You mean he reneged? That after agreeing to participate, he didn't drink his port at all?"

"That's it."

She kept on staring at me, but her index finger kept tapping slower and slower until it shortly stopped altogether, and I thought I could see in her eyes certain signs that we might be entering a heavenly era of madness, delirium, and irresistibility.

"Well," she said, "I can see that I called the wrong man an old so and so."

"That's all right," I said. "Would you care for an ambrosia highball?"

"I think I would," she said. "I need it."

THE BEST-FRIEND MURDER

•

Donald E. Westlake

Pity the poor detective. He must detect, and having de-
tected, like all true artists, he dare not be satisfied. Catching
someone for a murder is not enough; this someone must
also be guilty of the crime.

Detective Abraham Levine of Brooklyn's Forty-
Third Precinct chewed on his pencil and glowered at
the report he'd just written. He didn't like it, he didn't
like it at all. It just didn't feel right, and the more he
thought about it the stronger the feeling became.

Levine was a short and stocky man, baggily-dressed
from plain pipe racks. His face was sensitive, topped by
salt-and-pepper gray hair chopped short in a military
crewcut. At fifty-three, he had twenty-four years of
duty on the police force, and was halfway through the
heart-attack age range, a fact that had been bothering
him for some time now. Every time he was reminded
of death, he thought worriedly about the aging heart
pumping away inside his chest.

And in his job, the reminders of death came often.
Natural death, accidental death, and violent death.

This one was a violent death, and to Levine it felt
wrong somewhere. He and his partner, Jack Crawley,
had taken the call just after lunch. It was from one of
the patrolmen in Prospect Park, a patrolman named
Tanner. A man giving his name as Larry Perkins had
walked up to Tanner in the park and announced that
he had just poisoned his best friend. Tanner went with
him, found a dead body in the apartment Perkins had

led him to, and called in. Levine and Crawley, having
just walked into the station after lunch, were given the
call. They turned around and walked back out again.

Crawley drove their car, an unmarked '56 Chevy,
while Levine sat beside him and worried about death.
At least this would be one of the neat ones. No knives
or bombs or broken beer bottles. Just poison, that was
all. The victim would look as though he were sleeping,
unless it had been one of those poisons causing muscle
spasms before death. But it would still be neater than
a knife or a bomb or a broken beer bottle, and the victim wouldn't look quite so completely dead.

Crawley drove leisurely, without the siren. He was a
big man in his forties, somewhat overweight, square-
faced and heavy-jowled, and he looked meaner than he
actually was. The Chevy tooled up Eighth Avenue, the
late spring sun shining on its hood. They were headed
for an address on Garfield Place, the block between
Eighth Avenue and Prospect Park West. They had to
circle the block, because Garfield was a one-way street.
That particular block on Garfield Place is a double
row of chipped brownstones, the street running down
between two rows of high stone stoops, the buildings
cut and chopped inside into thousands of apartments,
crannies and cubbyholes, niches and box-like caves,
where the subway riders sleep at night. The subway to
Manhattan is six blocks away, up at Grand Army
Plaza, across the way from the main library.

At one p.m. on this Wednesday in late May, the sidewalks were deserted, the buildings had the look of long
abandoned dwellings. Only the cars parked along the
left side of the street indicated present occupancy.

The number they wanted was in the middle of the
block, on the right-hand side. There was no parking
allowed on that side, so there was room directly in
front of the address for Crawley to stop the Chevy. He
flipped the sun visor down, with the official business
card showing through the windshield, and followed
Levine across the sidewalk and down the two steps to
the basement door, under the stoop. The door was

propped open with a battered garbage can. Levine and Crawley walked inside. It was dim in there, after the bright sunlight, and it took Levine's eyes a few seconds to get used to the change. Then he made out the figures of two men standing at the other end of the hallway, in front of a closed door. One was the patrolman, Tanner, young, just over six feet, with a square and impersonal face. The other was Larry Perkins.

Levine and Crawley moved down the hallway to the two men waiting for them. In the seven years they had been partners, they had established a division of labor that satisfied them both. Crawley asked the questions, and Levine listened to the answers. Now, Crawley introduced himself to Tanner, who said, "This is Larry Perkins of 294 Fourth Street."

"Body in there?" asked Crawley, pointing at the closed door.

"Yes, sir," said Tanner.

"Let's go inside," said Crawley. "You keep an eye on the pigeon. See he doesn't fly away."

"I've got some stuff to go to the library," said Perkins suddenly. His voice was young and soft.

They stared at him. Crawley said, "It'll keep."

Levine looked at Perkins, trying to get to know him. It was a technique he used, most of it unconsciously. First, he tried to fit Perkins into a type or category, some sort of general stereotype. Then he would look for small and individual ways in which Perkins differed from the general type, and he would probably wind up with a surprisingly complete mental picture, which would also be surprisingly accurate.

The general stereotype was easy. Perkins, in his black wool sweater and belt-in-the-back khakis and scuffed brown loafers without socks, was "arty." What were they calling them this year? They were "hip" last year, but this year they were—"beat." That was it. For a general stereotype, Larry Perkins was a Beatnik. The individual differences would show up soon, in Perkins' talk and mannerisms and attitudes.

Crawley said again, "Let's go inside," and the four of them trooped into the room where the corpse lay.

The apartment was one large room, plus a closet-size kitchenette and an even smaller bathroom. A Murphy bed stood open, covered with zebra-striped material. The rest of the furniture consisted of a battered dresser, a couple of armchairs and lamps, and a record player sitting on a table beside a huge stack of long-playing records. Everything except the record player looked faded and worn and second-hand, including the thin maroon rug on the floor and the soiled flower-pattern wallpaper. Two windows looked out on a narrow cement enclosure and the back of another brownstone. It was a sunny day outside, but no sun managed to get down into this room.

In the middle of the room stood a card table, with a typewriter and two stacks of paper on it. Before the card table was a folding chair, and in the chair sat the dead man. He was slumped forward, his arms flung out and crumpling the stacks of paper, his head resting on the typewriter. His face was turned toward the door, and his eyes were closed, his facial muscles relaxed. It had been a peaceful death, at least, and Levine was grateful for that.

Crawley looked at the body, grunted, and turned to Perkins. "Okay," he said. "Tell us about it."

"I put the poison in his beer," said Perkins simply. He didn't talk like a Beatnik at any rate. "He asked me to open a can of beer for him. When I poured it into a glass, I put the poison in, too. When he was dead, I went and talked to the patrolman here."

"And that's all there was to it?"

"That's all."

Levine asked, "Why did you kill him?"

Perkins looked over at Levine. "Because he was a pompous ass."

"Look at me," Crawley told him.

Perkins immediately looked away from Levine, but before he did so, Levine caught a flicker of emotion in the boy's eyes, what emotion he couldn't tell. Levine glanced around the room, at the faded furniture and the card table and the body, and at young Perkins, dressed like a Beatnik but talking like the politest of polite young men, outwardly calm but hiding some strong emotion deep inside his eyes. What was it Levine had seen there? Terror? Rage? Or pleading?

"Tell us about this guy," said Crawley, motioning at the body. "His name, where you knew him from, the whole thing."

"His name is Al Gruber. He got out of the Army about eight months ago. He's living on his savings and the GI Bill. I mean, he *was*."

"He was a college student?"

"More or less. He was taking a few courses at Columbia, nights. He wasn't a full-time student."

Crawley said, "What was he, full-time?"

Perkins shrugged. "Not much of anything. A writer. An undiscovered writer. Like me."

Levine asked, "Did he make much money from his writing?"

"None," said Perkins. This time he didn't turn to look at Levine, but kept watching Crawley while he answered. "He got something accepted by one of the quarterlies once," he said, "but I don't think they ever published it. And they don't pay anything anyway."

"So he was broke?" asked Crawley.

"Very broke. I know the feeling well."

"You in the same boat?"

"Same life story completely," said Perkins. He glanced at the body of Al Gruber and said, "Well, almost. I write, too. And I don't get any money for it. And I'm living on the GI Bill and savings and a few home-typing jobs, and going to Columbia nights."

People came into the room then, the medical examiner and the boys from the lab, and Levine and Crawley, bracketing Perkins between them, waited and watched for a while. When they could see that the M.E. had completed his first examination, they left

Perkins in Tanner's charge and went over to talk to him.

Crawley, as usual, asked the questions. "Hi, Doc," he said. "What's it look like to you?"

"Pretty straightforward case," said the M.E. "On the surface, anyway. Our man here was poisoned, felt the effects coming on, went to the typewriter to tell us who'd done it to him, and died. A used glass and a small medicine bottle were on the dresser. We'll check them out, but they almost certainly did the job."

"Did he manage to do any typing before he died?" asked Crawley.

The M.E. shook his head. "Not a word. The paper was in the machine kind of crooked, as though he'd been in a hurry, but he just wasn't fast enough."

"He wasted his time," said Crawley. "The guy confessed right away."

"The one over there with the patrolman?"

"Uh-huh."

"Seems odd, doesn't it?" said the M.E. "Take the trouble to poison someone, and then run out and confess to the first cop you see."

Crawley shrugged. "You can never figure," he said.

"I'll get the report to you soon's I can," said the M.E.

"Thanks, Doc. Come on, Abe, let's take our pigeon to his nest."

"Okay," said Levine, abstractedly. Already it felt wrong. It had been feeling wrong, vaguely, ever since he'd caught that glimpse of something in Perkins' eyes. And the feeling of wrongness was getting stronger by the minute, without getting any clearer.

They walked back to Tanner and Perkins, and Crawley said, "Okay, Perkins, let's go for a ride."

They walked back to Tanner.

"You're going to book me?" asked Perkins. He sounded oddly eager.

"Just come along," said Crawley. He didn't believe in answering extraneous questions.

"All right," said Perkins. He turned to Tanner. "Would you mind taking my books and records back to the library? They're due today. They're the ones on the chair. And there's a couple more over in the stack of Al's records."

"Sure," said Tanner. He was gazing at Perkins with a troubled look on his face, and Levine wondered if Tanner felt the same wrongness that was plaguing him.

"Let's go," said Crawley impatiently, and Perkins moved toward the door.

"I'll be right along," said Levine. As Crawley and Perkins left the apartment, Levine glanced at the titles of the books and record albums Perkins had wanted returned to the library. Two of the books were collections of Elizabethan plays, one was the *New Arts Writing Annual,* and the other two were books on criminology. The records were mainly folk songs, of the bloodier type.

Levine frowned and went over to Tanner. He asked, "What were you and Perkins talking about before we got here?"

Tanner's face was still creased in a puzzled frown. "The stupidity of the criminal mind," he said. "There's something goofy here, Lieutenant."

"You may be right," Levine told him. He walked on down the hall and joined the other two at the door.

All three got into the front seat of the Chevy, Crawley driving again and Perkins sitting in the middle. They rode in silence, Crawley busy driving, Perkins studying the complex array of the dashboard, with its extra knobs and switches and the mike hooked beneath the radio, and Levine trying to figure out what was wrong.

At the station, after booking, they brought him to a small office, one of the interrogation rooms. There was a bare and battered desk, plus four chairs. Crawley sat behind the desk, Perkins sat across the desk and facing him, Levine took the chair in a corner behind and to the left of Perkins, and a male stenographer, notebook in hand, filled the fourth chair, behind Crawley.

Crawley's first questions covered the same ground already covered at Gruber's apartment, this time for the record. "Okay," said Crawley, when he'd brought them up to date. "You and Gruber were both doing the same kind of thing, living the same kind of life. You were both unpublished writers, both taking night courses at Columbia, both living on very little money."

"That's right," said Perkins.

"How long you known each other?"

"About six months. We met at Columbia, and we took the same subway home after class. We got to talking, found out we were both dreaming the same kind of dream, and became friends. You know. Misery loves company."

"Take the same classes at Columbia?"

"Only one. Creative Writing, from Professor Stonegell."

"Where'd you buy the poison?"

"I didn't. Al did. He bought it a while back and just kept it around. He kept saying if he didn't make a good sale soon he'd kill himself. But he didn't mean it. It was just a kind of gag."

Crawley pulled at his right earlobe. Levine knew, from his long experience with his partner, that that gesture meant that Crawley was confused. "You went there today to kill him?"

"That's right."

Levine shook his head. That wasn't right. Softly, he said, "Why did you bring the library books along?"

"I was on my way up to the library," said Perkins, twisting around in his seat to look at Levine.

"Look this way," snapped Crawley.

Perkins looked around at Crawley again, but not before Levine had seen that same burning deep in Perkins' eyes. Stronger, this time, and more like pleading. Pleading? What was Perkins pleading for?

"I was on my way to the library," Perkins said again.

"Al had a couple of records out on my card, so I went over to get them. On the way, I decided to kill him."

"Why?" asked Crawley.

"Because he was a pompous ass," said Perkins, the the same answer he'd given before.

"Because he got a story accepted by one of the literary magazines and you didn't?" suggested Crawley.

"Maybe. Partially. His whole attitude. He was smug. He knew more than anybody else in the world."

"Why did you kill him today? Why not last week or next week?"

"I felt like it today."

"Why did you give yourself up?"

"You would have gotten me anyway."

Levine asked, "Did you know that before you killed him?"

"I don't know," said Perkins, without looking around at Levine. "I didn't think about it till afterward. Then I knew the police would get me anyway—they'd talk to Professor Stonegell and the other people who knew us both and I didn't want to have to wait it out. So I went and confessed."

"You told the patrolman," said Levine, "that you'd killed your best friend."

"That's right."

"Why did you use that phrase, best friend, if you hated him so much you wanted to kill him?"

"He was my best friend. At least, in New York. I didn't really know anyone else, except Professor Stonegell. Al was my best friend because he was just about my only friend."

"Are you sorry you killed him?" asked Levine.

This time, Perkins twisted around in the chair again, ignoring Crawley. "No, sir," he said, and his eyes now were blank.

There was silence in the room, and Crawley and Levine loked at one another. Crawley questioned with his eyes, and Levine shrugged, shaking his head. Something was wrong, but he didn't know what. And

Perkins was being so helpful that he wound up being no help at all.

Crawley turned to the stenographer. "Type it up formal," he said. "And have somebody come take the pigeon to his nest."

After the stenographer had left, Levine said, "Anything you want to say off the record, Perkins?"

Perkins grinned. His face was half-turned away from Crawley, and he was looking at the floor, as though he was amused by something he saw there. "Off the record?" he murmured. "As long as there are two of you in here, it's *on* the record."

"Do you want one of us to leave?"

Perkins looked up at Levine again, and stopped smiling. He seemed to think it over for a minute, and then he shook his head. "No," he said. "Thanks, anyway. But I don't think I have anything more to say. Not right now anyway."

Levine frowned and sat back in his chair, studying Perkins. The boy didn't ring true; he was constructed of too many contradictions. Levine reached out for a mental image of Perkins, but all he touched was air.

After Perkins was led out of the room by two uniformed cops, Crawley got to his feet, stretched, sighed, scratched, pulled his earlobe, and said, "What do you make of it, Abe?"

"I don't like it."

"I know that. I saw it in your face. But he confessed, so what else is there?"

"The phony confession is not exactly unheard of, you know."

"Not this time," said Crawley. "A guy confesses to a crime he didn't commit for one of two reasons. Either he's a crackpot who wants the publicity or to be punished or something like that, or he's protecting somebody else. Perkins doesn't read like a crackpot to me, and there's nobody else involved for him to be protecting."

"In a capital punishment state," suggested Levine, "a

guy might confess to a murder he didn't commit so the state would do his suicide for him."

Crawley shook his head. "That still doesn't look like Perkins," he said.

"Nothing looks like Perkins. He's given us a blank wall to stare at. A couple of times it started to slip, and there was something else inside."

"Don't build a big thing, Abe. The kid confessed. He's the killer; let it go at that."

"The job's finished, I know that. But it still bothers me."

"Okay," said Crawley. He sat down behind the desk again and put his feet up on the scarred desk top. "Let's straighten it out. Where does it bother you?"

"All over. Number one, motivation. You don't kill a man for being a pompous ass. Not when you turn around a minute later and say he was your best friend."

"People do funny things when they're pushed far enough. Even to friends."

"Sure. Okay, number two. The murder method. It doesn't sound right. When a man kills impulsively, he grabs something and starts swinging. When he calms down, he goes and turns himself in. But when you *poison* somebody, you're using a pretty sneaky method. It doesn't make sense for you to run out and call a cop right after using poison. It isn't the same kind of mentality."

"He used the poison," said Crawley, "because it was handy. Gruber bought it, probably had it sitting on his dresser or something, and Perkins just picked it up on impulse and poured it into the beer."

"That's another thing," said Levine. "Do you drink much beer out of cans?"

Crawley grinned. "You know I do."

"I saw some empty beer cans sitting around the apartment, so that's where Gruber got his last beer from."

"Yeah. So what?"

"When you drink a can of beer, do you pour the

beer out of the can into a glass, or do you just drink it straight from the can?"

"I drink it out of the can. But not everybody does."

"I know, I know. Okay, what about the library books? If you're going to go kill somebody, are you going to bring library books along?"

"It was an impulse killing. He didn't know he was going to do it until he got there."

Levine got to his feet. "That's the hell of it," he said. "You can explain away every single question in this business. But it's such a simple case. Why should there be so many questions that need explaining away?"

Crawley shrugged. "Beats me," he said. "All I know is, we've got a confession, and that's enough to satisfy me."

"Not me," said Levine. "I think I'll go poke around and see what happens. Want to come along?"

"Somebody's going to have to hand the pen to Perkins when he signs his confession," said Crawley.

"Mind if I take off for a while?"

"Go ahead. Have a big time," said Crawley, grinning at him. "Play detective."

Levine's first stop was back at Gruber's address. Gruber's apartment was empty now, having been sifted completely through normal routine procedure. Levine went down to the basement door under the stoop, but he didn't go back to Gruber's door. He stopped at the front apartment instead, where a ragged-edge strip of paper attached with peeling scotch tape to the door read, in awkward and childish lettering, SUPERIN-TENDENT. Levine rapped and waited. After a minute, the door opened a couple of inches, held by a chain. A round face peered out at him from a height of a little over five feet. The face said, "Who you looking for?"

"Police," Levine told him. He opened his wallet and held it up for the face to look at.

"Oh," said the face. "Sure thing." The door shut,

and Levine waited while the chain was clinked free, and then the door opened wide.

The super was a short and round man, dressed in corduroy trousers and a grease-spotted undershirt. He wheezed, "Come in, come in," and stood back for Levine to come into his crowded and musty-smelling living room.

Levine said, "I want to talk to you about Al Gruber."

The super shut the door and waddled into the middle of the room, shaking his head. "Wasn't that a shame?" he asked. "Al was a nice boy. No money, but a nice boy. Sit down somewhere, anywhere."

Levine looked around. The room was full of low-slung, heavy, sagging, over-stuffed furniture, armchairs and sofas. He picked the least battered armchair of the lot, and sat on the very edge. Although he was a short man, his knees seemed to be almost up to his chin, and he had the feeling that if he relaxed he'd fall over backward.

The super trundled across the room and dropped into one of the other armchairs, sinking into it as though he never intended to get to his feet again in his life. "A real shame," he said again. "And to think I maybe could have stopped it."

"You could have stopped it? How?"

"It was around noon," said the super. "I was watching the TV over there, and I heard a voice from the back apartment, shouting, 'Al! Al!' So I went out to the hall, but by the time I got there the shouting was all done. So I didn't know what to do. I waited a minute, and then I came back in and watched the TV again. That was probably when it was happening."

"There wasn't any noise while you were in the hall? Just the two shouts before you got out there?"

"That's all. At first, I thought it was another one of them arguments, and I was gonna bawl out the two of them, but it stopped before I even got the door open."

"Arguments?"

"Mr. Gruber and Mr. Perkins. They used to argue

all the time, shout at each other, carry on like monkeys. The other tenants was always complaining about it. They'd do it late at night sometimes, two or three o'clock in the morning, and the tenants would all start phoning me to complain."

"What did they argue about?"

The super shrugged his massive shoulders. "Who knows? Names. People. Writers. They both think they're great writers or something."

"Did they ever get into a fist fight or anything like that? Ever threaten to kill each other?"

"Naw, they'd just shout at each other and call each other stupid and ignorant and stuff like that. They liked each other, really, I guess. At least they always hung around together. They just loved to argue, that's all. You know how it is with college kids. I've had college kids renting here before, and they're all like that. They all love to argue. Course, I never had nothing like this happen before."

"What kind of person was Gruber, exactly?"

The super mulled it over for a while. "Kind of a quiet guy," he said at last. "Except when he was with Mr. Perkins, I mean. Then he'd shout just as loud and often as anybody. But most of the time he was quiet. And good-mannered. A real surprise, after most of the kids around today. He was always polite, and he'd lend a hand if you needed some help or something, like the time I was carrying a bed up to the third floor front. Mr. Gruber come along and pitched right in with me. He did more of the work than I did."

"And he was a writer, wasn't he? At least, he was trying to be a writer."

"Oh, sure. I'd hear that typewriter of his tappin' away in there at all hours. And he always carried a notebook around with him, writin' things down in it. I asked him once what he wrote in there, and he said descriptions, of places like Prospect Park up at the corner, and of the people he knew. He always said he wanted to be a writer like some guy named Wolfe, used to live in Brooklyn too."

"I see." Levine struggled out of the armchair. "Thanks for your time," he said.

"Not at all." The super waddled after Levine to the door. "Anything I can do," he said. "Any time at all."

"Thanks again," said Levine. He went outside and stood in the hallway, thinking things over, listening to the latch cli.. in place behind him. Then he turned and walked down the hallway to Gruber's apartment, and knocked on the door.

As he'd expected, a uniformed cop had been left behind to keep an eye on the place for a while, and when he opened the door, Levine showed his identification and said, "I'm on the case. I'd like to take a look around."

The cop let him in, and Levine looked carefully through Gruber's personal property. He found the notebooks, finally, in the bottom drawer of the dresser. There were five of them, steno pad size loose-leaf fillers. Four of them were filled with writing, in pen, in a slow and careful hand, and the fifth was still half-blank.

Levine carried the notebooks over to the card table, pushed the typewriter out of the way, sat down and began to skim through the books.

He found what he was looking for in the middle of the third one he tried. A description of Larry Perkins, written by the man Perkins had killed. The description, or character study, which it more closely resembled, was four pages long, beginning with a physical description and moving into a discussion of Perkins' personality. Levine noticed particular sentences in this latter part: "Larry doesn't want to write, he wants to be a writer, and that isn't the same thing. He wants the glamour and the fame and the money, and he thinks he'll get it from being a writer. That's why he's dabbled in acting and painting and all the other so-called glamorous professions. Larry and I are both being thwarted by the same thing: neither of us has anything to say worth saying. The difference is, I'm trying to find something to say, and Larry wants to make it on glibness alone. One of these days, he's going to find out he won't get anywhere that way. That's going to be a terrible day for him."

Levine closed the book, then picked up the last one, the one that hadn't yet been filled, and leafed through that. One word kept showing up throughout the last notebook. "Nihilism." Gruber obviously hated the word, and he was also obviously afraid of it. "Nihilism is death," he wrote on one page. "It is the belief that there are no beliefs, that no effort is worthwhile. How could any writer believe such a thing? Writing is the most positive of acts. So how can it be used for negative purposes? The only expression of nihilism is death, not the written word. If I can say nothing hopeful, I shouldn't say anything at all."

Levine put the notebooks back in the dresser drawer finally, thanked the cop, and went out to the Chevy. He'd hoped to be able to fill in the blank spaces in Perkins' character through Gruber's notebooks, but Gruber had apparently had just as much trouble defining Perkins as Levine was now having. Levine had learned a lot about the dead man, that he was sincere and intense and self-demanding as only the young can be, but Perkins was still little more than a smooth and blank wall. "Glibness," Gruber had called it. What was beneath the glibness? A murderer, by Perkins' own admission. But what else?

Levine crawled wearily into the Chevy and headed for Manhattan.

Professor Harvey Stonegell was in class when Levine got to Columbia University, but the girl at the desk in the dean's outer office told him that Stonegell would be out of that class in just a few minutes, and would then be free for the rest of the afternoon. She gave him directions to Stonegell's office, and Levine thanked her.

Stonegell's office door was locked, so Levine waited in the hall, watching the students hurrying by in both directions, and reading the notices of scholarships, grants and fellowships thumb-tacked to the bulletin board near the office door.

The professor showed up about fifteen minutes later, with two students in tow. He was a tall and slender man, with a gaunt face and a full head of gray-white hair. He could have been any age between fifty and seventy. He wore a tweed suit jacket, leather patches at the elbows, and non-matching gray slacks.

Levine said, "Professor Stonegell?"

"Yes?"

Levine introduced himself and showed his identification. "I'd like to talk to you for a minute or two."

"Of course. I'll just be a minute." Stonegell handed a book to one of the two students, telling him to read certain sections of it, and explained to the other student why he hadn't received a passing grade in his latest assignment. When both of them were taken care of, Levine stepped into Stonegell's crowded and tiny office, and sat down in the chair beside the desk.

Stonegell said, "Is this about one of my students?"

"Two of them. From your evening writing course. Gruber and Perkins."

"Those two? They aren't in trouble, are they?"

"I'm afraid so. Perkins has confessed to murdering Gruber."

Stonegell's thin face paled. "Gruber's dead? Murdered?"

"By Perkins. He turned himself in right after it happened. But, to be honest with you, the whole thing bothers me. It doesn't make sense. You knew them both. I thought you might be able to tell me something about them, so it *would* make sense."

Stonegell lit himself a cigarette, offered one to Levine, but Levine declined. He'd given up cigarettes shortly after he'd started worrying about his heart.

"This takes some getting used to," said Stonegell after a minute. "Gruber and Perkins. They were both good students in my class, Gruber perhaps a bit better. And they were friends."

"I'd heard they were friends."

"There was a friendly rivalry between them," said Stonegell. "Whenever one of them started a project, the other one started a similar project, intent on beating the first one at his own game. Actually, that was more Perkins than Gruber. And they always took opposite sides of every question, screamed at each other like sworn enemies. But actually they were very close friends. I can't understand either one of them murdering the other."

"Was Gruber similar to Perkins?"

"Did I give that impression? No, they were definitely unalike. The old business about opposites attracting. Gruber was by far the more sensitive and sincere of the two. I don't mean to imply that Perkins was insensitive or insincere at all. Perkins had his own sensitivity and his own sincerity, but they were almost exclusively directed within himself. He equated everything with himself, his own feelings and his own ambitions. But Gruber had more of the—oh, I don't know—more of a *world-view*, to badly translate the German. His sensitivity was directed outward, toward the feelings of other people. It showed up in their writing. Gruber's forte was characterization, subtle interplay between personalities. Perkins was deft, almost glib, with movement and action and plot, but his characters lacked substance. He wasn't really interested in anyone but himself."

"He doesn't sound like the kind of guy who'd confess to a murder right after he committed it."

"I know what you mean. That isn't like him. I don't imagine Perkins would ever feel remorse or guilt. I should think he would be one of the people who believes the only crime is in being caught."

"Yet we didn't catch him. He came to us." Levine studied the book titles on the shelf behind Stonegell. "What about their mental attitudes recently?" he asked. "Generally speaking, I mean. Were they happy or unhappy, impatient or content or what?"

"I think they were both rather depressed, actually," said Stonegell. "Though for somewhat different reasons. They had both come out of the Army less than a year ago, and had come to New York to try to make their mark as writers. Gruber was having difficulty with subject matter. We talked about it a few times. He couldn't find anything he really wanted to write about, nothing he felt strongly enough to give him direction in his writing."

"And Perkins?"

"He wasn't particularly worried about writing in that way. He was as I say, deft and rather clever in his writing, but it was all too shallow. I think they might have been bad for one another, actually. Perkins could see that Gruber had the depth and sincerity that he lacked, and Gruber thought that Perkins was free from the soul-searching and self-doubt that was hampering him so much. In the last month or so, both of them have talked about dropping out of school, going back home and forgetting about the whole thing. But neither of them could have done that, at least not yet. Gruber couldn't have, because the desire to write was too strong in him. Perkins couldn't, because the desire to be a famous writer was too strong."

"A year seems like a pretty short time to get all that depressed," said Levine.

Stonegell smiled. "When you're young," he said, "a year can be eternity. Patience is an attribute of the old."

"I suppose you're right. What about girl friends, other people who knew them both?"

"Well, there was one girl whom both were dating rather steadily. The rivalry again. I don't think either of them were particularly serious about her, but both of them wanted to take her away from the other one."

"Do you know this girl's name?"

"Yes, of course. She was in the same class with Perkins and Gruber. I think I might have her home address here."

Stonegell opened a small file drawer atop his desk, and looked through it. "Yes, here it is," he said. "Her name is Anne Marie Stone, and she lives on Grove Street, down in the Village. Here you are."

Levine accepted the card from Stonegell, copied the name and address onto his pad, and gave the card back. He got to his feet. "Thank you for your trouble," he said.

"Not at all," said Stonegell, standing. He extended his hand, and Levine, shaking it, found it bony and almost parchment-thin, but surprisingly strong. "I don't know if I've been much help, though," he said.

"Neither do I, yet," said Levine. "I may be just wasting both our time. Perkins confessed, after all."

"Still—" said Stonegell.

Levine nodded. "I know. That's what's got me doing extra work."

"I'm still thinking of this thing as though—as though it were a story problem, if you know what I mean. It isn't real yet. Two young students, I've taken an interest in both of them, fifty years after the worms get me they'll still be around—and then you tell me one of them is already wormfood, and the other one is effectively just as dead. It isn't real to me yet. They won't be in class tomorrow night, but I still won't believe it."

"I know what you mean."

"Let me know if anything happens, will you?"

"Of course."

Anne Marie Stone lived in an apartment on the fifth floor of a walk-up on Grove Street in Greenwich Village, a block and a half from Sheridan Square. Levine found himself out of breath by the time he reached the third floor, and he stopped for a minute to get his wind back and to slow the pounding of his heart. There was no sound in the world quite as loud as the beating of his own heart these days, and when that beating grew too rapid or too irregular, Detective Levine felt a kind of panic that twenty-four years as a cop had never been able to produce.

He had to stop again at the fourth floor, and he remembered with envy what a Bostonian friend had told him about a city of Boston regulation that buildings used as residence had to have elevators if they were more than four stories high. Oh, to live in Boston. Or, even better, in Levittown, where there isn't a building higher than two stories anywhere.

He reached the fifth floor, finally, and knocked on the door of apartment 5B. Rustlings from within culminated in the peephole in the door being opened, and a blue eye peered suspiciously out at him. "Who is it?" asked a muffled voice.

"Police," said Levine. He dragged out his wallet, and held it high, so the eye in the peephole could read the identification.

"Second," said the muffled voice, and the peephole closed. A seemingly endless series of rattles and clicks indicated locks being released, and then the door opened, and a short, slender girl, dressed in pink toreador pants, gray bulky sweater and blond pony tail, motioned to Levine to come in. "Have a seat," she said, closing the door after him.

"Thank you." Levine sat in a new-fangled basket chair, as uncomfortable as it looked, and the girl sat in another chair of the same type, facing him. But she managed to look comfortable in the thing.

"Is this something I did?" she asked him. "Jaywalking or something?"

Levine smiled. No matter how innocent, a citizen always presumes himself guilty when the police come calling. "No," he said. "It concerns two friends of yours, Al Gruber and Larry Perkins."

"Those two?" The girl seemed calm, though curious, but not at all worried or apprehensive. She was still thinking in terms of something no more serious than jaywalking or a neighbor calling the police to complain about loud noises. "What are they up to?"

"How close are you to them?"

The girl shrugged. "I've gone out with both of them, that's all. We all take courses at Columbia. They're both nice guys, but there's nothing serious, you know. Not with either of them."

"I don't know how to say this," said Levine, "except the blunt way. Early this afternoon, Perkins turned himself in and admitted he'd just killed Gruber."

The girl stared at him. Twice, she opened her mouth to speak, but both times she closed it again. The silence lengthened, and Levine wondered belatedly if the girl had been telling the truth, if perhaps there had been something serious in her relationship with one of the boys after all. Then she blinked and looked away from him, clearing her throat. She stared out the window for a second, then looked back and said, "He's pulling your leg."

Levine shook his head. "I'm afraid not."

"Larry's got a weird sense of humor sometimes," she said. "It's a sick joke, that's all. Al's still around. You haven't found the body, have you?"

"I'm afraid we have. He was poisoned, and Perkins admitted he was the one who gave him the poison."

"That little bottle Al had around the place? That was only a gag."

"Not any more."

She thought about it a minute longer, then shrugged, as though giving up the struggle to either believe or disbelieve. "Why come to me?" she asked him.

"I'm not sure, to tell you the truth. Something smells wrong about the case, and I don't know what. There isn't any logic to it. I can't get through to Perkins, and it's too late to get through to Gruber. But I've got to get to know them both, if I'm going to understand what happened."

"And you want me to tell you about them."

"Yes."

"Where did you hear about me? From Larry?"

"No, he didn't mention you at all. The gentlemanly instinct, I suppose. I talked to your teacher, Professor Stonegell."

"I see." She got up suddenly, in a single rapid and

graceless movement, as though she had to make some motion, no matter how meaningless. "Do you want some coffee?"

"Thank you, yes."

"Come on along. We can talk while I get it ready."

He followed her through the apartment. A hallway led from the long, narrow living room past bedroom and bathroom to a tiny kitchen. Levine sat down at the kitchen table, and Anne Marie Stone went through the motions of making coffee. As she worked, she talked.

"They're good friends," she said. "I mean, they *were* good friends. You know what I mean. Anyway, they're a lot different from each other. Oh, golly! I'm getting all loused up in tenses."

"Talk as though both were still alive," said Levine. "It should be easier that way."

"I don't really believe it anyway," she said. "Al—he's a lot quieter than Larry. Kind of intense, you know? He's got a kind of reversed Messiah complex. You know, he figures he's supposed to be something great, a great writer, but he's afraid he doesn't have the stuff for it. So he worries about himself, and keeps trying to analyze himself, and he hates everything he writes because he doesn't think it's good enough for what he's supposed to be doing. That bottle of poison, that was a gag, you know, just a gag, but it was the kind of joke that has some sort of truth behind it. With this thing driving him like this, I suppose even death begins to look like a good escape after a while."

She stopped her preparations with the coffee, and stood listening to what she had just said. "Now he did escape, didn't he? I wonder if he'd thank Larry for taking the decision out of his hands."

"Do you suppose he asked Larry to take the decision out of his hands?"

She shook her head. "No. In the first place, Al could never ask anyone else to help him fight the thing out in any way. I know, I tried to talk to him a couple of times, but he just couldn't listen. It wasn't that he didn't want to listen, he just couldn't. He had to figure it out for himself. And Larry isn't the helpful sort, so Larry would be the last person anybody would go to for help. Not that Larry's a bad guy, really. He's just awfully self-centered. They both are, but in different ways. Al's always worried about himself, but Larry's always proud of himself. You know. Larry would say, 'I'm for me first,' and Al would say, 'Am I worthy?' Something like that."

"Had the two of them had a quarrel or anything recently, anything that you know of that might have prompted Larry to murder?"

"Not that I know of. They've both been getting more and more depressed, but neither of them blamed the other. Al blamed himself for not getting anywhere, and Larry blamed the stupidity of the world. You know, Larry wanted the same thing Al did, but Larry didn't worry about whether he was worthy or capable or anything like that. He once told me he wanted to be a famous writer, and he'd be one if he had to rob banks and use the money to bribe every publisher and editor and critic in the business. That was a gag, too, like Al's bottle of poison, but I think that one had some truth behind it, too."

The coffee was ready, and she poured two cups, then sat down across from him. Levine added a bit of evaporated milk, but no sugar, and stirred the coffee distractedly. "I want to know why," he said. "Does that seem strange? Cops are supposed to want to know who, not why. I know who, but I want to know why."

"Larry's the only one who could tell you, and I don't think he will."

Levine drank some of the coffee, then got to his feet. "Mind if I use your phone?" he asked.

"Go right ahead. It's in the living room, next to the bookcase."

Levine walked back into the living room and called the station. He asked for Crawley. When his partner came on the line, Levine said, "Has Perkins signed the confession yet?"

"He's on the way down now. It's just been typed up."

"Hold him there after he signs it, okay? I want to talk to him. I'm in Manhattan, starting back now."

"What have you got?"

"I'm not sure I have anything. I just want to talk to Perkins again that's all."

"Why sweat it? We got the body; we got the confession; we got the killer in a cell. Why make work for yourself?"

"I don't know. Maybe I'm just bored."

"Okay, I'll hold him. Same room as before."

Levine went back to the kitchen. "Thank you for the coffee," he said. "If there's nothing else you can think of, I'll be leaving now."

"Nothing," she said. "Larry's the only one can tell you why."

She walked him to the front door, and he thanked her again as he was leaving. The stairs were a lot easier going down.

When Levine got back to the station, he picked up another plainclothesman, a detective named Ricco, a tall, athletic man in his middle thirties who affected the Ivy League look. He resembled more closely someone from the District Attorney's office than a precinct cop. Levine gave him a part to play, and the two of them went down the hall to the room where Perkins was waiting with Crawley.

"Perkins," said Levine, the minute he walked in the room, before Crawley had a chance to give the game away by saying something to Ricco, "this is Dan Ricco, a reporter from the *Daily News*."

Perkins looked at Ricco with obvious interest, the first real display of interest and animation Levine had yet seen from him. "A reporter?"

"That's right," said Ricco. He looked at Levine.

"What is this?" he asked. He was playing it straight and blank.

"College student," said Levine. "Name's Larry Perkins." He spelled the last name. "He poisoned a fellow student."

"Oh, yeah?" Ricco glanced at Perkins without much eagerness. "What for?" he asked, looking back at Levine. "Girl? Any sex in it?"

"Afraid not. It was some kind of intellectual motivation. They both wanted to be writers."

Ricco shrugged. "Two guys with the same job? What's so hot about that?"

"Well, the main thing," said Levine, "is that Perkins here wants to be famous. He tried to get famous by being a writer, but that wasn't working out. So he decided to be a famous murderer."

Ricco looked at Perkins. "Is that right?" he asked.

Perkins was glowering at them all, but especially at Levine. "What difference does it make?" he said.

"The kid's going to get the chair, of course," said Levine blandly. "We have his signed confession and everything. But I've kind of taken a liking to him. I'd hate to see him throw his life away without getting something for it. I thought maybe you could get him a nice headline on page two, something he could hang up on the wall of his cell."

Ricco chuckled and shook his head. "Not a chance of it," he said. "Even if I wrote the story big, the city desk would knock it down to nothing. This kind of story is a dime a dozen. People kill other people around New York twenty-four hours a day. Unless there's a good strong sex interest, or it's maybe one of those mass killings things like the guy who put the bomb in the airplane, a murder in New York is filler stuff. And who needs filler stuff in the spring, when the ball teams are just getting started?"

"You've got influence on the paper, Dan," said Levine. "Couldn't you at least get him picked up by the wire services?"

"Not a chance in a million. What's he done that a few hundred other clucks in New York don't do every year? Sorry, Abe, I'd like to do you the favor, but it's no go."

Levine sighed. "Okay, Dan," he said. "If you say so."

"Sorry," said Ricco. He grinned at Perkins. "Sorry, kid," he said. "You should of knifed a chorus girl or something."

Ricco left and Levine glanced at Crawley, who was industriously yanking on his ear-lobe and looking bewildered. Levine sat down facing Perkins and said, "Well?"

"Let me alone a minute," snarled Perkins. "I'm trying to think."

"I was right, wasn't I?" asked Levine. "You wanted to go out in a blaze of glory."

"All right, all right. Al took his way, I took mine. What's the difference?"

"No difference," said Levine. He got wearily to his feet, and headed for the door. "I'll have you sent back to your cell now."

"Listen," said Perkins suddenly. "You know I didn't kill him, don't you? You know he committed suicide, don't you?"

Levine opened the door and motioned to the two uniformed cops waiting in the hall.

"Wait," said Perkins desperately.

"I know, I know," said Levine. "Gruber really killed himself, and I suppose you burned the note he left."

"You know damn well I did."

"That's too bad, boy."

Perkins didn't want to leave. Levine watched dead-pan as the boy was led away, and then he allowed himself to relax, let the tension drain out of him. He sagged into a chair and studied the veins on the backs of his hands.

Crawley said, into the silence, "What was all that about, Abe?"

"Just what you heard."

"Gruber committed suicide?"

"They both did."

"Well—what are we going to do now?"

"Nothing. We investigated; we got a confession; we made an arrest. Now we're done."

"But—"

"But hell!" Levine glared at his partner. "That little fool is gonna go to trial, Jack, and he's gonna be convicted and go to the chair. He chose it himself. It was *his* choice. I'm not railroading him; he chose his own end. And he's going to get what he wanted."

"But listen, Abe—"

"I won't listen!"

"Let me—let me get a word in."

Levine was on his feet suddenly, and now it all came boiling out, the indignation and the rage and the frustration. "Damn it, you don't know yet! You've got another six, seven years yet. You don't know what it feels like to lie awake in bed at night and listen to your heart skip a beat every once in a while, and wonder when it's going to skip two beats in a row and you're dead. You don't know what it feels like to know your body's starting to die, it's starting to get old and die and it's all downhill from now on."

"What's that got to do with—"

"I'll tell you what! They had the *choice!* Both of them young, both of them with sound bodies and sound hearts and years ahead of them, decades ahead of them. And they chose to throw it away! They chose to throw away what I don't have any more. Don't you think I wish *I* had that choice? All right! They chose to die, let 'em die!"

Levine was panting from exertion, leaning over the desk and shouting in Jack Crawley's face. And now, in the sudden silence while he wasn't speaking, he heard the ragged rustle of his breath, felt the tremblings of nerve and muscle throughout his body. He let himself carefully down into a chair and sat there, staring at the wall, trying to get his breath.

Jack Crawley was saying something, far away, but Levine couldn't hear him. He was listening to something else, the loudest sound in all the world. The fitful throbbing of his own heart.

MIKE SHAYNE MYSTERIES
by Brett Halliday

More than 30 million Mike Shayne mysteries have been printed in Dell Book editions alone!

- ☐ **ARMED DANGEROUS** 0299-26
- ☐ **AT THE POINT OF A .38** 3152-00
- ☐ **LAST SEEN HITCHHIKING** 4683-06
- ☐ **MURDER IN HASTE** 5970-21
- ☐ **MURDER SPINS THE WHEEL** 6123-25
- ☐ **SIX SECONDS TO KILL** 8001-10
- ☐ **TARGET MIKE SHAYNE** 8492-32
- ☐ **THE VIOLENT WORLD OF MIKE SHAYNE** 9334-32

DELL BOOKS 95¢ each

BESTSELLERS
FROM DELL

fiction

"Why don't you ask your wife?"

He turned to stare at Helen Cooper, who raised her chin and refused to meet his gaze.

"He'd been lying there dead for three days?" he asked slowly.

"Uh-huh," I said.

The woman screamed at me, "You're lying!"

Cooper put his hands to his ears and walked half-way across the room to sink into a chair. His wife stared after him, then shifted her gaze back to me when he looked at her.

In a tense, but lower-toned voice she said, "Why do you think he had been dead three days?"

I said, "The coroner's physician says so."

"He made a mistake."

"Hardly," I said. "Marks's body lay in your house all that time. Don't try to make us believe you didn't notice it."

Nervously she worked her hands together, trying to think of a way out. "I just had the day wrong, is all. George killed him on Friday. In all the excitement, I just—"

Her voice trailed off, when we both unbelievingly shook our heads.

I said, "Why don't you save time by telling us about it, lady?"

She looked hopelessly from one to the other of us. Finally she said in a whisper, "I didn't mean to do it. Honest I didn't."

We waited.

"It was spur-of-the-moment. When he said—" Her voice failed.

"When he said what?" I prompted.

Drearily, all hope now gone, she said, "He told me he was going back to her."

"His wife?" Sam asked.

"Yes. That plain little nothing. After all we'd been to each other, he said I was just an interlude. He said he *loved* her."

"Then what?" I asked.

"That little vixen, Viola Marks. She's so jealous, she'd even slander her own husband to get even."

"Even for what?" I asked.

"For being better looking than she is. She hates me for it."

Sam and George Cooper came back from the water cooler. Cooper said, "If I ever take another drink, I'll kick myself—hard."

"Feel better?" Sam asked.

"Not yet. It takes a while."

I said, "I was just telling your wife about some new developments, Mr. Cooper."

Helen Cooper said loudly, "Don't you dare repeat that slander!"

Cooper winced and gave his wife an irritated look. "Do you have to yell?" He turned to me. "What slander?"

"It's hardly slander," I said. "We've pretty well established that your wife was carrying on an affair with Henry Marks."

Mrs. Cooper got an outraged expression on her face, but her husband's reaction seemed to surprise her out of saying anything. Instead of showing either astonishment or indignation, he merely gave an interested nod.

"You knew?" I inquired.

"Oh, no," he said. "Merely suspected. I've caught him in the house a time or two. Helen insisted he's been passing at her and she's been resisting him. She's begged me not to make an issue of it because she didn't want trouble with neighbors. She said she could handle him all right. I guess I'm a henpecked husband. I let her think I believed her, when I really didn't at all."

"George!" she said in a shocked voice. "How can you say that?"

He ignored her.

I said, "Another development was that Marks had been dead three days at the time you were supposed to have your fight."

This managed to surprise him. "Three days?" he said without understanding. "How could that be?"